"I was so self-righteous when we broke up," she continued. "So stupid."

"Don't bring it up, Cece." He stroked her hair, let the fine strands slide through his fingers. "Let's start over. Now. Tonight. We've both been through some rough times the last couple of years. Let's not dig up hard feelings that are even farther in the past."

"Yes," she said, still wondering if that was possible. Car headlights stabbed through the open window and brought Cece back to reality. "I have to go."

"I'll see you again." She knew he didn't mean professionally.

"I'll think about it," she hedged in a sudden attack of cowardice. "I'll see myself out."

"Don't think about it, Cece," she heard him say as she hurried down the hall, her mind in turmoil. "Don't think. Just feel the way you used to."

Special thanks and acknowledgment to Marisa Carroll
for her contribution to the Tyler series.

Special thanks and acknowledgment to Joanna Kosloff
for her contribution to the concept for the Tyler series.

Published December 1992

ISBN 0-373-82510-2

CROSSROADS

CROSSROADS

MARISA CARROLL

Harlequin Books

TORONTO • NEW YORK • LONDON
AMSTERDAM • PARIS • SYDNEY • HAMBURG
STOCKHOLM • ATHENS • TOKYO • MILAN
MADRID • WARSAW • BUDAPEST • AUCKLAND

TYLER

WHIRLWIND
Nancy Martin

BRIGHT HOPES
Pat Warren

WISCONSIN WEDDING
Carla Neggers

MONKEY WRENCH
Nancy Martin

BLAZING STAR
Suzanne Ellison

SUNSHINE
Pat Warren

ARROWPOINT
Suzanne Ellison

BACHELOR'S PUZZLE
Ginger Chambers

MILKY WAY
Muriel Jensen

CROSSROADS
Marisa Carroll

COURTHOUSE STEPS
Ginger Chambers

LOVEKNOT
Marisa Carroll

TYLER

American women have always used the art quilt as a means of expressing their views on life and as a commentary on events in the world around them. And in Tyler, quilting has always been a popular communal activity. So what could be a more appropriate theme for our book covers and titles?

CROSSROADS

Many small settlements sprang up at the intersection of frontier trails where settlers flocked to exchange goods and gossip. The careful combination of squares and triangles in the Crossroads pattern conveys the vitality of those early communities, suggesting sunny fields of prosperous farmland and Sunday drives along country roads.

Dear Reader,

Welcome to Harlequin's Tyler, a small Wisconsin town whose citizens we hope you'll come to know and love. Like many of the innovative publishing concepts Harlequin has launched over the years, the idea for the Tyler series originated in response to our readers' preferences. Your enthusiasm for sequels and continuing characters within many of the Harlequin lines has prompted us to create a twelve-book series of individual romances whose characters' lives inevitably intertwine.

Tyler faces many challenges typical of small towns, but the fabric of this fictional community created by Harlequin has been torn by the revelation of a long-ago murder, the details of which are evolving right through the series. This intriguing crime will culminate in an emotional trial that profoundly affects the lives of the Ingallses, the Barons, the Forresters and the Wochecks.

Folks in town have a lot on their minds these days. Amanda Baron is busy preparing the defense for her grandfather Judson's trial, Cece Hayes has been pressed into volunteering to conduct childbirth classes at the free clinic, Liza Forrester is due to deliver her baby anytime now, and poor Alyssa has been plagued by strange recurring nightmares, mysteriously linked to Margaret Ingalls's death so many years ago.

So join us in Tyler, once a month for the next three months, for a slice of small-town life that's not as innocent or as quiet as you might expect, and for a sense of community that will capture your mind and your heart.

Marsha Zinberg
Editorial Coordinator, Tyler

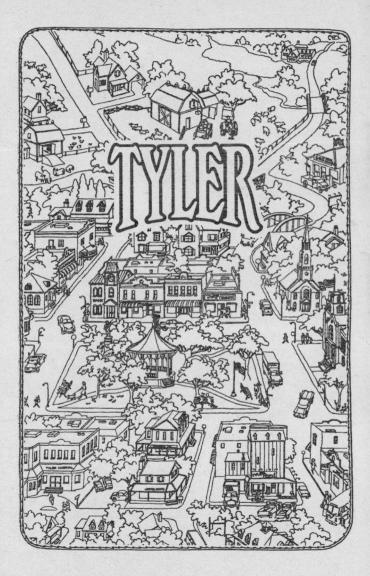

CHAPTER ONE

"MRS. HAYES! Please hurry! Something's terribly wrong with Mr. Badenhop."

Cecelia Scanlon Hayes, R.N., known to everyone in Tyler, Wisconsin, as Cece, shoved the metal-backed patient chart she'd been studying into the circular file on the counter of the nurses' station. "What is it?" she asked, her crepe-soled shoes making little sound on the vinyl-tiled floor of Worthington House Retirement Center's extended care unit as she hurried along. "What's wrong?" She moved past the agitated nurse's aide who had called her and into the patient's room.

"I don't know," the young woman responded. She looked scared, unsure of herself, the way Cece felt so often inside her soul these days but couldn't let show.

She took a moment to give the aide a calming smile as she moved toward Wilhelm Badenhop's bed, her practiced eye taking in details of his condition as she spoke. "Take a deep breath and start at the beginning."

"He was resting comfortably when I looked in on him half an hour ago. When I came back to check his intravenous line, I noticed he was barely breathing. Has he had a stroke or something?" the aide asked very quietly as she watched Cece rapidly examine the old man.

"I can't tell yet," Cece admitted, being careful not to let any of her own anxiety creep into her words. She wasn't seeing any of the expected symptoms of pneumonia and advanced arthritic deterioration, the medical problems that had brought Wilhelm to the unit, and it threw her off balance. "He's having a lot of trouble breathing. I'm going to increase his oxygen flow." Cece opened the valve on the metal cylinder at the head of the bed. Respiratory distress wasn't unusual in a patient suffering from pneumonia, but Wilhelm Badenhop's breathing was unusually slow and deep, not quick and shallow as she'd expected.

"Is he going to die?"

"Raise his head," Cece instructed, ignoring the question. "Then get the charge nurse to bring the emergency med tray and get Dr. Phelps on the phone. I don't like his color or his pulse rate."

"He looks like he's going to die." The young woman, Tracie, a part-time employee and second-year nursing student from the university, stood frozen at the end of the bed.

"Not if I can help it," Cece assured her, but she felt far less confident than she sounded. "We may have to get a breathing tube down his throat. Be sure there's one ready when Dr. Phelps gets here." She kept her fingertips on the old man's thready pulse. "Mr. Badenhop," she said loudly. "This is Cece Hayes. Can you tell me how you're feeling?"

No response.

"Tracie, do as I said," Cece ordered.

"Dr. Phelps isn't a-available," Tracie stuttered, as Cece pulled her stethoscope out of the oversize pocket of her white lab coat and prepared to slip the tabs in her ears. "Didn't you hear?" Her pale blue eyes fixed themselves on Cece's face. "He eloped with Marge Peterson—you know, from Marge's Diner—over the weekend."

"I was out of town over the weekend," Cece said, checking Wilhelm's IV setup. The bag of fluid was nearly empty but the unit seemed to be functioning properly. In any case, the only medication in the fluid was an antibiotic, nothing that would cause the perilous condition her patient was in at the moment. She glanced down at the old man once more. His color was slightly improved since she'd increased the flow of oxygen through the mask covering his mouth and nose, but his lips and the flesh beneath his fingernails were still dangerously blue.

"Then you missed the excitement," Tracie went on, making no move to leave the room. "No one knows for certain where they've gone."

"Someone's got to be covering for Dr. Phelps at Tyler General," Cece snapped. She was only half listening to Tracie. Most of her attention was focused on Wilhelm's labored breathing. "Who is it?" Cece turned on Tracie, her gray eyes flashing. There was no time for this. The aide was going to have to learn that when a superior gave her an order, she should carry it out immediately. "Someone has to be on call. It doesn't matter who, just get them."

"It's Dr. Baron," Tracie said. She finally moved to do the nursing supervisor's bidding. "Dr. Jeff Baron."

"Great. That's all I need—Jeff Baron," Cece muttered. She took a deep, steadying breath. Now wasn't the time to worry about awkward meetings with the boy she'd once thought she loved more than life itself. She took a deep, steadying breath. "Get moving, Tracie." She made the words an order. "Get someone from the hospital over here. Stat! There's no more time to waste—he's going into arrest."

DR. JEFFREY BARON pulled out of the staff parking lot at Tyler General Hospital and headed home. It had been a long, hot Sunday night in the emergency room. They'd been understaffed, as usual, and busy with sunburns, a case of food poisoning, two minor car accidents and a stab wound victim from a fight outside a bar on Michigan Street. Even in a town as small as Tyler, there was a wrong side of the tracks. And since the recession had begun, it seemed to take in more and more of the town.

He rubbed the back of his neck and rolled down the car window to let in the still-cool morning air. He was dead tired, but he only had time for a shower and shave before he'd have to head back across town to see George Phelps's morning patients. He made a mental note to have George's receptionist, Anna Kelsey, rearrange the appointments after today, move them back to afternoons, or he'd be dead on his feet before Wednesday.

Jeff didn't mind doing George a favor; he just wished the older doctor had let him in on his plans to elope with Marge Peterson so he could have shifted his own duty schedule around to balance the load. Thank God someone else would have to be responsible for George's administrative duties at the hospital. As it was, Jeff didn't know whom he'd find to fill in for him at the free clinic tomorrow. He didn't like the idea of his patients there having to go all the way to Sugar Creek for care. But if he didn't get some financial help for the clinic—and soon—they'd be making the drive on a regular basis, not just for the two or three weeks that Doc Phelps would be out of town.

Life seldom worked out exactly as you planned it. And then again, Jeff decided with a wry twist of his lips that just missed being a smile, if you were as much in love as Doc and Marge you didn't always look as far ahead as you should. He certainly hadn't wanted to listen to anyone or anything but his heart four years earlier, when both his grandfather and his mother had warned him that his marriage to a wealthy Chicago socialite would never work out.

It hadn't. In spades.

And he'd learned the hard way about never letting your heart overrule your head.

The emergency channel radio scanner under the dashboard crackled to life. Jeff listened to the tersely worded request for emergency help at Worthington House and realized with a jolt that the patients at the retirement center were his responsibility as well, until George returned from his honeymoon.

"Hell, what a day," he muttered under his breath. "It isn't even nine o'clock in the morning."

He made a U-turn in the middle of Elm Street to head back toward the old brick mansion that housed Tyler's only retirement home. By cellular phone he informed the Emergency Medical Service that he would need an ambulance and wondered just what kind of situation he was going to find at Worthington House.

He could handle just about anything they threw at him from a medical standpoint; he had no qualms about that. He wasn't so sure he could handle being face-to-face with the facility's new nursing supervisor. So far during the course of the summer he'd been able to avoid one Cece Scanlon Hayes. This Monday in August it looked as if his luck had run out.

CECE PULLED the sterile wrap off an endotracheal tube and made preparations to insert it in Wilhelm Badenhop's airway. He'd stopped breathing almost a minute earlier. She knew if she didn't attempt to resuscitate him immediately, his heart would stop beating.

"Help me," she ordered Juanita Pelsten, when the charge nurse joined her uncertainly at the old man's bedside.

"You're not authorized to intubate." Juanita made no move to assist her.

"I know that," Cece said, positioning the old man's head herself.

"None of the nurses at Worthington House have that authority, including the nursing supervisor," Juanita went on in an agitated whisper.

Cece tried to hold on to her fraying temper and her fear. Inside she was shaking like a leaf; outside she was solid as a rock. This was her first real emergency situation since the earthquake that had leveled the hospital where she'd worked in Nicaragua, killing her husband. She knew she was operating outside the boundaries of her authority just as Juanita did, but she couldn't stop to consider the consequences of her actions now. Her patient's life was all that mattered. Mrs. Pelsten was twenty-five years older than Cece. She'd been trained at a time when a nurse never questioned a doctor's order or acted on her own initiative. It wasn't her fault she was hesitant to take the responsibility now.

"Mrs. Hayes, you'll lose your job. Maybe your license," the woman cautioned, putting her hand on Cece's arm in gentle restraint. "We both will. He's old and sick. People come to Worthington House to die. Let him go in peace."

"No!" Cece hissed. "Not as long as there's a chance to save him."

"Step back and let her work, Mrs. Pelsten."

It was a man's voice—deeper and more mature, perhaps, but a voice she'd know anywhere, any time, even though she hadn't heard it in ten years. Cece didn't look up when a pair of strong, well-shaped male hands reached forward and helped her secure a breathing bag to the tube.

"Bag him," Jeff Baron instructed. "Mrs. Pelsten, get that emergency med tray over here. What have we got, Cece?"

She ignored the use of her first name. She'd always liked the way he said it. She still did.

"One of the nursing assistants came in to check on his IV meds and found him unresponsive and in respiratory distress. He arrested about ninety seconds ago."

Cece took a moment to glance up from her patient. Jeff was frowning as he surveyed the array of medications on the wheeled tray Juanita pushed toward him. She'd only seen Jeff a time or two in the weeks she'd been back in Tyler. From a distance, he'd looked much the same as he had a decade before. Now she could see the subtle changes time had worked on his features, turning a handsome, earnest boy into a man.

"We can't give up on him, Doctor."

Jeff turned his head. She could feel him watching her from eyes so dark a blue they were almost black.

Lord, how she remembered those eyes, achingly blue, with absurdly thick black lashes that had set her adolescent heart beating so wildly all those years ago.

She looked him straight in the eye and felt not a twinge of reaction; her heart was already beating so rapidly she thought it might burst.

"Get me an ampoule of epinephrine," he directed over his shoulder to Juanita Pelsten.

He gave Cece look for look. She broke eye contact first, glad for the excuse to keep her attention fastened on her patient and the situation at hand. She went back to counting respirations, gently forcing air into Wilhelm's lungs, certain that Jeff would do everything he could to bring their patient back from the brink of death. He grabbed the syringe Juanita held out to him and injected the contents directly into the IV tubing running into Wilhelm's arm.

"Mrs. Pelsten, get a bag of glucose and start it running. We don't want to lose this vein if we can help it. We might need it later. Come on, you old geezer," he said under his breath. "Breathe!"

"He's not responding," Juanita said, although she picked up a plastic bag of intravenous solution and moved around the bed, behind Cece, to make the transfer.

"Don't give up on him yet," Jeff answered gruffly. "Keep it up, Cece, until he comes around. Then watch out. He'll probably make a grab for the breathing tube."

"Yes, Doctor." For one of the first times in her life she was grateful for the protocols they'd drilled into her in nurses' training. It helped not to have to address Jeff by his given name, the name she'd scribbled in countless notebooks all through high school. *Jeff. Jeffrey.* And the most exciting, wonderful of all, *Mrs. Dr. Jeffrey Baron.* How silly and foolish—and so very much in love—she'd been then. Thank God she'd gotten over him a long time ago.

Wilhelm Badenhop's eyes fluttered open. He began to claw weakly at his throat with his one free hand. Jeff reached past Cece to restrain him and their hands brushed, for only a second, but long enough for

Cece to realize what she'd been thinking just moments before wasn't altogether true. When he touched her her whole body tingled with awareness, just as it had the first time they'd kissed, after the homecoming football game their sophomore year at Tyler High. She'd come alive that night, in her heart and soul, in a way that no other man, not even Steve, had been able to reproduce. She certainly wasn't happy to know the chemistry between them, at least from her point of view, was still potent and alive.

She didn't want anything to do with Dr. Jeffrey Baron, personally or professionally. The latter circumstances she could do nothing about, as long as she was working at Worthington House; the former, she had every intention of accomplishing.

"The ambulance is here, Dr. Baron," the aide, Tracie, announced in a not-quite-steady voice, as she stuck her head through the doorway.

"Tell them to wait." Cece relinquished her place by the bedside so that Jeff could remove the breathing tube now that Wilhelm was breathing on his own. "Dr. Baron will let you know when it's safe to transport Mr. Badenhop."

"I want to make sure he's stabilized first." Straightening, he caught Cece's eye, his wry look telling her more clearly than words that he knew what she was doing—hastily erecting barriers of professionalism and medical etiquette between them.

"Yes, Doctor," Tracie replied and disappeared down the hall.

"Mrs. Pelsten, will you check Wilhelm's vital signs while Mrs. Hayes and I try to figure out exactly what happened here?"

"Yes, Doctor," the older nurse said, just as meekly as Tracie.

"Will?" Jeff asked in a gruff but friendly voice, a man-to-man kind of voice, as he bent over the bed rail and patted the old man's shoulder. "Did you wake up feeling bad this morning?"

"No." Wilhelm shook his head weakly. "Throat hurts like hell now, though."

"We had to put a tube in to help you breathe for a while. Do you remember anything about what you did this morning?"

Wilhelm closed his eyes, thinking. Cece reached over the railing from her side of the bed and smoothed his wispy white hair back off his high forehead. "He's very alert mentally," she said, interpreting the slight frown between Jeff's straight dark brows to mean he wasn't certain of their patient's ability to recall the morning's events with any clarity.

"I know that," Jeff responded, again catching her eye for a brief, disconcerting moment. "I've known Wilhelm all my life, just like you have, remember?"

"Pulse and blood pressure returning to normal," Juanita announced as she removed the cuff from Wilhelm's arm. Cece looked away from Jeff's compelling gaze, spared from making an attempt at a halfhearted apology by the older nurse's interruption.

"Wilhelm?" Jeff said more loudly. He gave the old man a gentle shake.

"Ate breakfast," Wilhelm answered immediately.

"Freddie Houser brought in his tray," Juanita informed Jeff. "She helped him with breakfast. She's slow, not quite right, you know, poor thing. But she's good at what she does. She would have come to me at once if he'd had any trouble eating, or choked on his food."

"Didn't choke," Wilhelm said in a thin, raspy voice. "Fed myself. Didn't spill anythin', even with my arm all wired up like it is. I ain't clear senile yet, Juanita Pelsten."

Jeff chuckled at the old man's show of spirit, and Cece bit her lip to keep from laughing out loud. Wilhelm took a deep breath, then another. Cece let out a tiny sigh of relief. It was a good sign.

"Do you remember anything else?"

"Got sleepy." The old man shook his head. "Sleepin' a lot, you know, since I got sick. Can't remember nothin' else. Just bad dreams. Couldn't breathe..." His words drifted off. He moved restlessly, looking up at Jeff with frightened, faded blue eyes. "What the hell happened to me? Is somethin' wrong with my heart?"

Jeff shook his head. "I don't think so, but for some reason you stopped breathing. I want to send you over to the hospital for a day or two so we can run some tests, try to find out what caused this to happen, okay?"

"I guess so." Wilhelm sounded uncertain. "Don't like hospitals much. You'd better check with my grandson, Bob. He's helpin' me take care of most everythin' since I got sick. Damned arthritis, ya know." He lifted one gnarled and twisted hand a few inches off the sheet. "Slows a man down somethin' fierce."

"I know, Wilhelm." Jeff patted his arm. "I'll talk to Bob as soon as I leave here. You get some rest now. It might be a bit of a bumpy ride getting you out of here on the gurney."

"Most excitement I've had in weeks," the old man said dryly, but he closed his eyes obediently. "You won't get too far away, will ya, Doc, in case I go off again?"

"I'll be right here," Jeff assured him. "Mrs. Hayes and I are going to be taking care of the paperwork to get you transferred."

"Helps a body rest a mite better, not being alone." Wilhelm's eyes drifted shut but his breathing was quicker, more regular, and Cece relaxed a little more.

"I think we're out of the woods," Jeff said, reading her thoughts. Straightening, he shoved his stethoscope into his traditional black bag.

Cece wondered if it had been given to him as a gift or if he'd bought it for himself. She'd always dreamed of buying him one when he was accepted into medical school—and he would have given her an engagement ring when she received her nursing degree. But when that day came they were hundreds of miles apart, completely estranged, and they'd never seen each other again. Steve had been the man who gave her a ring and his heart, but she'd lost him after only six years together. Jeff had married, also, although from what her mother said, the marriage had been short and unhappy. She was sorry for that. Life seldom turned out the way you thought it would.

"You're certain there was nothing unusual to report about Wilhelm's condition over the weekend?" Jeff asked, as he flipped through the pages of the old man's chart.

"Nothing that I'm aware of. It was my weekend off," Cece explained, pushing the intrusive memories of the past out of her thoughts to concentrate on matters at hand. "I was in Chicago, visiting my...visiting Steve's parents."

Jeff shut the chart with a snap. He looked at her and she couldn't break away from the compelling blue of his eyes. "I was sorry to hear about your husband's death," he said a bit stiffly, formally. "I...I was having some problems myself when it happened, but that was no excuse for not sending my condolences. I apologize."

"Please don't," Cece replied, more harshly than she'd meant to. Her throat ached with the effort not to cry. She couldn't seem to help it when people mentioned her husband's death, although in the past few months the horror of the earthquake and the pain of his loss were slowly fading away. "I know you meant well. And the mail is very erratic in the rural areas of Nicaragua. It's possible your letter might never have reached me."

"Still, you have my sympathy."

"Thank you." The words hung awkwardly in the air between them.

The sounds of voices and movement in the hall saved her from any further difficult conversation about Steve's death, or Jeff Baron's divorce, because she was certain that was the problem he'd been referring to. And she certainly didn't want the subject to progress into a discussion of their own past history.

She wondered what Jeff might think if he knew just how familiar she was with the events of his life. Her mother had made certain of that. Annabelle Scanlon, Tyler's postmistress, had inordinate faith in the ability of the United States mail to be delivered to the farthest reaches of the globe, and she'd bombarded Cece with long, chatty letters about Tyler's residents. Jeff's whirlwind courtship of a Chicago socialite and the short doomed marriage that followed had been the talk of the town, paralleling as it did some of the scandalous aspects of his grandfather's ultimately tragic marriage to Margaret Lindstrom a half century before.

Suddenly Cece found herself wanting to tell Jeff how sorry she was about his grandfather's ordeal following the discovery of Margaret's long-dead body. It was hard to imagine Judson Ingalls being in jail. It was even harder to believe he was a murderer. The idea didn't mesh with the image of the tall, dynamic, white-haired man she remembered so vividly from her girlhood. But the opportunity to mention it passed as the paramedics wheeled the gurney into the room.

In the bustle and confusion of the next thirty minutes, she didn't have a chance to speak privately with Jeff again. And perhaps it was better that way. What, after all, did they really have to say to each other beyond a few polite, strained pleasantries? Jeff seemed just as happy as she was to have the familiarity of medical routine keep a small distance between them. He asked that copies of Wilhelm's chart and medication schedule be sent over to the hospital, took a few minutes to help her explain the situation to her boss, Worthington House's administrator, Cecil Kellaway, and then he was gone. Back to Dr. Phelps's office to see his patients, he said.

It was only later, as she sat in her cubbyhole of an office beneath the carved walnut staircase on the main floor, filling out yet more reports, that Cece recalled how tired he had looked. He must have been on duty at the hospital all night, she realized, and by now would have been on his feet nearly twenty-four hours straight.

That was like him, she decided, chewing the end of her pen. He had always been earnest and trustworthy, handsome, smart, the all-American boy. It was only when it came to the dream they'd shared, or she'd thought they shared, that he had let her down and broken her heart.

"I BROUGHT YOU something to eat. I thought you might be hungry." Alyssa spoke from the open doorway of her son's bedroom.

"Sandwiches and lemonade. Great. Thanks, Mom, I'm starved." Jeff turned away from the window, tucking his shirttail into his jeans as he talked. He was barefoot and his hair was still damp from the shower. He smiled.

He looked a lot like his father when he smiled. He had Ronald's thick, slightly curly chestnut hair, which he never remembered to have trimmed unless she or Amanda reminded him, and his father's dark blue eyes. His nose—commanding, she liked to call it; big, Jeff always insisted—and strong, obstinate chin were exact duplicates of her own father's features. His personality was also more like Judson Ingalls's—bluff, direct, no-nonsense. Ronald had been more outgoing and fun-loving than his son, at least until near the end of his life. Jeff, like most children, was very much a mixture of his parents, and at the same time, very much his own man.

"Clara insisted I bring them up." Alyssa smiled, a little apologetically, in return. Clara Myers was her father's housekeeper. She and her husband, Archie, had been with Judson as long as Alyssa could remember. Clara had been almost a mother to her when she was growing up and was still trying to mother her now that she had moved back under her father's roof.

"Tell her thanks," Jeff said, eyeing the chicken salad sandwich on the tray appreciatively. "I don't think I have the energy to make it down to the kitchen. I'm beat."

"George Phelps should never have expected you to take over his practice on such short notice. You've got more than enough patients of your own to take care of."

"People don't generally plan elopements weeks in advance," Jeff pointed out, moving across the big, high-ceilinged room in three quick strides. "If you do that, it's a wedding, not an elopement, and you know what kind of a to-do weddings cause in this town. Everyone goes a little crazy. You ought to have figured that out yourself by now. Tyler has had more than its share of them lately," he added as he picked up half a sandwich and took a bite.

Alyssa ignored his comments on weddings in general. "I can't imagine what those two were thinking of," she said with a shake of her head. "They ought to know better at their age."

"I never knew there was an age limit on falling in love," Jeff said, sitting down on his bed. He reached up and took the tray from her hands, to place it carefully on the bedspread in front of him. He was watching her with a teasing sparkle in his eyes, but she continued to refuse the bait he dangled in front of her. Her feelings for Edward Wocheck were far too complicated and uncertain to qualify as anything even close to love. Not now, not yet.

"There's certainly no age limit on showing poor judgment," she responded tartly, moving forward to shut the drapes at the big double windows to block out the bright August sun so Jeff could sleep when he'd finished eating.

"C'mon, Mom. Admit it. No one in this town thought George Phelps had a romantic bone in his body until he fell in love with Marge Peterson."

"Well, no," she admitted with a smile, as she settled herself carefully at the foot of the four-poster cherry bed. "You'd think he'd shy away from becoming involved again so soon. But that's neither here nor there. I hope they're very happy together." She tucked one foot up under her skirt and watched her son eat. "Lord knows he spent a lot of unhappy years with Mary. Still, I hope they get themselves back here soon so you can get a decent night's sleep."

"I can't disagree with that," Jeff said, taking a long swallow of lemonade. "I could sleep for a week. But I have to be back on duty at the emergency room at eleven and I want to stop by the clinic before I go." He ran his hand through his hair. "And I want to get to the hospital early enough to check up on old Wilhelm Badenhop, too."

"Oh, dear," Alyssa said, frowning slightly. "What happened to Wilhelm?" She'd known the old man all her life. He was only a few years older than Judson. "Has he had a relapse? I thought he was recovering from his bout with pneumonia."

"It seems he was, until this morning. He nearly died of respiratory arrest. If it hadn't been for Cece Scanlon . . . I mean, Cece Hayes." He grinned ruefully, but the teasing glint had gone out of his eyes, leaving them dark and cold as a midnight sky. "She's a hell of a nurse. If it hadn't been for her quick thinking, we'd be paying our last respects to old Wilhelm at the funeral home tonight, instead of me checking over his lab tests, trying to figure out what went wrong.''

"I hope everything turns out well. I like old Wilhelm," Alyssa said. "And I agree, Cece's an excellent nurse. Worthington House is lucky to have her. But it must be quite different from the work she did as a midwife in Nicaragua.''

"Midwife?" Jeff scowled, his dark brows pulled together in a frown that was so like Judson's, Alyssa had to lower her head to hide her smile. "I didn't know she was a midwife.''

"You don't spend enough time at the post office. Annabelle keeps the whole town up to date on Cece's life.''

"Well, for once Annabelle isn't exaggerating," Jeff said, taking a last swallow of lemonade before setting the empty glass on the tray. "She's smart and savvy and cool as ice under pressure. She's sure as hell wasting her professional skills at Worthington House. We could really use someone like her at the clinic.''

"Worthington House's residents deserve excellent nursing care also," Alyssa reminded him, picking up the tray as she rose from the bed.

Jeff lay down and pulled a pillow onto his chest. He folded his arms around it, just as he had from the time he was a boy. He looked up at the ceiling. Alyssa looked at him.

"Why don't you ask if she's willing to volunteer a few hours of her time at the clinic each week?" she couldn't resist asking.

"No. And don't you go asking her on my behalf either, the next time you see her. I've got enough problems on my mind without adding Cece Hayes to the list." He closed his eyes deliberately, ending the conversation.

It was the first time he'd mentioned Cece since she'd been back in town. They'd been very much in love when they were younger. Alyssa often wondered what had happened to end the romance. Jeff had never talked about it, although she was certain in her own mind that it was his father's suicide and the financial hardships that followed that had been the cause of it all.

Wisely, she decided not to question her son further. He was a grown man, after all—thirty years old; he could look out for himself where matters of the heart were concerned.

At least she hoped he could.

His divorce had hurt Jeff deeply, Alyssa knew, although he tried to pretend that it hadn't. She hoped it hadn't scarred him so badly he wouldn't take the chance on falling in love again. Not that she had any intention of trying to act as a matchmaker for her son and Cece Hayes. She knew better than that. And she'd make sure Annabelle Scanlon didn't get the idea into her head to do so, either.

"I'll wake you at ten," she said, preparing to close the door behind her.

"Better make that nine-thirty," Jeff answered, his voice already husky with sleep. "I've got to juggle a few accounts around at the clinic to keep the wolves from the door another month.''

''Nine-thirty,'' she repeated, shutting the door. He was asleep before the latch clicked shut. ''Pleasant dreams,'' she whispered, starting down the stairs. Those were the words she'd spoken to her children every night when they were small, a talisman to protect them from the darkness and the unknown. It was still her wish for them now that they were grown.

Her own dreams were seldom pleasant, especially these past few nights since her father had been sent to jail. The reality of Judson's being accused of her mother's murder still carried the quality of nightmare. She couldn't believe it was true, yet she remembered so little of the night Margaret Ingalls had disappeared. She could barely distinguish actual memory from childhood fantasy and recent snatches of recollection. She had been so young then, and it was so long ago; she only wanted to forget. But that wasn't possible. Her father's future happiness, perhaps his very life, depended on her remembering everything she could about that terrible night.

Alyssa paused at the bottom of the stairway. She set down the empty tray on the walnut pedestal table that had sat in the foyer for almost a century and lifted her hand to her temple to rub away the dull ache of tension that echoed every beat of her heart. Most of the time she couldn't remember enough about the night her mother disappeared to answer anyone's questions, including her own. But sometimes, sometimes, she was afraid she would remember too much.

In her dreams the past few nights, dreams that had kept her awake for hours after their passing, she had seen a man. No one she knew or recognized, only a shadowy masculine figure running away from her mother's bedroom. Running away from her. Because in her dream she also saw herself, the child Alyssa, standing at the foot of her mother's bed, and that other, long-ago Alyssa was holding a gun.

CHAPTER TWO

"HERE, LET ME do that for you, Ms. Hayes." Frederica Houser, better known as Freddie, rushed toward Cece, her hands held out to take the armload of patient charts she was carrying. The charts were heavy and ungainly to transfer. The last thing Cece wanted to do was hand them over to another person not fifteen feet from the nurse's station.

"It's okay, Freddie," she said with a smile. "I can manage."

"But I want to help. I've picked up all the breakfast trays. I don't have anything to do," Freddie complained, her plump, childish features puckering into an unattractive frown.

"All right," Cece said, changing her mind. "You hold the charts for me and I'll return them to the desk file. How's that?"

"Great." Freddie made an awkward grab for the stack of metal-backed charts and cradled them against her chest. "I'll read you the names," she insisted.

"That will be helpful." Cece pretended not to see the annoyed frown on Juanita Pelsten's face as the charge nurse scooted her chair over to make room for Cece and her helper.

"Dr. Phelps spoils that girl," Juanita muttered.

Freddie was a long way from being a girl. She was nearly forty, but Juanita—indeed, almost everyone in Tyler—referred to Freddie as a girl. She was still a child in mind and spirit, if not in body. "She has no business being at the nurses' station," Juanita complained, but under her breath, so that Freddie couldn't overhear.

"It's all right, Mrs. Pelsten. She's helping me."

"I am," Freddie said proudly, thrusting the heavy armload of charts forward for Juanita to see. They began to slide and she clutched them fiercely against her mint green smock.

"Don't drop them," Juanita ordered in the same voice she would use to scold an eight-year-old child.

"I won't." Freddie sniffed, her feelings hurt.

"Whose chart is first?" Cece asked to prevent tears.

"Elmo Schw...Elmo Schwiebert," Freddie said, beaming up at Cece, her flyaway red hair standing out around her head like a halo.

"Schwiebert," Cece confirmed, sliding the chart back into the carousel file. "I found very few charting errors this week, Juanita," she said, taking a second patient record from Freddie's eager hands. "I'll go over them with you and the evening-shift nurses during afternoon report. I'll catch up with the night-shift nurses before they go off duty in the morning." She wasn't really listening to Freddie's droning voice stumbling over the names on the chart as she discussed procedures with Juanita.

"Who's this, Ms. Hayes?" Freddie interrupted imperiously. "I can't read this one."

"Violet Orthwein," Cece said, pointing out the letters that would clue Freddie in to the name. Cece had been told by Dr. Phelps that Freddie couldn't really read, although she knew her letters. She had a very good memory and was a talented mimic, qualities that made her seem more functional than she actually was.

"One more," Freddie said with a flourish as Cece took the Orthwein chart from her hands. "This one says Wil...Wilhelm Bad..." She stopped trying to pronounce the name. "Where is he?"

"In the hospital," Cece said gently, when she saw the stricken look on Freddie's face.

"Is he dead?"

"No." Cece slid the chart into the file and patted Freddie's plump hand, still held out in front of her. "He became very ill yesterday morning, don't you remember?"

"I thought he died," Freddie said, her normally ruddy complexion pasty white. "Miss Peterson died and went to heaven when she got sick like that."

"Miss Peterson was very, very sick already," Juanita said, looking up at Cece with a shrug. Cece had been told that Luetta Peterson, an elderly shirttail relation of Marge Peterson, had been a special friend to Freddie and her mother. It was to be expected the woman's sudden death would have upset Freddie.

"Not everyone who gets ill dies, even at Worthington House," Cece said gently. "Dr. Baron is very good. He saved Wilhelm's life."

"My mom died. Miss Peterson died." Freddie screwed up her face in a frown. "I have to go. It's time to pass ice water," she said suddenly. She walked past Cece, lumbering off toward the elevator and the independent living quarters on the main floor of the old brick mansion as quickly as her short, heavy legs would carry her.

"Oh dear," Cece said, biting her lower lip. "She's very upset. Should I go after her and try to explain again?"

"It won't do any good." Juanita stared over the counter at Freddie's retreating figure. "She doesn't understand. Her mother's death was so hard on her." She shook her head in gruff sympathy. "I could just kick myself when I forget that and let my impatience with the girl get the better of me. Phyllis Houser was all Freddie had in this world to love, but she's been gone for more than a year. Freddie should be coming to terms with her mother's death by now."

"Everything comes hard for Freddie," Cece said softly, feeling her own ever-present sorrow stir restlessly inside her heart. "Being healed of her grief won't come any easier than the rest."

"No, I suppose not." Juanita bent to her charting once more. "And Luetta's death recently didn't help matters."

"Good morning, ladies."

Cece whirled around to find Jeff Baron coming down the second-floor corridor from the direction of the main staircase.

"Good morning," Juanita said with a nod.

"Good morning, Doctor." Cece noticed dark stubble on his chin and shadows under his eyes. This morning she didn't have to guess if he'd been up all night—she knew. The hospital emergency room had sent over a copy of his duty schedule so that the Worthington House staff could locate him more quickly if they needed him.

"Good morning, Cece. Don't you think it's time you started calling me Jeff again?"

"I don't think that's wise." Cece hated herself for sounding so straitlaced.

"You two have known each other all your lives," Juanita said with a chuckle. "Don't tell me you're going to start standing on ceremony now!"

"Mrs. Hayes is a very conscientious nurse," Jeff said with the same quirky grin that had set her pulse racing since she was fifteen years old.

"Dr. Baron," she said, emphasizing the title ever so slightly, "has always had a certain disregard for the conventions." Two could play at this game as easily as one, she was discovering. "I distinctly remember the night after the pep rally for the Belton game our senior year in high school, when he went out to the lake and—"

"Never mind, Cece. Juanita gets the picture." His quirky smile was replaced by a frown that failed to reach the teasing light in his blue eyes.

"I get the picture all right," Juanita said, shutting the cover on her chart with a bang. "Would you like me to accompany you on rounds this morning? Or would you prefer Mrs. Hayes go with you?"

Cece held her breath. If Jeff said or did anything to make Juanita suspicious that they had been more than just friends who'd dated in high school, she'd never forgive him. It was hard enough coming back to Tyler after all these years without the rumor mill gearing up to grind her private life to fine dust.

"You, of course, Juanita. Mrs. Hayes has only been here a few weeks herself. I'm not familiar with a lot of the patients. You can take me through rounds with one hand tied behind your back and we'll still both come out smelling like roses."

"Thank you, Dr. Jeff." Juanita beamed.

Cece narrowed her eyes. Jeff stared back at her in feigned innocence as he shrugged into the white lab coat Cece handed him from the closet directly behind her. He'd been able to charm every female he met since the day he was born. Juanita was no exception. Cece would do well to remember how potent his sex appeal still was or she knew she'd find herself falling back under his spell, no matter how unwilling she was to do so.

"Will you be in your office when I'm done up here, Cece?" he asked, suddenly all business. "I'd like to fill you in on Wilhelm Badenhop's condition before I leave."

"Of course. I'll be waiting."

"Good." He turned away. "C'mon, Juanita, let's get going. I'm already forty minutes behind schedule. It was another wild night in ER."

"The duty nurse will be back from her break in just a few minutes. Will you stay at the station until she does return, Mrs. Hayes?"

"Yes," Cece said as she turned back from shutting the closet door. "I can stay." She needn't have bothered answering. Jeff and Juanita were already halfway down the corridor and she was alone.

"COULD I INTEREST YOU in a cup of coffee?" Jeff propped his shoulder against the doorframe and gave Cece his best smile. He was determined not to feel like a fifteen-year-old jock whenever she looked at him with that smoky gray gaze, but it wasn't easy. Her eyes seemed to change color with her every change of mood; funny how he'd forgotten that about her until just now. She did something to his thought processes, not to mention his pulse rate, and she always had. He suspected she always would.

"I'm afraid I don't have time for coffee at the moment," Cece replied in a very businesslike manner. She wasn't looking directly at him, but at a point just past his left ear. "I've got a ton of paperwork to finish before I leave today."

"I wanted to discuss Wilhelm Badenhop's condition with you," Jeff said, shamelessly manipulating the situation. He didn't know why, or at least he didn't want to admit the reason to himself, but he needed to talk to her, to hear her voice and see her smile, and Wilhelm offered the perfect excuse.

"Oh." She looked down at the paperwork on her desk. He knew duty would win out over inclination and he was right. "Couldn't we discuss Wilhelm here?" She indicated the hard wooden chair in front of her desk. The metal desk dwarfed the small office tucked underneath the main staircase. A fan stirred the warm air from atop the filing cabinets that stretched from wall to wall at the other end of the closet-size room.

"Can't," Jeff said, shaking his head. "I'm claustrophobic. This place gives me the creeps."

"You aren't claustrophobic," Cece answered, with another wave of her hand toward the straight-backed, uncomfortable-looking chair. Jeff could see she regretted the taunting response and the opening it gave him to reply in kind almost as soon as the words left her mouth.

"I'm surprised you remember."

"I remember a great deal," she said softly, "but it was a long time ago."

"Yes, it was." He shoved his hands into his pockets. He wondered why he was trying so hard to keep the conversation alive. All he had to tell her was that Wilhelm had spent a quiet night and that he didn't have any more of an explanation today for what had caused the old man's emergency than he'd had when it happened. "All right. If I can't get you to fall for that one, how about the fact that I haven't seen the sun in three days?"

Her frown was as enchanting as her smile, he decided. "I don't see the connection."

"Is the staff lounge still in the back corner of the solarium?"

Cece nodded. She twirled her pen between her fingers nervously. She didn't want him in her office, it was plain to see. He forged ahead, regardless of her wariness.

"Come, have a cup of coffee with me while we talk. It'll be the only chance I have all week to get some sun."

She rearranged the paperwork spread out on the metal desktop. "I really should stay here and get this done."

"C'mon," he said, making it a challenge. "I know how much you always liked the sun. Or have you changed more than I thought?"

"*I* haven't changed," she said, looking straight at him for the first time since he'd shown up in the doorway.

Jeff rubbed his hand along his jaw, unsure of how to reply. This wasn't the time or place to delve into the past too deeply. He wasn't sure if there would ever be a right time or place. He'd hurt Cece badly all those years ago. Since then, he'd been hurt badly in return and he knew how it felt. He fell back on protocol. "I do need to talk to you about Wilhelm and I do need a cup of coffee." He didn't add that he'd been on his feet nearly twelve hours straight.

"Of course, Doctor." She stood up and preceded him out of her office. She was wearing a dark green cotton skirt and a pink-and-green flowered blouse beneath her white lab coat. Her hair was brushed back off her face, tucked behind her ears, and she looked soft and cool as a summer morning. He was about to object to her insistence on the use of his title when he saw her lips quirk in the ghost of a reluctant smile. The smile did something to his central nervous system and he didn't feel nearly as tired as he had just moments before. "I see no reason we can't confer on Mr. Badenhop's condition in the staff lounge."

"Thanks," he said and meant it. "I'm beat."

"I can see that."

Moments later she held open the door to the small, partitioned-off section of the glass-walled solarium, which had been the talk of Tyler when it was built ninety years before.

"It shows, huh?" he asked ruefully, running his hand across the stubble on his face. "I haven't had a chance to shave yet today."

"You look just like Steve used to when he'd get back to the hospital after delivering a baby," she said, moving across the Italian tile floor, another extravagance of Worthington House's original owners, to draw woven blinds across the expanse of glass and soften the direct rays of the August sun.

"I thought your husband was an administrator." He poured himself a cup of coffee from the insulated thermos sitting on a table behind the door.

"He was." She turned away to look out over the large side yard, where residents could sit and feed the birds, tend small garden plots or grow flowers if they chose. "But he was also a damn good nurse. In a little out-of-the-way place like Santa Rosita you had to wear more than one hat. He was the hospital administrator, chief fund-raiser, and the plumber, electrician and general handyman, too." He could tell she was smiling, even though he couldn't see her face.

"I know what you mean," he said unthinkingly.

"I doubt it," she replied, turning around, the smile erased from her lips and her tone of voice, "unless you've been there. Nicaragua is a beautiful place but the poverty and need are appalling. I can't begin to describe it."

Jeff held his coffee cup between his hands and waited for her to continue. He could see her anger, sense her loss and her grief, but he didn't know what to say next, just as he hadn't known what to say yesterday when the subject of her husband's death was raised.

"Who told you about our work in Santa Rosita?" she asked suddenly, throwing him a curve.

"My mother, and your mother," he answered, dropping down on the cushioned wicker couch facing the glass wall.

"I should have known. What else did Mom tell you, and the rest of the town?" She began picking dead fronds off a fern standing in a brass container at the other end of the couch.

"That he died from injuries he suffered when the hospital where you were both working collapsed after the big earthquake they had down there last year."

"Yes," she said, closing her eyes briefly as if to keep her emotions under control, "that's what happened. I'd rather not talk about it, if you don't mind. I loved my husband very much. It's hard to believe he's gone."

"Of course." He took a long swallow of his coffee and stood up, setting down the cup on the table by the thermos. It was only lukewarm but almost strong enough to give him the caffeine jolt he needed. Cece remained standing behind him, silent, lost in her thoughts. She wasn't going to make it easy on him and he couldn't blame her. He'd walked out on her without an explanation all those years ago. She had a right to be wary of becoming involved with him again, for whatever reason. Especially if he kept making the mistake of bringing up the subject of her dead husband.

"I've gone over all the nursing notes on Wilhelm's chart for the past several days," she said, abruptly and purposefully returning the subject to professional concerns. "I've also questioned the night nurses and the rest of the staff. Nothing unusual occurred that any of them noticed or remember. His pneumonia was responding to IV antibiotic therapy. He ate well, slept well, was alert and cooperative right up until Tracie walked into his room and found him in such distress."

"You're cutting the ground from under my feet," Jeff said with a wry twist of his lips as he turned to face her once more. He shoved his hands into his pockets. "You knew I was going to ask you to give me an evaluation of the nursing care here before I asked, didn't you?"

She nodded. "I wouldn't expect anything less. I take it nothing unusual turned up in any of the tests you ran at the hospital?"

"No. It didn't help that we had no idea what we were looking for."

"I'm meeting with the whole nursing staff today and tomorrow. I want to evaluate our emergency procedures and review the signs and symptoms of cardiac and respiratory distress with the aides. I don't know of any other way to be better prepared. Do you have any suggestions, Doctor?"

"No. You seem to be right on top of the situation." Any headway he might have been making with her personally was eroded by the renewed tension in their professional relationship.

Cece's beeper sounded. She reached into the pocket of her lab coat and shut it off. "That's my page," she said unnecessarily, obviously as relieved as he was to have their conversation end.

"I have to be going, too. I have patients to see in George's office in less than an hour." It wasn't much of an excuse for hightailing it out of there but at least it was the truth. If there was one uncomfortable fact he was learning from his renewed acquaintance with Cecelia Scanlon Hayes, it was that she had the ability to turn his thought processes topsy-turvy. If he were honest with himself, she'd always been able to work that particular piece of sorcery. He felt as confused and out of his depth around her as he had at sixteen when he'd held her in his arms for the very first time.

At least now, at thirty, he had the option of staying away, of disregarding the urges of mind and body that had held sway over both of them when they were teenagers. He could do it if Cece could. And looking at her cool, composed features, he didn't see any sign of a struggle. She didn't seem to be feeling any of that old magic at all. It was over. Their affair had been ashes for a decade. All he had to do was remember that simple fact and everything would be just fine.

JEFF WAS TALKING to Edward Wocheck and his father, Phil, in the main lobby as Cece left her office a few minutes later. The message on her beeper had been a trivial one, but a welcome distraction nonetheless. She couldn't feel comfortable around Jeff Baron no matter how many times she told herself that there was no reason for the way she felt. Anything between them had been over and done ten years ago. She only felt this way because her heart was awakening from its long healing sleep and Jeff Baron was a very attractive man. That was all. There was nothing more to it.

Yet, when she walked into the reception area to find him still in the building, her pulse raced and she felt her breath catch in her throat, just as it always had.

"Miss Cece," Phil Wocheck called out from his wheelchair. "You have heard the good news that my friend Wilhelm is soon to be returning to us."

"Yes, it's very good news, indeed," Cece agreed with a smile for the white-haired old man. Jeff was frowning slightly, and she wondered what subject of conversation she'd interrupted between the men, but pretended not to notice. "We were all very worried about him."

"He was well when I spoke to him as he ate his breakfast," Phil continued, "yesterday morning, as I took my walk past his room with that Cossack of a therapist you employ here." The rich remnants of his

Polish accent became more pronounced as he warmed
to his tale. "Then *pfft,* he is whisked away to hospital. Almost dead, they tell me at lunch."

Cece hid a smile at the old man's description of
Worthington House's therapist. He did have a domi-
neering personality. He was also excellent at his job.
"Dr. Baron just told me that Wilhelm is recovering
very rapidly."

"I like it that you did not say 'for a man his age and
in his condition,'" Phil said, with a nod in his son's
direction. "This is one very smart lady, Eddie."

"You'll get no argument from me. Good morning,
Mrs. Hayes." Edward Wocheck held out his hand. He
was wearing a white shirt and dark, pleated slacks,
casual, well tailored and very expensive. Beside him,
in a creased and wrinkled blue plaid shirt and jeans
that had seen better days, Jeff looked more over-
worked and disheveled than ever.

"Good morning, Mr. Wocheck," Cece replied.
Edward's grip was firm and strong like his voice.
"Have you and your father been for a walk?"

"He walks. I ride in this metal cage with wheels,"
Phil said, with a scowl that matched Jeff's in intensity.

"Give your hip another week or two to heal and
you'll be dancing up a storm," Jeff said, clapping the
elderly man on the shoulder.

"I don't care to dance. Only to walk out of here
under my own steam," Phil said, still frowning.

"Don't rush things, Dad." Now Edward was
frowning, too.

"I want to go home."

"I thought you were pleased with your new room, Mr. Wocheck," Cece said, signaling Edward that she would push his father's chair now. "I distinctly remember you saying that being on the main floor was a hell of an improvement over the Extended Care wing."

"Ha! Anything with a roof would be an improvement, and I did not say 'hell.' I do not say such words in front of ladies."

"My apologies," Cece said very sweetly and was rewarded with a crooked, grudging smile.

"Perhaps the word did slip out," Phil admitted. "But it is not good that you repeat it."

"I'll remember to be more careful," Cece promised. "Would you like to lie down for a little while before the Cossack arrives to take you upstairs?"

"Ahh. He comes again today?" Phil shook his white head. "There is no rest for the wicked."

"That's a perfect exit line if I ever heard one," Jeff said, looking at his watch. "It's been nice talking to you, Edward. Phil, go easy on the therapist, you hear? I'll be back to check up on you in a day or two."

"No hurry," the old man grumbled. "I'm going nowhere important anytime soon."

"Please let me know if there's any way I can be of help," Edward said.

"The most important thing right now is to get my grandfather cleared of suspicion." Jeff's words were harshly spoken.

Cece's eyes flew to his face but he wasn't looking at her, or at anybody else for that matter. His expression was hard and set. "I don't know what that damned district attorney thinks he's up to, trying to pin a forty-year-old murder rap on a man his age."

"I plan to be in town the rest of the week," Edward said, ignoring Jeff's angry tone. "Call me if you need me."

Phil was sitting very straight in his chair, his bony shoulders stiff beneath his shirt. "Hurry," he said to Cece, interrupting Edward's last remark. "I'm tired. I want to rest."

The tension in the air among the three men was so strong it was tangible. The rumors flying around Tyler about the odds for and against Judson Ingalls being indicted for murder were too numerous to count. Yet Edward Wocheck and his father seemed even more interested than most. Cece's mother had been hinting recently that Edward and Alyssa Baron were falling in love again, more than thirty years after Judson had refused to let his daughter marry the son of an immigrant laborer. What did Jeff and his sisters think of that possibility? Cece couldn't help but wonder.

Evidently some of those old, hard feelings were surfacing between the two families again today. Or was it something even more sinister? Those same rumors hinted that an important piece of evidence regarding Margaret's death had been found in Phil's room at the Kelsey Boardinghouse—evidence the old man had been hiding to blackmail Judson through the years, as punishment, some said, for his breaking young Eddie's heart. But it was evidence more damning than that, according to Cece's mother, who believed she was always correct where whispered confidences of such import were concerned. Annabelle had heard that it was a gun they'd found in Phil's room. An odd English make. And it was the gun the D.A. was going to use to prove that Judson Ingalls had murdered his wife.

"ALYSSA WILL NEVER HAVE you as long as that young buck has anything to do with it."

Edward's father sat propped up on his hospital bed in the cheerful, well-furnished room he'd been transferred to several days before. He was looking out the window as if he, too, could see Jeff Baron driving away, although he could not. Edward turned away from the window and glanced at the door to see if it was closed.

"This is not the old country. No one is listening outside the door," Phil scoffed.

"I don't want to talk about myself and Alyssa today, Dad," Edward said with more patience than he felt. He watched his father carefully as the old man smoothed a knitted afghan across his knees. Phil looked up, watching him in return, although the bright sunlight coming in the window behind Edward made the old man blink. Edward stepped to the side, out of the direct rays of the August sun. "I want to talk to you about Judson Ingalls. About Margaret's murder."

"Too long ago," Phil snapped, laying his head back against the pillow. "I do not recall."

"You have to try, Dad." His father looked old and frail. Edward felt like a bastard pushing him this way, but the stubborn old man had to be made to understand he could end up in as much trouble as Judson Ingalls if he didn't make some kind of statement to the D.A. and soon.

"Too many years," Phil mumbled as if he was falling asleep. Only the tension in his gnarled hands, tightly clenched on the blanket, alerted Edward that he was feigning sleep.

"You have to tell me what happened that night. You must have been the one to put Margaret's suitcase in the potting shed. And why did you keep that gun all these years? It's Judson's gun, isn't it?"

"I don't remember." There was steel in the old man's voice. He stared at Edward with an obstinate lack of expression in his faded gray eyes.

"You know the district attorney will try and prove to the grand jury that that was the gun that killed Margaret Ingalls."

"It cannot be helped." Phil closed his eyes again.

"They found the gun in your room, Dad." Edward felt as if he were beating his head against a wall. "You could be accused just as easily as Judson."

"I have done nothing wrong." There was finality in the old man's voice. "Leave me now. I need to sleep."

Edward turned back to the window. His father remembered what had happened that long-ago night at the lodge, he was certain of that. But what exactly had the old man seen that night? Was he trying to protect himself? Or someone else?

CHAPTER THREE

"You're Cece Scanlon, aren't you?"

Cece looked up from the envelope she was addressing at the Formica-topped table in the lobby of the Tyler post office. Outside it was hot and muggy, but in the lobby of the century-old brick building it was blessedly cool. The price of that coolness was the noisy operation of the outdated air conditioner, which chose that moment to rattle into service.

"Yes," she responded with a polite smile, speaking loud enough to make herself heard over the air conditioner. "I'm Cece Hayes."

"Right." The very tall, blond young woman before her smiled back, but without apology. She was wearing a pale yellow maternity top and cutoff shorts, her hair pulled up in a haphazard knot on top of her head. She looked healthy and happy and very sure of herself. "I forget your married name. Do you remember me?"

"You're Liza, Jeff Baron's sister, aren't you?" Cece guessed.

"Yes, but it's Liza Forrester now. The black sheep of the Baron family come back to Tyler. You probably know how that feels." She laughed easily, but Cece caught a ragged edge of defiance in the sound. "I mean, coming back to the old hometown, not the black sheep part.''

"It does seem strange after being away so many years,'' Cece admitted, then found herself adding, "in some ways it's almost as if time stood still while I was gone.'' She gestured to their surroundings and the view of the town square beyond the windows. "But then again, there are a lot of changes as well.''

"Some big ones,'' Liza laughed, patting her rounded stomach.

"Congratulations,'' Cece said, responding to the happiness in her smile.

"Yes,'' Liza said, more softly. "I am happy.''

Cece smiled again, but it was only a courtesy, a reflex. She and Steve had planned to start a family of their own, but she hadn't been lucky enough to conceive before his death.

"I didn't just happen in here, you know,'' Liza disclosed before Cece had a chance to speak again. "I followed you.''

"Why?'' Cece asked, slightly taken aback at the admission. She licked a stamp and fixed it carefully to the corner of the envelope. Two young boys rushed through the glass doors and pelted up to the counter, demanding stamps in loud, careless voices.

"I want to talk to you,'' Liza said abruptly, taking no notice of the boys. She propped her elbow on the high tabletop and eyed Cece speculatively.

"Talk to me? About what, may I ask?'' *Good heavens, not Jeff,* Cece thought in momentary panic. Even in Tyler rumors had to have some basis in fact to get started this fast. Liza, who was three years younger than her brother and Cece, had only been a freshman or sophomore in high school when she and Jeff broke up. Surely Liza had forgotten what an item they'd been a dozen years before.

"It's about a part-time job," Liza responded unexpectedly.

"I'm sorry, I already have a job," Cece told her, now completely at a loss to understand. "I've taken over as nursing supervisor at Worthington House."

"Oh, I know that. My brother told me," Liza went on, as blithely aggressive as before. "The job I'm referring to is more in the nature of volunteer work."

"Volunteer work?" Cece wished she could think of something on her own to say instead of parroting Liza's phrases back at her. She suspected it would be difficult. Liza Baron Forrester seemed to be the kind of person who usually had the upper hand in a conversation.

"Yes. At the free clinic over on Indiana Street." She gave Cece a sharp look from beneath carefully darkened eyebrows pulled together in a faint frown. "Don't you know about the clinic?"

"No, I'm afraid I don't." Cece stood a little straighter. She wasn't used to having to tip her head up to look at other women. At five eight, she had always thought herself tall. Liza was at least three inches taller.

"I'll fill you in," Liza offered, but didn't get the chance.

"Oh, Cece, it is you. I thought I heard your voice out here." Annabelle Scanlon poked her head around the six-foot-high divider that separated the lobby from the working area of the post office. "Who are you talking with?"

"It's me, Mrs. Scanlon," Liza said with a wave. "I've finally caught up with your daughter."

"Good." Annabelle came out from behind the wood-and-glass partition. She was wearing a dark blue jumper and a gray-and-white-striped blouse that made her look younger than her nearly sixty years. She folded her plump arms beneath her breasts and gave Cece a charged look. "Listen to this young woman," she said with a nod that sent her short, dark curls bouncing around her face. "I think you'll be interested in what she has to say."

"Mother," Cece said in exasperation, "I don't have time—"

"Of course you have time," Annabelle interrupted. "You sit at home alone every night."

"I work hard during the day. I'm tired at night," Cece began helplessly. The last thing she wanted to discuss with Jeff's sister was her lack of a social life.

"Nonsense. You're half my age and I manage to get out once in a while in the evening. You can't mourn Steve forever." A phone rang somewhere behind Annabelle. She opened her mouth as if to press her point further, then closed it with a snap. "I have to answer that," she said unnecessarily. "Listen to what she has to say, Cece." It was the same tone of voice she'd used when Cece was eight and being stubborn about practicing the piano. "Please," she added, disappearing again behind the tall partition.

Cece stared at the spot where Annabelle had been standing. Her mother never asked, she commanded. This must be an unusual situation. "Goodness," Cece said aloud before she could stop herself. She swung her head around to find Liza Forrester smiling again, but this time the smile didn't reach her intense blue eyes. "I'm sorry. My mother worries about me more than she should."

"Mothers have a tendency to do that."

Cece remembered just then that Annabelle had said Liza and Alyssa Baron hadn't gotten along well for a while before Liza returned to Tyler.

"Please, go on." She guided the conversation back to the original topic. It wouldn't hurt to hear what Liza had to say.

"We need a nurse to teach the prenatal classes at the free clinic two evenings a week for the next four weeks. Our regular instructor slipped in the shower and hurt her back. She's going to be laid up for at least six weeks."

"I'm sorry to hear that." Cece had stepped across the narrow lobby to slip her letter into the Out of Town slot. She hesitated just a fraction of a second before dropping it, not long enough for Liza to notice how much the request had surprised and dismayed her. But underneath it all it excited her, too. Her heart began to beat a little faster. Her hands trembled ever so slightly. She pushed them into the pockets of her slacks.

"I know you're a trained midwife," Liza continued. "Your mother told me so."

"Yes," Cece said. That was all. She wasn't ready to admit, even to herself, how badly she wanted to return to her nursing specialty.

"Surely you taught classes like that in..." Liza threw up her hands, unable to recall where Cece and Steve had worked.

"Yes, I did teach classes in Nicaragua, but..." Cece wished they weren't in so public, so central a place. Several people had already passed them in the granite-floored lobby. She could hear her mother's voice and that of a clerk coming from behind the dark wooden partition. She was beginning to think she might as well say yes to Liza Forrester's proposition and get it over with.

"Then you shouldn't have any trouble at the clinic."

Cece made one last attempt to refuse. "Surely there are similar classes at Tyler General that your free clinic parents could attend."

"Oh, there are," Liza agreed readily. "But there's also a fifty-dollar fee. And the next class doesn't start for almost a month." She looked down at her burgeoning stomach with a touch of disbelief. "Some of us can't wait that long. What do you say?" she coaxed with a wide, cajoling smile that reminded Cece, just a little, of Jeff's sexy grin. "Please, help us out."

"All right. When are the classes and where exactly is the clinic?" Cece asked, bowing to a stubborn determination that was stronger than her will to resist.

"That means I've convinced you," Liza said with satisfaction. "Great. Cliff and I were just starting to get the hang of our breathing exercises."

"I had no idea you were involved with...a project like the free clinic." Cece nodded politely to Reverend Haley from the First Methodist Church as he deposited a fistful of envelopes in the Local delivery slot.

"Oh, I am," Liza said, giving the minister a wave and a smile as he passed. "At least I have been for the past few months. Since my marriage. I'm not the only Baron who's into good works in the old hometown, just the last one to get the call to serve."

Cece felt a chill along her spine that had nothing to do with the functioning of the antiquated air conditioner. She should have expected this.

"Whom do I report to when I arrive for the class?" she asked, unable for some reason she didn't want to confront just then to request outright the name of the clinic's attending physician. Somehow she was certain Liza wouldn't say it was Dr. Phelps, or one of the other Tyler physicians.

"Why, my brother, of course," Liza replied, long gold-tipped lashes sweeping down to cover her blue eyes for the space of a heartbeat. When she glanced up again she looked as innocent as a baby. "Jeff works part-time at the clinic, too. Didn't you know that?"

"YOU'LL GET WRINKLES in that classically handsome Baron forehead if you keep frowning like that," Liza predicted, propping her hip on the scarred and dusty library table that served as a desk in the office at the free clinic.

"I'll risk it," Jeff muttered, running his eyes down the columns of figures in the ledger before him.

"It doesn't matter how many times you add them up," Liza said with real sympathy neatly hidden beneath amusement. "They keep coming out the same. The clinic's in the red, just like my checkbook has been for the past five years."

"We're not just in the red, we're hemorrhaging money." Jeff closed the ledger in disgust. "There's no way I can stop it. We've cut expenses to the bone. Services, too, dammit. We were barely making ends meet with the sliding-fee scale when the economy around here was in good shape." He slammed down his pen beside the ledger.

"I've solved one of your problems," Liza said, one leg swinging free. "I've got a teacher for the prenatal classes. Gratis."

If he'd been more alert, Jeff would have been put on his guard by the smug satisfaction he heard in his sister's voice. "Who is it?"

"Cece Hayes."

"Cece Hayes!" He sat up straight, his wooden swivel chair protesting loudly at the sudden change of position.

"That got your attention," Liza said, pleased with his response.

"Why in hell did you ask her?"

"You gave me the idea." Liza was unmoved by his outburst. "You told me yourself she's a trained midwife. And practically a missionary, from what her mother said.''

"She isn't a missionary. She and her husband worked for one of the smaller international relief agencies," Jeff corrected. He wasn't looking at Liza and missed the interested look she shot him.

"My mistake. Anyway, she's agreed to teach the class."

"You should have consulted me first." It never did much good to try sounding like an authority figure around Liza. She never listened to anyone but Cliff.

"The class is scheduled to start in less than an hour. Anyway, you were sleeping and Mom wouldn't let me wake you up, so when I saw Cece Hayes in the post office I asked her and she said yes."

"Just like that?"

"Of course not *just like that,*" Liza said with a gusty sigh of impatience. "I talked till I was blue in the face." She slid her hip off the desktop and stood up, her hand going to the small of her back. "I thought you'd be pleased. You know you'd have ended up teaching the class yourself if I hadn't asked Cece to do it. And that's the last thing you need right now—another responsibility to shoulder."

"I have broad shoulders." Jeff leaned back in his squeaky chair, deliberately relaxed.

"Every one of the single women in this burg, and most of the married ones, will agree with you on that point," Liza said wickedly.

"Liza!" He felt the back of his neck grow warm, embarrassed himself by blushing, and spoke more sharply than he'd intended. "Cut the crap. I've got enough to worry about down here without you dragging Cece Hayes into the fold, that's all. I can just about guarantee she won't thank you for it."

"Hey, big brother, I thought I was doing you a favor." She gave her long blond hair a toss. "I did it for myself, too. I just don't feel like lumbering into classes at the hospital with all those supremely boring, terribly domestic...witches—" she made a face "—I went to high school with. It's like an epidemic. Everyone I know is pregnant." She threw her hands wide in a gesture of frustration. "I like it here, Jeff. I like Mary and Danny, and Tom and Bette Wilson. Tanya and her mother are a scream. And Cliff feels more at ease here." The last statement was made with finality, as if that settled the matter. And for his sister, Jeff supposed, it did.

"Okay, okay. I appreciate your trying to help me out, but Cece Hayes is the last person I would have thought to ask, that's all." It was also a lie. He'd thought about it. He hadn't had the courage to do it. He laced his fingers behind his head and tipped back his chair, studiously nonchalant.

"That's hard to believe," Liza said, folding her hands across her stomach. "I always thought you two were a real hot item in high school."

"Who was a real hot item in high school?"

Jeff looked up to find their sister, Amanda, standing in the doorway. She was dressed conservatively in a gray suit and pale yellow blouse. Her chestnut brown hair fell in an intricate French braid down her back, and her Baron blue eyes were assessing as she advanced into the small office. "Let me guess. You must be discussing Cece Scanlon for one reason or another."

"Good Lord, I can't believe you two," Jeff said in exasperation. He hadn't felt this ganged up on by his sisters since they were all in their teens. "I haven't been in contact with the woman for more than ten years, or spoken a word to her until three days ago." .

"Don't get your stethoscope in a knot," Amanda retorted with a wink in Liza's direction. "I was listening outside the door for a moment. I only said that to tease you. I'm sure no one else in town remembers you two were quite an item all those years ago. Right up until Dad died—" She broke off abruptly, waving her hand to change the subject. "I didn't stop by to talk about your old love affairs," she announced, commanding their attention with one speaking glance. "I've arranged bail for Granddad. He's on his way home with Mom right now."

"Great, Counselor," Jeff said, coming out from behind his desk to give Amanda a hug. "We knew you could do it."

"It's barbaric keeping a man his age in jail," Liza said, giving Amanda's free hand a quick squeeze. "This is wonderful. How is he? Is he feeling well?" Judson had refused to see any of his grandchildren except Amanda since his incarceration. While Liza's relationship with her mother had been stormy and painful, she had always been close to Judson. "Will it be all right if Cliff and I drop by the house after class?''

"He's fine," Amanda assured her younger sister. "And I know he wants to see you. Just don't keep him up late."

"As if Mother would allow it," Liza shot back as she headed for the door. "I have to go find Cliff. He's somewhere fixing a light switch or something."

"At least she isn't rushing off to search for more clues to what really happened the night Margaret died." Jeff found it hard to call the woman he'd never known and who had caused his family such heartache "Grandmother."

"Liza identifies so strongly with her," Amanda said, shaking her head. She looked up at him with solemn, worried eyes. "She wants to see Granddad free. She wants to have the mystery cleared up. I just hope I can oblige her."

"C'mon, sis. You're a hell of a lawyer."

"In Tyler, maybe. If the case goes to trial there's talk of the state bringing in a real hotshot to prosecute."

"A ringer?" Jeff asked, frowning. Amanda's frown matched his own. She nodded. "Who?"

"Rumor says Ethan Trask."

"Cripes," Jeff muttered, sitting down on the edge of his desk. "Even I've heard of him."

"Six convictions out of his last seven trials. And in the one he didn't win the defendant plea-bargained down to a lesser offense by promising to turn state's evidence to help solve another murder."

Jeff heard the uncertainty, the raw fear underlying Amanda's words. He pretended not to. "Let's not worry too much about it yet. After all, the grand jury hasn't even agreed to hear the evidence against Granddad. Maybe they'll throw the case out of court."

"Sure," Amanda said, but without much conviction. She squared her shoulders and changed the subject. "I'm starved. Want to come down to Marge's Diner with me and get a burger and fries?"

"I had a sandwich earlier. And I think I'd better hang around here for an hour or so. Just to make sure Cece doesn't run into any problems with the childbirth class."

"Maybe I should hang around, too, just to make sure you don't run into any problems with Cece," Amanda said slyly, sounding a lot like Liza, although they were exact opposites in almost every respect.

"Enough already with this Cece Hayes business! That was over with ten years ago. I barely know the woman anymore."

"You don't have to prove anything to me," his sister said with a chuckle. "I'm a lawyer, remember? All my clients are presumed innocent." She tilted her head and watched his reaction from the corner of her eye. "Until they're proved guilty."

"HOW DID IT GO?"

Cece looked up from the folder of notes and pamphlets she'd been scanning. Jeff was standing in the doorway, one shoulder propped against the frame. He was wearing a brown, short-sleeved shirt, open at the throat, and old, faded jeans that fit him like a glove.

"Fine," she said, making no attempt to hide her welcoming smile. "Just like old times. Breathing exercises are the same all over, but this time we panted in English and not in Spanish." She looked down at the manila folder she was holding. It hadn't been that easy, not really, but it hadn't been as hard to return to the old routine as she'd feared. What she did fear, however, was going home alone to her memories. "Can you tell me where to put this for safekeeping? Liza was anxious to leave and I forgot to ask. I think I have everything else put back where it belongs."

"Just put it on the desk. Mary Skibicki, our head nurse, will clear up when she comes in tomorrow. She's the only full-time employee this operation has. She knows where everything belongs."

"Okay." Cece tilted her head. "But how will I be able to find it if I need it again Thursday evening and Mary isn't here to ask?"

"Good point." He motioned toward the single section of metal filing cabinets at the back of the room. "Try the top drawer. I think that's where it goes."

"If it isn't the right drawer and Mary reads you the riot act you can blame it on me," Cece offered magnanimously.

"I'll remember that." He grinned, the quick upward lifting of one corner of his mouth had always set Cece's pulse pounding in the past. It still did. He leaned both hands on the desk as Cece stood up and slid the file into the drawer. "I want you to know how much I appreciate... Let me rephrase that—how much the clinic directors," he corrected hurriedly, "appreciate your helping out this way."

"I'm glad to do it." Cece slammed the file drawer shut. She turned and found herself staring down at his hands as they rested on the wood—strong hands, with long, tapered fingers and short, blunt nails; a doctor's hands... a lover's hands.

"I won't hold you to it," he said after a moment's silence. "I've been on the receiving end of some of Liza's requests for assistance. There isn't a court in the land that would convict you for backing out." It was an unfortunate choice of words. They both realized it the moment he said it. Jeff's face darkened like a thundercloud. Cece couldn't find the right words to sympathize about his grandfather's predicament, so she answered his first statement instead.

"I wasn't coerced. I can hold my own in a discussion, even with Liza." She smiled to show she was teasing him a little, only to get his mind off his family troubles, nothing more. "I wanted to help."

"It's what you're trained for, after all," he said very quietly, but with more than a hint of a challenge in the words.

"Among other things." Cece picked up a stack of colored pamphlets on family planning and tapped them into order on the desktop.

"Okay," Jeff said, still softly, but no longer challenging. "We'll let it go at that. I'm too grateful for your help to push for explanations that are none of my business." He smiled, but the expression didn't reach his eyes. "If you opt out on us, I'll have to teach this class myself."

"We can't have that, Doctor," Cece said in her best head-nurse voice. She was too off balance to be alone with him like this. She didn't know how to handle herself around him anymore.

"No, indeed we cannot, Nurse Hayes." Jeff straightened but didn't take his eyes from hers. Cece found it hard to breathe all of a sudden. The building was quiet, the room silent, the atmosphere charged. She took one deep, steadying breath, then another, just to make sure her voice wouldn't come out all squeaky and high-pitched. She felt as wobbly and scared and excited in his presence as she had when she was sixteen and he'd whispered in her ear that he wanted to make love with her for the very first time.

Oh God, what had made her think of that after all these years?

"I have to be going," she said. "My mother's picking me up. I don't have a car," she added needlessly, helplessly. She grabbed her sweater off the back of the chair. "It's getting late."

"It's only a little after nine," Jeff pointed out, stepping back from the desk, watching her, studying her reactions, making her more nervous—and aware of him—than ever. "I thought you might like to see the rest of the facilities before I lock up for the night."

"Oh." Cece had no idea what she had expected him to say next. "Yes, sure." She had control of herself once more. There was no reason in the world to act this way. There was no way she could change the fact that Jeff Baron was the first man she'd ever made love with. They had been young and inexperienced and had learned about passion and sex together. It was natural; it had seemed very, very right and very, very wonderful. But it had also been a very long time ago. There was no reason it should have any bearing on the here and now. "I would like to look around. How long has the clinic been operating? Is it privately funded? I can't imagine why my mother didn't write me about it when it opened." She shut her mouth, biting her lower lip between her teeth. She was babbling like an idiot.

"A little over a year and a half. We receive very little public money, sorry to say. And I don't know why your mother didn't write you about it, either," he said, smiling, really smiling as he answered her questions one after the other. "C'mon." He held out his hand. "Let's start the tour."

If she didn't take his hand he'd think she was still angry over their clash at Worthington House. If she did take it, he'd be able to feel her trembling. Trembling because she could feel something happening inside her. It was as if her memories of Steve, the years they'd been together, had started to seal themselves away inside a silken cocoon, leaving her unprotected by the familiar numbness of grief. The feeling was frightening and exhilarating—and all Jeff's fault. Cece stuck her hands in the pockets of her long cotton sweater. Jeff narrowed his eyes but made no attempt to touch her again. He led the way out of the room.

"We have two examination rooms," he told her as they walked. "Anybody who's really sick or badly injured we send over to Tyler General and I work on them there. But most everything else we can do here." He showed her the two side-by-side, sparsely furnished examination rooms, which reminded her a little of the clinic in Santa Rosita. The equipment was secondhand, the metal dressing carts dented, the examining tables old-fashioned and unwieldy, covered with black leather. The glass-fronted medicine cabinets held the barest minimum of supplies and a lone fluorescent light fixture hung from a chain fastened to the ceiling.

"How many patients do you see on average a week?"

"Fifty. Sixty. It depends on the time of year and how bad the unemployment figures are."

She stepped up to the examining table, ran her hands over the cold metal surface of the stirrups. "This is all so very familiar," she said, more to herself than to the man standing beside her.

"People need help the world over," Jeff said quietly.

She didn't want to think about the other world she'd known. "Are you privately funded?" she asked again. Money, or something like it, had come between them once before. It was still an effective barrier. He'd stepped up behind her. He was so close she could feel the heat of his body in the small, cool room.

Jeff laughed, but there was little amusement in the sound. It sounded more like a growl of frustration and anger, but she refused to analyze it further. "We're privately funded, like I said. At least for the time being.''

She spun around, interested in spite of herself. ''You're losing your backing?''

He shrugged, as reluctant, it seemed, to discuss money as she was. ''We'll survive. Isn't that something else that's the same wherever you go? If there are enough people who want to help those less fortunate, they usually find a way to get it done.''

''Yes,'' she replied in a voice that was so low it was barely more than a whisper. ''Thank God they do.'' She ought to apologize, come right out and tell him she'd been mistaken for thinking he didn't care about people anymore. She had been wrong about that, she could see now, very wrong. And she was ashamed, ashamed of herself because it wasn't any easier to apologize now than it had been ten years ago.

''Shh, Cece. Don't say anything else. Don't start one of your save-the-world lectures. Don't stir up the past. It's too close to us tonight. Can't you feel it?''

''Yes.''

He reached out, took her in his arms, pulled her near, and after a moment's hesitation she came into his embrace, but not willingly. He felt her resistance and looked at her for a long time. She closed her eyes.

He lowered his head and kissed her. Thoughts of noble, self-sacrificing apologies flew out of her mind, leaving her unpleasantly aware of the loss of her sustaining grief. Instead, she felt a surge of need and desire that made her dizzy and weak. And it was Jeff's fault. She made a protesting, desperate little sound at the back of her throat, and he lifted his head to look down at her once again, bracketing her head between his hands.

"I've wanted to do that since the first time I saw you back in town," he said. His breath was warm on her lips, his body hard and strong against hers.

"I didn't want you to."

"Why not?" He traced the outline of her lips with the tip of his thumb. She let him, bewildered by her body's betrayal of her mind's direction. Her body felt reckless and desirable and she knew she was alive again inside in places she thought had died of grief.

"It's hard not to remember that the last time you kissed me you left town the next day, without saying goodbye." Surely he hadn't forgotten he'd run out on her? Surely he didn't think she would stand here like a confused teenager and let him kiss her anger and betrayal away without explaining himself?

"I'm sorry," he said, as though that was enough. "I'm sorry as hell." He kissed her again and she kissed him back. Kissing Jeff was like old times, as well as totally new and unexpected, and that realization was even more frightening than the first. He was a man today, not a boy. She was a woman, not a girl. That was the difference. But she knew enough, now, not to let herself be hurt by this man again.

This time when he stopped kissing her, let her breathe and think again, she stepped out of his arms. "Saying you're sorry isn't enough, Jeff. I want to know why you walked out on me all those years ago."

"Don't, Cece." He didn't attempt to take her in his arms again. Instead, he lifted his hand and stroked her hair, let the fine strands slip through his fingers. "Let's start over. Now. Tonight." His eyes were dark, with pain and anger like her own. She closed her eyes, refusing to recognize his regret. "We've both been through some rough times the past couple of years. Let's not dig up hard feelings that are even further in the past."

She didn't think that was possible. "All I want to know is why you acted the way you did."

"You really don't know, do you?" he said, shaking his head. He touched her cheek. His hand was trembling, but not from passion. "Cece, please. My father's death . . . his suicide is still hard to talk about. Don't ask me about it tonight. I don't—"

Car headlights stabbed through the window. Jeff turned his head, looked away, and when he looked back the naked vulnerability in his eyes was gone. He was in control of himself once more.

"My mother's here," she stated needlessly. What had Jeff been going to say? She wished Annabelle was far away, anywhere but in the parking lot of the free clinic, honking the horn of her sedan.

"Caught us smooching on the porch again," he said, sounding relieved, not embarrassed. He didn't smile. "Look, Cece. I apologize for taking advantage of the moment like this. Let's just chalk it up to old times' sake and forget it, okay?"

"No." Cece refused to be distracted. "My mother can wait. What were you going to tell me, Jeff? I want to know."

"Nothing. I was a heel ten years ago. I walked out on you and broke your heart."

"You didn't break my heart." It hurt her to see him this way, his jaw hard, his eyes bleak with self-loathing.

"No." He moved his hand as if to touch her again, then stuck his thumb in the waistband of his jeans instead. "You found Steve. I never knew him, but I know if you loved him, he was a great guy."

"He was," she whispered around a lump in her throat.

"And I found Caroline. Believe me, being married to her was punishment enough for breaking off with you. She avenged you just fine." He turned away.

Cece put her hand on his arm. "Don't say that. I'm sorry your marriage couldn't have been as happy as mine." He was hurting and she didn't know how to make it better. Letting him kiss her had only made it worse. When he'd left her, all those years ago, she'd mentally accused him of selling out their youthful ideals. But he'd always been a caring person. She should have known he wouldn't change. "Jeff, about what just happened . . . it shouldn't have." She had to start somewhere. She reached out and put her hand on his arm to stop him from leaving.

He stopped but didn't turn around. "It was my fault, Cece. I kissed you first."

"I kissed you back."

A muscle in his jaw jumped and the corner of his mouth twisted into a smile. "Then let's call it a draw. A mistake. A whimsy. Just forget it." He started walking. "C'mon. Your mom's honking the horn again. She must be getting antsy out there."

"Jeff." She was as angry and confused as he was, only she wasn't ready to walk away. She wasn't a girl anymore. She was a woman and determined to have her say. "I think—"

His voice was soft; his words were steel, but their meaning was unclear and tempered with her dismay. "Don't think. Just feel . . . the way you used to."

"Mom, what are you doing up this late?" Jeff could barely discern Alyssa's slim figure sitting in the big wing chair near the fireplace. He'd only stepped into the huge formal living room to turn off a table lamp that had been left burning.

"I couldn't sleep very well," she said, not rising from her chair. "I might ask the same question of you."

"It always takes me a day or two to get my internal clock reset after coming off a round of night duty. I've been out at the lake, sitting on the dock, swatting mosquitoes." It was a version of the truth. He'd been swatting mosquitoes and thinking of Cece Hayes.

"Are you hungry?"

Jeff shook his head. It was nearly two. He didn't like the idea of his mother being awake at this hour—she needed her rest. They all did, if they were going to face Judson's probable indictment and trial with a minimum of stress. "Do you want me to get you something to help you sleep?"

"Will it stop my dreams?" she asked in such a sad voice that his heart squeezed painfully.

"If you want." He came closer and she stood up, looking up at him without a trace of her usual delicate smile.

"No." She shook her head very slightly. "If I dream perhaps I'll remember something about the night my mother disappeared. Something that will help me put the pieces back together, not just cause me to ask more questions of myself."

"Don't force yourself, Mom." His voice was rough and grated a little on the words. He hated to see her hurting this way. She'd had enough trouble and heartache the past few years. "It was a very long time ago. You were just a little girl."

"But I was there. I know I was. I just can't remember anything else that will be of any help to Dad." She lifted her hand to her temple, rubbing the skin as if she were in pain.

"Give it time. C'mon. Let's have a snack, raid the refrigerator and give Clara something to get into a snit about tomorrow. Then go to bed, rest, put Margaret's disappearance out of your mind for the time being." He made his tone deliberately brisk and physicianlike.

"Yes, Doctor," she said with a proud little smile. "I only wish it was that easy." She sighed as she stood up, the top of her head coming level with his chin. She linked her arm in his as they walked out of the big, high-ceilinged room in the house where Alyssa had spent her lonely childhood, and where she'd returned after she was widowed.

"Me, too, Mom." He patted her hand, not knowing what else to say.

Their lives seemed to be going around in circles, between the house and the lodge on the lake, between the night more than forty years ago when Margaret Ingalls had died and the present. Even though Margaret's remains had been laid to rest in Tyler Cemetery weeks ago in a private family funeral, there had been no sense of peace or closure in the ceremony. All of the questions surrounding her murder still remained. Jeff didn't see any way to break the cycle, unless the truth about his grandmother's death was finally revealed. But he wasn't like Liza, rushing headlong to uncover old secrets, or even like Amanda, dealing with evidence as it arose. Like his mother, part of him didn't want to know the truth. As far as he was concerned, it could only hurt his family more: another circle, a noose of innuendo and circumstantial evidence tightening around his grandfather's neck, threatening at the same time to strangle them all.

CHAPTER FOUR

"OKAY, CECE, what's going on?" Jeff came striding into the emergency room, heading straight for the curtained cubicle where Violet Orthwein lay in a stupor, already connected to monitors. Blood samples were being drawn by a nurse as Cece and the paramedics watched from nearby.

"We found her like this about fifteen minutes ago," Cece explained, stepping out of his way. She had no authority here at Tyler General, but it was hard to remain passive on the sidelines. Violet was her patient, in her charge. "She was fine when she had her bath this morning, but when the aide stopped by her room to help her get ready for breakfast, she was like this. I knew you were on duty so we had the paramedics bring her straight here."

"Good." He nodded tersely, then bent to examine the frail old lady lying on the high, hard bed. She looked small and childlike against the white sheet, and very still. "Nothing unusual happened, you said?" He gestured to the nurse for a lighted scope to peer into Violet's eyes as he spoke.

"Nothing," Cece replied sharply, shoving her hands into the pockets of her skirt to keep herself from pushing forward, shouldering the emergency room nurse aside to assist Jeff herself. She wanted to help Violet, not just answer questions about her for Jeff's benefit.

"Can you get me a list of her medications?"

"I know them." Cece reeled them off as Jeff continued his exam.

"No injectable drugs?" He stood up, looking at her with a frown between his dark brows, not a hint of what had passed between them a few days earlier evident in his expression or his tone.

"None." Cece hoped her voice and face were equally dispassionate. Inside she was anything but unmoved. Her heart was hammering against her ribs, not only because of her anxiety over Violet's condition, but because she was with Jeff again.

"Are you certain?"

"Yes, Doctor." Cece stood a little taller, spoke a little more forcefully. "I'm positive."

"Then what's this?" He indicated a small reddened area on the old lady's leg where her nightgown had ridden up on her thigh. "It's a needle puncture. It can't be anything else." Cece moved forward, past the openly curious paramedics and the nurse, who'd stopped what she was doing to look also.

"I—I don't know how it got there." She hated having to say that, but there was no denying Jeff's observation. Her own eyes told her he was right. The puncture mark was recent and couldn't be mistaken for anything else.

"Who's on duty this morning?"

"Juanita Pelsten in extended care, and I'm filling in on the assisted-living floor."

Jeff nodded but didn't say anything else. He handed the blood samples to the nurse. "Get those down to the lab and run a full scan on them." He glanced at the monitors beeping and flashing on shelves just above eye level. "And if we find what I think we're going to find—" He broke off to check his patient once more. "Violet," he said, shaking her shoulder gently but firmly. "Violet, wake up!"

The elderly woman groaned slightly, shook her head feebly as if to answer, or perhaps deny, his request.

The nurse hurried off to do Jeff's bidding. Cece stepped forward quickly, a little defiantly, to take her place. "Violet," she called, taking the tiny cold hand in her own. "It's Cece. Talk to me."

"No," came the whispered response. Violet opened confused, faded brown eyes and stared up at Cece. "No."

"It's Cece, Violet. Can you answer the doctor?"

"Too sleepy," the woman mumbled.

"What happened?"

Violet seemed confused but at least she was attempting to respond to the questions. "I'm so tired."

Cece patted her hand. "Then sleep. We'll talk later."

"Okay." She drifted off again. Cece glanced up at the monitors anxiously, but the readings had leveled out and remained steady.

"That doesn't tell us much," Jeff said, still frowning as he, too, scanned the monitors.

"No," Cece admitted. "Only that she's tired."

The emergency room nurse came back and handed Jeff a computer readout. Cece watched and waited as she read the results of Violet's preliminary blood tests.

"We'll keep her here for the time being," he said gruffly. "I want to keep a close eye on her. Have a narcotic antagonist ready to go. I mean at the bedside, not on a cart somewhere. Check her vital signs every five minutes and let me know if there's any change." He turned away from the nurse to face Cece head-on. Their eyes met and Cece felt the contact as if it had been physical. If he was still angry with her, still sorry he'd kissed her that night at the clinic, it didn't show. "Come into my office. I want to talk to you."

"What did you order a narcotic antagonist for?" Cece demanded the moment they were inside the small, glass-walled cubicle. If he could be all-business, so could she.

Glancing around, she noticed nothing marked the room as belonging to him except a photograph of his family. Taken recently, possibly at Cliff and Liza's wedding, it showed them all smiling and happy. At another time Cece would have examined it carefully; now she paid it scant attention.

"Because of her symptoms. And because of this." He offered her the readout. Cece took it reluctantly. She was certain she didn't want to learn what it had to tell her. Her brain was already in a whirl, with so many questions demanding to be answered she didn't even know which to ask first.

"Morphine sulfate?"

"Computers don't lie." Jeff flicked the paper with the tip of his finger. "Whoever injected Violet this morning gave her morphine." His voice told her he was certain of the facts. "She has all the symptoms. I don't have to repeat them to you. You probably know them as well as I do."

Better, she thought wildly. She'd given Steve morphine to ease the terrible pain of his injuries before he died, trapped in the wreckage of their small hospital.

"It's impossible."

"It isn't impossible. It happened."

His words hit her like a blow. For a moment she was afraid she might be ill. She stared down at the paper in her hand so hard the figures danced and blurred before her eyes, but they didn't change.

"We can't rule out the possibility that the same drug caused Wilhelm Badenhop's respiratory arrest, as well."

"No!" She couldn't accept the point she knew he was going to make.

"Cece, we have to proceed on that assumption. I have no alternative but to recommend an investigation of your nursing staff and drug-dispensing policies."

"Worthington House follows every state and federal guideline in our nursing procedures." She wasn't about to let him see how badly his accusations had shaken her. Had she been lax? Had some terrible mistake been made that she could have prevented? "We inventory all restricted medications and narcotics each shift. There's no way a mistake like that could be made." She spoke instinctively, from the heart.

"It did happen, Cece," Jeff said without heat or anger, but with complete conviction.

He was watching her closely and she realized her shock and anguish must show plainly on her face. She made her clenched hands relax, tried to make her voice as even and steady as his. "At the moment I can't dispute your findings or your conclusions." She caught her lower lip between her teeth. "If you think Violet's out of danger, I'll return to Worthington House. I'll have to discuss this matter with Mr. Kellaway."

"Certainly. I'll talk to Cecil myself, as soon as I can get away from here. There's no need to have this go any further than the three of us for the time being."

"Thank you." Her words were stiff and formal, the way she felt. Jeff looked like a stranger, sounded like a stranger. Only two days ago he'd held her in his arms, kissed her, made her remember, despite the bitterness of their breakup, all the joyous wonder of first love.

"I have to do what's best for the residents, Cece."

Her thoughts were in turmoil. She didn't hear the unspoken plea for understanding in his words.

"I wouldn't expect you to do less," she replied tonelessly. He looked hard and angered, a professional healer determined to find out who had betrayed the helpless patients they were sworn to protect. It didn't matter who stood in his way, she realized, and that included herself.

Cece turned without another word. She wanted to get to the bottom of this matter as badly as Jeff. She'd come to the defense of her nurses automatically, but the truth was she didn't know some of them all that well. Could there be a potential killer among them? Would they ever know for sure unless they caught someone in the act of administering a not-prescribed drug to a patient? She couldn't be everywhere at once. How could she keep this from happening again?

JEFF CLIMBED the front steps of Worthington House almost as slowly as one of the residents might. It had been a long day and it wasn't over yet. He wished George Phelps was back in town. If he'd never left, Jeff wouldn't have gotten this mess dumped in his lap. George was on the board of directors of Worthington House, as well as being resident physician. To Jeff it seemed unlikely that anyone could have knowingly injected Violet and Wilhelm with potentially fatal doses of morphine unless the nursing procedures were criminally lax. That just didn't seem possible. Tyler was too small a town, the families of residents too involved in their care and vigilant of their well-being to allow any abuses to occur. But the alternative... That someone was purposely injecting innocent old people with potentially fatal doses of narcotic was even harder to believe. He didn't expect Cecil Kellaway to shed any light on the mystery. He just hoped the administrator would cooperate with an investigation and not take it into his head to fight him all the way.

Jeff walked down the hall, past the main-floor nurses' station by the staircase, and knocked on the door to Cecil's office, which was situated between the dining room and kitchen. The door opened and the tall, heavysct, very nervous administrator stood aside so Jeff could enter the office. The walls, lined with glass-fronted cabinets, and a wide marble shelf along the back wall, now dotted with plants, photos and small statues, made Jeff decide this long narrow room must have been the butler's pantry when the house was new.

"Jeff, come in." Cecil waved him to a seat. "You know Cece Hayes, don't you?" He waved at Cece, too.

"Yes. We went to high school together."

"Did you?" Cecil sat down behind his desk, paying no attention to how Cece and Jeff greeted each other.

Jeff was glad of that. All he got from her was a polite nod and the faintest of smiles. He couldn't expect much more after the way he'd behaved the other night. Damn, why did she have to affect him like that? Why couldn't he have told her the truth about why he'd walked out on her? His dad had been dead for ten years now. He'd thought the hurt was healed, but it wasn't. When he saw her again, it had all come back, and he realized he wasn't ready to deal with it yet, even for Cece.

"You'd think after eight years in Tyler I'd remember everyone has known everyone else from the cradle."

Cecil liked to affect a slight British accent. Most people ignored it; a few made fun of him behind his back. Jeff knew, because George Phelps had told him that the man had been born and raised in Akron, Ohio. Jeff had never paid much attention to the harmless charade, until now. Was there a more sinister motive behind the administrator's playacting? Had Wilhelm or Violet agreed to turn over their assets to Worthington House in return for care and residence at the facility for as long as they lived? Was Cecil hoping to make a profit from their early demise?

And what about Juanita Pelsten? She was getting on in years. With his own ears he'd heard her tell Cece to let Wilhelm Badenhop "go." Had she truly thought the old man was beyond medical help...or had she been responsible for his condition in the first place?

He wondered what Cece's thoughts on the matter were. Did landing in the middle of this kind of situation make you suspect everyone involved? If it did, he was glad he hadn't decided on a career as a private investigator.

"I imagine Cece has filled you in on the details," Jeff began.

"Yes, she has." Kellaway nodded in Cece's direction as he took his seat behind the desk. "We've discussed the possibility of a connection between the incidents, and frankly, I'm having a hard time believing any of this."

"Well, believe it," Jeff said.

"We've inventoried our narcotics. Every dose is accounted for."

On cue, Cece passed Jeff a sheaf of medication inventories. He glanced through them. They were all signed and initialed, double-checked. Indeed, everything looked to be in order in that respect. But if Kellaway was responsible for the attacks, he'd have made sure they were. Jeff put his nagging suspicions aside and concentrated on the facts at hand.

"We can't rule out the possibility that your supply is tainted, adulterated—that it's been tampered with," he concluded bluntly.

Cecil looked shocked, then angry. His mouth opened and closed with a snap.

"It makes sense, Mr. Kellaway." Cece spoke up for the first time, fixing her attention on her superior, ignoring Jeff as she had since he entered the room. "*If* someone on staff is responsible for these . . . incidents, it would follow that they would try to cover their tracks. I suggest we return all our narcotics to the pharmacy and have them replaced with a new supply."

"I want all the morphine sent to a lab in Madison to be analyzed first," Jeff broke in.

Both heads swung in his direction. Cecil looked as if he'd like to throw him bodily out of the office. Cece looked angry but resigned.

"Of course," she said. "We should have thought of that ourselves."

Kellaway gave her a murderous look. Obviously he didn't appreciate his new nursing supervisor siding with the enemy. "Is that really necessary?" he asked. "Neither Wilhelm nor Violet remembers anything suspicious happening. We don't know for sure the two incidents are even connected. Or that in Violet's case the injection wasn't merely an unfortunate accident."

"We can't go on that assumption," Jeff retorted.

"Why not?" Cecil leaned back in his chair, looking as though he'd scored a point.

"Because it's too dangerous. Look, just keeping this investigation among the three of us is skirting the limits of the law. By rights, I should have turned this over to the appropriate authorities. You know that, Kellaway."

"You have no proof that anything other than a mistake in medication has been made. There's no grounds for criminal action, or even disciplinary measures at this time. I give you my word, there will be no more incidents." Cecil leaned forward once more, looking earnest, and folded his hands on the desk.

"That's not good enough." Jeff didn't give him a chance to retaliate. It was time to drop his bombshell. "I've been doing some checking myself today. It's possible there's been a third incident."

"A third incident?" Cecil's face grew red. From the corner of his eye Jeff saw Cece's hands tighten on the arms of her chair.

"Luetta Peterson?" she asked in a voice that was steady but held a great deal of strain.

"Good God, man, are you crazy? That woman was terminally ill with cancer."

"But by all reports her condition at the time was stable. She died of respiratory arrest, just as Wilhelm Badenhop almost did."

"That's right." Cecil subsided into his chair once again. "But the entire course of her illness was very sudden. She'd only been diagnosed three months earlier."

"I understand Dr. Phelps didn't hesitate to sign the death certificate," Cece interjected, still sounding strained but in control, still looking past him, through him, as if he weren't there. Jeff wondered briefly, with a stab of almost physical pain, if she would ever forgive him for doing this to her.

"I agree, at the time there was no cause for suspicion." He wasn't certain George Phelps would have noticed if there had been something suspicious about Luetta's death. Mary had been making his life hell just about then. "I'm saying that now, in the light of what's happened in the past few days, the circumstances surrounding Luetta's death should be reviewed."

"We'll see to it at once." Kellaway was pale as a ghost. All the bluster and bombast had seeped out in a hissing sigh of worry and disbelief. "This whole thing is absolutely unbelievable."

"Cece, I suggest you start requiring two licensed nurses to be on hand if and when any narcotic is given," Jeff suggested.

"I've already done that. Actually, that's why I'm here this late at night, to brief the third-shift nurses on the new regs."

"Good." He wanted to say something more—praise her initiative and professionalism, ask her to be on his side, help him solve this mess—but he didn't say anything else, only nodded his head once in approval.

"Just let us solve this…problem…from within our own ranks, Baron," Cecil said, regaining his equilibrium. He got to his feet, signaling an end to the discussion. "As I said before, the only proof you have that anything's happened is the incident today. I think you're out of line trying to connect Wilhelm's episode to Violet's and I think you're downright crazy trying to link Luetta Peterson's death with either of them."

Jeff stood, too. He'd taken just about all he was going to from the officious administrator. "I don't need any more proof to turn you in to the state nursing home examiners, Kellaway," he said, doing nothing to hide the menace in his voice.

Kellaway stood his ground. "You have nothing but your own suspicions. You're the only one who thinks some kind of crazed murderer is running around loose in Worthington House—because that's obviously what's on your mind, due to your own family situation."

"You jackass!" It might just be worth the scandal, Jeff thought, to come around the desk and punch Cecil Kellaway in the mouth.

Cece remained seated. "Dr. Baron, Mr. Kellaway, please. The only issue of consequence here is the fact that our patients are at risk and we need to take every precaution to ensure their safety. At the moment that also requires us to keep this among ourselves. Do you agree?"

"Yes." Kellaway sat down, straightening his tie with hands that weren't quite steady. He cleared his throat. "Sorry, Baron. That comment was out of line."

Jeff remained standing, one hand on the back of his chair, the other shoved into the pocket of his slacks. "Forget it," he said gruffly. He'd thought that over the past few weeks he'd gotten used to the snide remarks, the innuendos about his grandfather's possible involvement in his wife's murder. But obviously he hadn't.

"Rest assured, my staff and I will do everything in our power to get to the bottom of this affair. You have my word, it won't happen again. Not if I can help it."

"And you have my word, Kellaway," Jeff said between his teeth, "that if anything at all suspicious does occur again I'll go to the authorities the moment I hear about it. Understood?"

"Understood. Good night, Baron."

"Kellaway." Jeff nodded curtly. "Good night, Cece."

"Goodbye, Dr. Baron." She stood up. "Is there anything else you wish to speak to me about, Mr. Kellaway?"

"No."

"Then I'll be in my office until it's time to meet with the night-shift nurses."

"Very well." He dismissed her and Jeff with a wave of his hand. He was already studying a sheaf of papers on his desk and didn't look up again as they left.

Jeff's right hand balled into a fist. "I should have popped him when I had the chance."

Cece glanced up at him, startled. "That wouldn't have helped matters at all."

He rubbed his hand across the stubble of beard on his chin. "Yeah, I guess you're right." He wondered what she'd say about his suspicion of Kellaway, or of Juanita Pelsten, for that matter.

"I know I am. It would be all over town by morning. And rumors of what's happened here would be thirty minutes behind."

"No argument there." He grinned, a rueful twist of his lips, no more. "You were always good at taking the long view."

"I don't have a long view on this," she admitted, steepling her fingers before her lips, looking down at the floor before lifting her eyes to his. "It's too close. I'm too personally involved."

She looked troubled. There were faint lines between her delicate brows. She was also uncomfortable in his presence. In a way, he'd become the enemy, personally and professionally. He didn't want her to feel that way. He wanted her back in his arms where she belonged. He wanted her close so that he could dream dreams of their future together. The future, he was beginning to realize, they should have been sharing for the past ten years. But there were things to settle between them, from the past as well as the present, before that could happen.

"Come outside on the porch with me." He wanted to have her alone with him, even if they had to go on talking about the drug overdoses. "Let's call it neutral territory." He tipped his head to indicate the surroundings of Worthington House, the duty nurse trying to appear not to listen to their stilted conversation. "We can talk this through. Compare notes."

"No." She shook her head. "Cecil would never permit that." She lowered her voice until it was little more than a haunting whisper. "If we talk, it will have to be about ourselves."

Was he ready to tell her the truth about why he'd left her at college in Ann Arbor and never returned? She knew his father had killed himself. She'd never known what that had done to him inside. He wasn't certain he could tell her yet. That was what ate at him, not his failed marriage or her memories of another man.

"All right," he temporized. "We won't talk about anything important."

Cece shook her head again. "No. I can't." Her tone held finality. Jeff felt a spasm of fear tighten his gut, then felt it overtaken by a determination to push past the new barriers she was erecting between them. He touched her arm, prepared to talk all night if he had to to overcome her resistance, but he never got the chance. A breathy, frightened voice called Cece's name from the doorway of the activity room just inside the main entrance.

"Cece. Ms. Hayes, can I talk to you?"

"What is it, Freddie?" The strain was gone from Cece's voice, hidden, pushed aside, as she gave Freddie her full attention.

"I...I want to talk to you, okay?" She looked at Jeff suspiciously. He smiled. And after a moment Freddie smiled back, but her eyes slid away from his. She hung her head. "Please, Cece."

"Would you like to come and sit on the porch with us?" Jeff asked, unwilling to let Cece go, almost certain she would have to second his idea if Freddie approved of the plan.

"Well..." She scuffed her foot on the floor. She was wearing a ratty terry-cloth robe, belted tightly around her stocky figure, and quilted boots that tied around her ankles. They were blue-and-green plaid and, like her robe, had seen better days. "Is it all right if I go outside in my jams?" she asked Cece.

"It's all right. C'mon." Cece held out her hand. Freddie took it, like the child she was inside. "I...I heard about Violet. I...how is she?"

Jeff was only half-listening to her stilted questions. He was more interested in Cece as she walked before him, in the sway of her hips beneath her skirt, the fall of light on her hair, the sweet, fresh scent of flowers that drifted around her.

"She's going to be all right," Cece said comfortingly as she and Freddie settled themselves in rocking chairs on the screened porch. Jeff leaned one hip against the porch rail and rested his shoulder against a supporting pillar. It was hot and sultry, the air thick with the sound of cicadas and the drone of mosquitoes.

"I don't know what happened. I got her breakfast tray. She was crying a little," Freddie said anxiously.

"She said she couldn't see good at all anymore. She almost spilled her juice. She wished she could go to heaven with the angels and saints."

"I'm sure she didn't mean that," Cece said, making her voice a soothing monotone as Freddie clung tightly to her hand. She leaned forward and patted the hand clutching hers. "Violet has been lonely since her husband died. You remember how hard it was for you when you first came here, don't you?"

"I missed my house. I missed my mom." Her face puckered up and Jeff thought she might start to cry, but she didn't. "I didn't want to come here but Dr. George said I'd like it. He said I could help people." Now Freddie was leaning forward too, earnestly. "I helped my mom and now I help people here."

"And you do very well," Cece said, disengaging her hand. "You are a great help to us."

"I try," Freddie said, shaking her head. "But sometimes it doesn't work right." She stood up. "I'd better go. It's time for 'Wheel of Fortune' on TV. I like the pretty dresses Vanna wears." She lumbered off down the porch, toward the door.

"Good night," she said, turning to look back at them from the doorway. "Good night, Cece." She gave a little wave. "Good night, Dr. Jeff."

"'Night, Freddie," Jeff answered, a little surprised she'd remembered his name. They had never spoken before.

"Sleep tight, Freddie." Cece stood up, too. "I have to get back inside, Jeff. Is there anything else you need to discuss with me before I go?" It was still there, the distance between them he'd hoped to breach. She wasn't going to let him get any closer. She looked cool and composed, unapproachable on every level.

A warning voice in his brain, or perhaps in his heart, told him to turn around and walk away. This Cece wasn't the sweet, shy girl he'd left behind at college when he'd returned to his shattered family, his upside-down world in Tyler. She was a woman, sure of herself and determined not to be hurt again. If they resumed a relationship, a love affair today, it would be very different from the love they'd shared a decade ago. He'd have to go slowly. He'd have to be sure of himself this time, not make the mistakes he'd made before.

"No. There's nothing else I want to discuss." He levered himself away from the pillar, making her tip her head slightly to look up at him. His eyes were drawn to the sweet, soft curve of her throat. His head spun and his body tightened with desire, and his heart raced with fear. He was afraid to admit he still loved her—had always loved her—because he might lose her again.

"Then I'll say good-night."

Jeff reached out a hand, preventing her from moving away. He couldn't seem to help himself. "Don't let this come between us, Cece."

"There is no 'us,' Jeff," she said softly. "There hasn't been for ten years."

"That's not how you reacted the other night when I kissed you."

She smiled sadly. "I wasn't thinking at all when you kissed me. You've always had that effect on me." She touched his cheek with the tip of her finger, so briefly he wondered if he'd imagined the fleeting caress. "But I've been thinking a lot since you sent me on my way that night."

"Damn it, Cece. I don't know what I said that night. Kissing you has always made me a little crazy." He wanted to pull her close. He wanted to run like hell. He did neither, just stood there, with his hands shoved into his pockets, waiting.

"You told me to remember how I felt . . . before."

"I wanted you to remember what a jackass I'd been."

"I know that." She smiled again, quickly, like summer lightning. "But I remembered the good times, too. And that's why I've decided not to let it happen again."

CHAPTER FIVE

ALYSSA TURNED AWAY from the glass-walled catwalk that looked down onto the factory floor. Both assembly lines were operating today, thanks to a contract with one of the big tractor manufacturers to make replacement parts. She'd just finished meeting with the plant manager and Johnny Kelsey, the foreman. For the time being everything at Ingalls Farm and Machinery was running smoothly. Judson would be glad to hear that. He hadn't set foot in the plant since he'd gotten out of jail. That worried Alyssa, but at the moment there was nothing she could do about it.

"How long will this new contract keep both lines running, Mom?" Amanda asked as they walked back into Judson's office and shut the door, muffling the sounds of metal presses and stamping machines sufficiently to allow conversation in a normal tone of voice.

"Two or three more weeks," Alyssa answered, folding her arms beneath her breasts. "After that, we're looking at another partial layoff."

"That will be the third one this year," Amanda remarked, looking up from the page full of figures she'd been studying with her usual intensity.

"I've been keeping count," Alyssa responded dryly. She crossed the familiar room to look out the window behind the desk. It wasn't much of a view. Beyond the graveled driveway and loading dock a high wire fence separated the factory grounds from the surrounding countryside. The grass looked a little brown and faded at the edges, the first sign that summer was almost over. In the cornfield that lay beyond, the stalks were tasseled and green and already heavy with an abundance of ears.

"What do you think, Mom?" Amanda asked suddenly, catching Alyssa off guard. "Should Granddad sell out to those Japanese investors that have been nosing around town?"

"No," Alyssa answered before she could think better of it. But, characteristically, she immediately qualified her response. "It isn't my decision to make." But it was too late. Amanda was already on the attack.

"Does this mean you're thinking of taking over the operation of Ingalls F and M yourself?"

Alyssa laughed, hoping she didn't sound as shaky, as unsure, as she felt inside. "Whatever gave you that idea?"

"I think you'd be good at it."

"Thank you, honey." She could always count on Amanda to champion her cause. How she loved her older daughter. She loved Jeff and Liza too, fiercely, but what she felt for their sister was different. They were much alike, she and Amanda. Sometimes Alyssa thought she might have been Amanda if she'd been born a generation later, been given the encouragement to pursue a career instead of rushing immediately into marriage and motherhood. "I don't agree with you, but thank you for the vote of confidence."

"I'm not just saying that to stroke your ego, Mom. You know I don't operate that way." Amanda laid the papers she'd been reading on top of Judson's desk. "I meant it."

"The thought frightens me to death," Alyssa said lightly with a smile, but her heart thumped inside her chest. Could she do it? Sometimes she wanted very much to try.

"I didn't say it would be easy. But you've got the brains and the skills—"

"I'd hardly call being president of the garden club and sitting on the town council sufficient preparation for running this place," Alyssa broke in.

"You can organize and delegate authority," Amanda went on, refusing to be derailed from her line of thought. "You can listen to advice, weigh the pros and cons, and you know enough to get expert help when you're in over your head. I'd say that gives you a running start at it."

"I'm good at organizing fund-raising dinners and chairing committees to plan the Fourth of July parade, or getting people to donate money to plant new trees in the park. It's not the same as running a multimillion-dollar business."

"I think Granddad would be the first to tell you that it isn't all that different, either." Amanda was sitting in one of the matching leather chairs that faced the desk.

Alyssa turned around to face her. "Your grandfather is my other big worry," she said, deliberately changing the direction of their conversation. She wasn't sure yet what she would do about her role in the plant's future. She would have to wait and see what tomorrow and the next day and the day after that had to bring before she made her decision. "He hasn't set foot outside the house since you brought him home from jail." The word nearly stuck in her throat. Her father in jail. Her father accused of murder—her mother's murder. It was so very hard to believe.

Sensing her distress, Amanda made her tone bracing. "He's a tough old bird. He'll be all right."

"I don't know." Alyssa shook her head, her own dark doubts and fears circling near again. "I don't know."

"Mom, if this case goes to trial, I'll get him the best lawyer I know."

This time it was Alyssa who noticed the faintest tremor of uncertainty in her daughter's voice. "You're going to represent your grandfather and you'll do a great job," she responded with conviction.

"I haven't said I'll take the case," Amanda said helplessly. "I'm a country lawyer, remember. Wills, child custody, divorces and alimony payments. I'm not a criminal lawyer and I'll be up against the best the state can throw at us."

"I have every confidence in you." Alyssa smiled. Her faith in Amanda was absolute. "Your grandfather won't hear of having another lawyer. I thought you understood that.''

"I understand it, all right." Amanda sighed. "I just hope to God I can live up to all your expectations. Especially if I have to go up against Ethan Trask. Let's talk about something else." Amanda rose from her chair. She glanced at her watch. "I'm starved. What are you doing for lunch?"

"I haven't made any plans," Alyssa began, but was interrupted by a knock on the door. "Come in," she called, raising her shoulders in a shrug in reply to Amanda's questioning look.

The door opened and Tisha Olsen walked into the room, her red hair piled high on her head, her eyes heavily made up, her generous mouth boldly outlined with crimson lipstick. She was almost exactly the same age as Alyssa, but looked as if she'd seen, and understood, more of life than Alyssa would ever know. Alyssa smoothed her hands over the soft linen weave of her slacks and stepped forward, halting at the corner of Judson's desk.

"Hello, Tisha, what can I do for you?"

"Hello, Alyssa," the other woman said, stopping short. She swiveled her head, smiled. "Hello, Amanda."

"Hi, Tisha. How did you manage to get away from the Hair Affair this early in the day?"

"I'm playing hooky," Tisha said with another big smile. "And I'm looking for Judson. I saw his car in the staff parking lot." For the first time she hesitated slightly. "I thought…I hoped…he'd decided to come back to work."

"No, he hasn't," Alyssa said, shaking her head.

"Mom drove Granddad's car out here. Hers is in the shop," Amanda offered, when the silence threatened to stretch out longer than it should.

"Well." Tisha lifted her hand to check the tendrils of hair escaping from her combs to curl along her neck. "I guess I'll just have to go up to the house and invite myself to lunch." She looked directly at Alyssa with a grin and a challenge in her eyes.

"Yes," Alyssa surprised herself by saying. "You do that. He needs to get out. He's barricaded himself inside that house as though it were a fortress." She'd never thought she'd find herself asking Tisha Olsen for help, even indirectly, never thought she'd be grateful for her interest and her friendship with Judson. It was just another indication of how much her life had changed over the past months—since the day Margaret's body had been discovered under the willow tree by the lake.

Tisha gave a disdainful sniff. "As if anyone in this town believes he could have done such a thing."

"There are some who do," Alyssa said, her head high, her blue eyes darkened with sadness.

Tisha looked at her sharply, then nodded. "There's always a few, anywhere you go, who like to see someone else suffer. People with small minds and smaller hearts. Listen," she said briskly, more her old self, "I know you don't approve of me seeing your old man."

"That isn't true," Alyssa said, and knew she'd spoken too quickly. "I can't recall ever doing anything or saying anything to give you that impression."

"Alyssa, honey, you don't have to do or say anything. All you have to do is look at me," Tisha said bluntly, without rancor. "It doesn't matter. I've been looked down on by better than you. But the truth of the matter is that I'm good for your father and he's good for me. He treats me like a lady, a lady with a brain and something to say about the world and what goes on in it. I like that. I like him . . . a lot. I'm going to stick by him through this thing, Alyssa Baron, and you can stand with me, or against me and put even more pressure on him."

"Tisha . . ." Alyssa didn't know what she meant to say. She looked down at her hands while she searched for words.

"Look," Tisha went on, "I'm sorry I barged in on you two like this, even if I'm not sorry for what I said. You must have work to do. I'll be on my way."

"If you hurry," Alyssa said before she could stop herself, "you might be able to coax my father out to lunch before Clara starts preparing a meal." She didn't particularly like Tisha Olsen, but Judson obviously enjoyed her company. For the time being that fact, and no other, would guide her conduct toward the woman.

"Okay," Tisha said after a moment or two. "I'll do that." She gave a jaunty little salute. "Goodbye, Amanda."

"Goodbye, Tisha."

"'Bye, Alyssa," she said, once again with a challenge in her voice.

"Goodbye, Tisha."

The door closed behind her.

"Hmm," Amanda said, eyeing her mother as sharply as Tisha had done. "What do you know about that?"

"I don't know what you're talking about," Alyssa said, aligning the desk blotter perfectly with the edge of the desk.

"Oh, come on, Mom. Everyone in Tyler knows Tisha is sweet on Granddad."

"So?" Alyssa managed to raise her head to meet Amanda stare for stare, but she was the first to look away.

"Don't tell me it doesn't bother you to see them together. She's almost your age."

"Do you think I'm so petty as to object to your grandfather's . . . friendships . . . on that basis alone?"

"No." Amanda shook her head and paused a moment. "Maybe she can make Granddad happy."

"The way my mother could not?" Alyssa looked past Amanda, into her memories. "He deserves to be happy. It's just that after all these years . . . alone . . ."

"Mom, it's not our decision," Amanda reminded her gently.

"Of course it isn't. Your grandfather has all his faculties, thank heaven. He can pick his own friends." She emphasized the last word ever so slightly so that Amanda would know she didn't intend to think of

Tisha Olsen as anything else, not now when she had so many other things on her mind.

Amanda didn't say anything for a long moment. "I know," she said, breaking the silence that was filled with the muted sounds of the assembly lines on the work floor below, "let's have a picnic. We can stop at the market and pick up some meat and fruit and cheese at the deli counter and take it out to the lake. We'll swing by the boathouse and collect Liza and maybe Cliff, and eat by the water. It's a great day, not too hot, not too humid. What do you say?"

"I don't know," Alyssa began, framing her refusal as she spoke so as not to hurt her daughter's feelings.

But Amanda wasn't so easily put off. "No excuses, Mom. You're beginning to look like skin and bones. You probably haven't been eating one good meal a day since this whole thing started."

"Clara and your brother make sure I eat." But it was true her appetite had been practically nonexistent for weeks. She ate what was put in front of her, but if food wasn't there she didn't miss it. "I really do have a hundred things to do this afternoon," she tried again.

"If you go home you're going to have to have lunch with Granddad and Tisha," Amanda said slyly. "You don't want to feel like the odd woman out, do you?"

Alyssa frowned, then smiled quickly when she saw the teasing glint in Amanda's blue eyes. "Okay, you win. I would like to get outside, sit in the sun. It's been so gloomy and overcast the past few days."

"And tomorrow it's going to be eighty-five degrees and humid as the devil. You'll be trapped back inside, sitting in front of the air conditioner, trying to keep cool."

"You know what they say about the weather in Tyler," Alyssa said, taking her purse from the desk as Amanda retrieved hers from the coatrack by the door.

"Stick around for twenty-four hours and it'll change."

They both laughed. It was an old joke, but it held more than a kernel of truth. "They have fresh lemonade at Marge's," Amanda said as they walked out the door. "And blueberry pie. The first of the season."

"Let's get one and take it along," Alyssa said with a smile. "Cliff loves blueberry pie."

"And Liza still can't cook worth a darn. I don't think we'll have to ask my new brother-in-law twice to join us."

"No, I don't suppose we will," Alyssa said with a giggle, linking her arm through her daughter's as they started down the wide, noisy metal stairs leading to the ground floor exit. "I don't suppose we will."

"Okay, Cece, taste this." Britt Hansen handed her friend a small dish of frozen yogurt. "It's Double Dutch Chocolate. What do you think?"

Cece took a bite, let the yogurt melt on her tongue, savored its richness, then took another bite.

"Well," Britt pointed out impatiently, "how is it?"

"My Lord, do you mean to tell me this stuff only has seventy calories a serving?" Cece asked, staring down at her dish with a disbelieving expression on her face. "It's great. It tastes . . ." Words failed her. "It tastes great."

"I take it that means you like it," Britt said, beaming with pride at her latest accomplishment. "Do you think there's a market for Yes! Yogurt's latest product?"

"I'll take a ton," Cece said and meant it. "What other flavors are you planning to bring it out in?"

"Strawberry and blueberry for starters," Britt said, picking up a spoon from the table between them to steal a taste from Cece's dish. "And vanilla, of course." Cece grabbed her dish away.

"Nothing doing. Get your own."

Britt laughed and sat back in the rocker, licking her spoon contentedly after Cece laughingly offered her another bite of yogurt.

"You'll be a millionaire by this time next summer if this takes off like I think it will."

Britt shook her head. "Don't count on it. Jake says the start-up costs alone will eat up the profits for the first two years, not to mention production and advertising costs, market research—"

"Enough," Cece said, lifting her spoon in a gesture of surrender. "I've heard enough. But I haven't tasted enough. How about another scoop? Please."

"You'll spoil your lunch and I've been slaving over a hot microwave all morning," Britt said, rising from her chair to do as Cece asked.

"Don't worry. I'll eat. I always eat when I'm upset." Now why had she said that? Cece wondered.

Britt had already opened the screen door. She turned around, closed it quietly and returned to her rocker. "Okay, spill it," she said, as she'd done so often through junior high and high school. "Something's bothering you. Otherwise you wouldn't be here in the middle of a workday, eating my yogurt and moping around on my porch."

"I'm not moping," Cece said, too abruptly. She scraped her spoon noisily over the bottom of her dish, then swallowed the last drops of melting yogurt.

"Okay, you're not moping, you're just...subdued," Britt said, brushing back a stray wisp of strawberry blond hair that had escaped her braid. "Is it Jeff?"

"No," Cece said. "I mean, yes and no." She sighed. "Yes, it's Jeff. And it's Worthington House." Quickly, with a minimum of words, she told Britt of the troubling incidents at the retirement center. There was no need to ask Britt to keep her revelations confidential. She had complete faith in her old friend's ability to keep a secret, big or small.

"And Jeff has jumped on his white horse and galloped off to do battle with this unknown enemy."

"Well, yes," Cece said, uncomfortable with Britt's assessment of his character. She'd always thought Jeff was a white knight, too. Until he'd left Ann Arbor, left her and returned to Tyler and his family business, family money, all those years ago. He'd known she couldn't follow him. She'd been on scholarship, the only way she could afford to attend college. He'd known that, but he hadn't cared enough to come back to her. That was what she'd thought then. That was what she thought now.

"That's not an answer," Britt pointed out, practical as ever.

"He's insisting on an investigation. Which is exactly what he should do. It's just that..." She broke off, finding it difficult to voice her doubts about her own abilities, even to Britt.

"You wonder if you've made some mistake, overlooked something or...someone...that might be causing the problem."

"Yes," Cece said, resting her head against the high back of the old-fashioned wooden rocker. "That's it exactly. I haven't slept for a week, going over procedures and evaluations in my mind. I know I haven't been nursing supervisor at Worthington House long. But I trust my nurses. I can't believe any of them are responsible for these terrible accidents."

"And, of course, there's also Jeff," Britt said softly.

Cece turned her head without lifting it from the back of the chair. "Yes, there's Jeff."

"You make him sound like a disease," Britt said with a gentle, teasing giggle. "Like you're having a relapse of something dreadful."

"Maybe I am," Cece said, staring out over the barnyard and the meadow beyond. She watched Britt's goats ambling about in the short-cropped grass for a long moment. "Sometimes I wish I were back in Santa Rosita, even if I did miss Steve every minute of the day and night. Britt?" she asked, keeping her voice even with a great deal of effort. "How long did it take you to get over losing Jimmy?"

"I don't think I'll ever get over losing him," Britt said matter-of-factly. "But the pain fades away and the good memories don't. And then I was lucky, so very lucky, to have found love again. Like you."

"I don't love Jeff," Cece said quickly, too quickly.

"All right, you aren't falling back in love with Jeff. But don't rule out the possibility. You didn't die in that earthquake with Steve, Cece. You're young and healthy and alive. You have a great deal of love to offer a man. Don't let guilt over what you can't change deny you happiness in the future."

"Is that what you think I'm doing? Denying my feelings for Jeff because I feel guilty that Steve is dead and I'm not?"

"I think there's a danger that might happen."

Cece winced. Britt had always been honest to a fault.

"Remember, I've been down that road before." Britt shaded her eyes with her hand, looked out over the meadow to the lake shimmering blue and gold in the August sun. "Here comes Jake and the kids," she said, and the happiness in her voice was plain to hear, painful to listen to in Cece's vulnerable state.

"I'm not falling in love with Jeff again," she insisted weakly.

"Yes, you are," Britt said bluntly, putting her hands on the arms of her chair, pushing herself to a standing position. "I'm in love again, too. I see the signs."

"No," Cece said, but without conviction. "That was kid stuff, over ten years ago."

"Then why do you look so miserable now?"

"I'm not falling in love with Jeff Baron again!"

"Okay," Britt said, shaking her head in defeat. "I won't argue with you anymore...today. But just remember what I said. I'll be only too happy to say, 'I told you so' at the wedding."

"Britt," Cece said miserably, "stop it."

"All right. I'll change the subject," Britt promised, taking pity on her confusion. "Come on inside. If you're a good girl and clean your plate I'll let you sample the blueberry frozen yogurt before you head back into town."

CHAPTER SIX

CECE WALKED down the steps of the Tyler library, blinking a little in the bright afternoon light. She fished around in her bag for her sunglasses but knew she wouldn't find them. In her mind's eye she pictured them right where she'd left them—on the dashboard of the car. She shifted the books she'd checked out of the library to her left arm and started walking. It was hot, very hot, and she almost turned around and went back inside the dim cool building to escape the blast-furnace effect of the August sun.

The books she'd collected were heavy. She stopped to put them inside the big canvas tote she had slung over her shoulder. The sun beat down on her uncovered head and in less than a minute she felt sweat begin to trickle down between her shoulder blades. She wished she were already home. And at the moment nothing sounded better than a big cool glass of lemonade and a good book. She had enough reading material to last the weekend.

She'd picked a murder mystery and a biography for herself, and a big glossy picture book of jungle animals for Freddie Houser that she intended to drop off at Worthington House on her way home. Freddie would pore over the colorful photographs for hours, and the book would keep her occupied over the weekend when there were fewer planned activities to keep her mind off her loneliness. Maybe Sunday afternoon, Cece thought, if her mother didn't need her car, she'd pick up Freddie and take her out for an ice cream sundae and a ride around the lake.

Cece crossed the street and stepped into the square, heading for Main Street and the post office, her thoughts having reminded her that she was supposed to meet her mother and drive her home at four-thirty. It was just a little past three but she wanted to look for a pair of shorts and a couple of tank tops at Gates Department Store's summer clearance sale before then. She had plenty of time to run her errands, but she really did have to think about getting a car of her own.

Did that mean she'd made the decision to remain in Tyler indefinitely? Or was she just tired of having to be chauffeured around town?

She couldn't live with her mother forever. She couldn't keep pretending the future would work itself out or that she would wake up one morning and find the past eighteen months had been a bad dream, that Steve was still alive and they could go on with their life together. The decision of what to do with the rest of her life was hers and hers alone.

"You look as if you're deciding the fate the world," Jeff said in her left ear.

She didn't turn her head right away. She was afraid it would show in her eyes, the excitement the mere sound of his voice caused in her brain and in her body.

Her heart kicked into overdrive inside her chest, but she recovered quickly enough to respond to his teasing remark before her confusion.

"Not the fate of the world. Just whether or not I need to buy a car of my own."

"Also a very weighty decision," he said, falling into step beside her.

Go away, Jeff, please, she wanted to say but did not. "Yes, it is, when your bank balance is as slim as mine." She hadn't expected their first encounter since the meeting at Worthington House with Cecil Kellaway to be so soon, or in so public a place. Perhaps that circumstance would turn out to be a blessing in disguise. Here, in the middle of the town square, it could only be casual and very, very brief.

"How well I know that feeling." He matched his long strides to hers, more in deference to the heat of the day than anything else.

Cece walked fast. She had no trouble keeping up with him and never had. At the moment she wished she had wings on her feet and could fly away. She glanced at him from the corner of her eye. He was wearing a light blue short-sleeved shirt and jeans. His sunglasses were sticking out of his shirt pocket, so she had no trouble reading his expression, which was comically sad.

Cece couldn't help laughing a little at the mournful sound of his words. "You're a doctor, for heaven's sake. Even in Tyler doctors make a good living. You don't expect me to believe you can't afford a new car if you need one. Not Jeffrey Judson Ingalls Baron,

scion of Tyler's two most important families.'' She
recalled the rumors of money troubles that had cir-
culated for a while after his father's suicide. It was true
that Tyler Elevator had been close to bankruptcy when
Ronald died, apparently, but none of the area farmers had lost their money and Alyssa had eventually
sold the business to the Sugar Creek Farm Co-op...for
a nice profit, Annabelle had said. Now Cece wondered if that were true, or only wishful thinking. She
wished she hadn't mentioned his family money, but
Jeff didn't seem to notice or pretended not to.

"Well, a good used one, maybe,'' he said with a grin
that looked perfectly ordinary on the surface but,
coupled with the set of his jaw and the nearness of his
lean, powerful body, made her heart jump erratically
yet again.

She took a deep breath and was immediately aware
of his scent, a mixture of soap and spicy shaving lo-
tion and sun-warmed male skin. The air came back
out of her lungs in a rush. There was nothing she
seemed able to do to school her body into disregarding the sensual fireworks that his presence set off inside her. She doubted even jumping into the chilly
waters of the lake fully clothed would cool the fire in
her veins.

"Poor you,'' she managed, clicking her tongue
against the roof of her mouth in mock sympathy. "If
you had a tin cup I'd put a quarter inside.'' She fished
in the pocket of her cotton skirt and pulled out a coin.

He held out his hand, palm up. "Put it here,'' he
said, his voice low and scratchy, all the teasing light

gone from his blue eyes, leaving them as dark and mysterious as the eastern sky at moonrise.

"Jeff," she said, pleading, stumbling a little over his name. It wasn't fair of him to keep pressuring her like this. She needed time, space, privacy to come to grips with her feelings for him and with the love she still felt for her husband, the memories of him she cherished and didn't want to let go. But how could she tell him that here, in the middle of the street, in the middle of Tyler, with half the town watching them?

He plucked the quarter from her nerveless fingers. "With the fifty cents I've got in my pocket we can pool our resources and have a cherry phosphate at Marge's," he said, his tone of voice no longer beckoning her to join him someplace lost and secret and theirs alone.

"I can't," she said helplessly, automatically.

"Why not?" His inflection was gentle, his searing gaze was not.

"I have errands to run."

"Not good enough."

He put his hand under her elbow, bare skin to bare skin, and steered her toward the side street where Marge's Diner was located. She shivered and tried not to recall how his hands had felt on her body when he kissed her at the clinic. Tried even harder not to remember how his hands had felt on her breasts when they'd made love those summer nights so long ago.

"I really don't have time for this," she insisted, pleased her voice sounded normal, not betraying the agitation she felt inside.

"Yes, you do. If you've got your mom's car, that means you're free until four-thirty, right?"

"Yes," she said, bowing to the inevitable. Everyone knew the post office hours. There was no use trying to lie to him. "But I need to stop at Gates's before then and pick up some things."

"No problem. We used to be able to get through a phosphate at Marge's in ten minutes flat, remember?" he asked.

"I remember," she said, realizing his thoughts, too, were in the past, their past, the one they'd shared together. "You had an old Volkswagen bug that barely ran under its own power."

"But it was a car."

"Yes," she admitted. "It was a car. Some nights you actually got me home before curfew."

"You were the only girl in the junior class who had to be home an hour after the game. It took me half that long to shower and change," he complained facetiously.

"Mom was awfully strict," she agreed, oblivious of the trap he was baiting for her.

"But by honing our technique with the phosphates at Marge's, we still managed to find twenty minutes to neck in the car in your driveway before the hour was up."

"Jeff," she said, laughing, but there was a catch in her voice and they both heard it. "Don't, please."

"All right." He was watching her closely. "I'll stop teasing you, but come with me to Marge's and have a phosphate. I think I can come up with enough cash for

you to have one of your own." Before she could protest he added, "That way you won't compromise your
reputation by sharing one with me."

"The grieving widow," she said, ashamed to let the
bitterness, the pain and confusion, show. "In need of
comforting by the handsome, eligible young doctor."

"I didn't mean it that way, Cece." His jaw tightened. For a moment he looked at her long and hard.

"I know." She sighed. "I need time, Jeff, and so do
you, or every conversation we have would end up in an
argument."

"Or a kiss."

"Exactly. That's why I don't think seeing each other
is a good idea."

"I don't agree." He held open the door of the diner.
He was playing with fire again but he didn't care. He'd
missed her too much the past few days to pass up the
opportunity to be with her, even in Marge's, the gossip center of Tyler. "But I won't argue with you. Not
today, anyway. I want to talk to you about Worthington House." He hated using the trouble at the retirement center as bait to keep her with him, but that
didn't stop him. "It may not be strictly by the book,
but I'd rather do it when Cecil isn't around."

"Oh, of course." She looked miserably confused,
and for a moment he wondered if he'd imagined her
initial reaction to him back in the park. The electricity in the air between them had been strong enough to
make the hair at the back of his neck stand on end.
Hadn't she noticed it? Of course she had, but she
wasn't letting it show.

"How can I help you?" she asked warily. He hadn't considered the ambivalence of her situation. Talking to him about the instances of possible overmedication at Worthington House could be seen as disloyalty to her employers. But he wanted to know if she had any suspicion of Kellaway or Juanita or anyone else. Cece was a hell of a nurse. Her loyalty, first and always, would lie with her patients' welfare and nowhere else.

"Kellaway told me yesterday that you hadn't turned up any discrepancies or errors in your charting and drug-dispensing records. Is that correct?"

"Yes." She nodded, sliding into a window booth. The thin mint green cotton fabric of her blouse pulled taut across her breasts and he felt it again, that stinging jolt of awareness deep in his gut that kept his mind and his body in an uproar whenever she was near enough to touch. The teenage waitress bounced across the room and he ordered two cherry phosphates. The diner was empty. They had the place to themselves.

Cece went on talking as soon as the waitress left. "Other than a few minor mistakes, the kind you see during any evaluation, there was nothing to be found."

"I was afraid of that." He took his sunglasses out of his pocket and opened and shut the earpieces, just to have something to do with his hands. Cece had folded hers on the tabletop. Now the right one clenched into a fist before she deliberately relaxed it again.

"What do you mean by that?"

He sighed. This was going to be harder than he thought. "I mean, if any or all of them were honest mistakes, you would have found something."

"Yes." She leaned her head against the high back of the booth, distancing herself subtly, perhaps unconsciously, from him. "Do you mean to say that you think these incidents were deliberate?"

"I don't know what to think," he said truthfully. "I do think we have to consider everyone employed at Worthington House a viable suspect."

"Except thee and me," she said with a quick, fleeting smile.

"Exactly."

"Have you obtained the results from the lab tests you ordered on our supply of morphine? Was it adulterated? There wasn't a drop missing from our inventory."

"I should hear in another day or two. If the solution was adulterated, though, we'll have a pretty good idea the acts were deliberate." He felt the muscles of his jaw tighten involuntarily. "It could be Kellaway. Or one of your nurses."

"What makes you think that?" She wasn't going to give him an inch. Cece was fiercely loyal to her nurses as well as her patients. She'd obviously decided to fight him just as hard in their professional relationship as in their personal one.

"Kellaway may be able to benefit by altering the victims' wills to make Worthington House their heirs, that is, if they've signed any agreements with the corporation that owns the place regarding lifelong care."

'Not likely," Cece pointed out. She digested the information for a moment. "But it's possible. So how's he doing it?"

"I didn't say he is. And I haven't the slightest idea how he'd go about it."

"I suppose there must be some way to check it out."

"I'll see what I can do."

"What else? Or should I say, who else do you suspect?"

"It could be Juanita Pelsten."

"I don't think so," Cece said after a minute of silence necessitated by the waitress's return with their soft drinks.

"You heard her remark about letting Wilhelm 'go' as well as I did."

"She was on duty the morning Violet almost died, as well," Cece admitted reluctantly. "She's been at Worthington House a long time."

"Maybe too long," Jeff said, stirring his drink with a straw. "Maybe she's seen too much illness and suffering. Maybe something snapped inside."

"Juanita's a good nurse. I've seen nothing to make me feel differently."

Jeff cupped his hands around the old-fashioned soda glass and counted to ten. All he'd wanted to do was spend some time with her, not argue. He shouldn't be venting his anger on Cece. She wanted to find out what was going on at Worthington House as badly as he did. He was letting his frustration with the legal system, engendered by the slow pace of the investigation into his grandmother's murder, color his approach to this other upsetting event in his life.

"You might as well blame this thing on Tracie, our nursing student, because she might have a messiah complex. Or on one of the other patients. I don't know what's happening but I have faith in my nurses," she said stubbornly.

"I hope you're right, but that doesn't explain away what's already happened. What might happen again tomorrow."

She'd bent her head to her glass, then lifted her gaze, her gray eyes blazing into his. "It won't happen again. I promise you. I'll spend every hour of every day there, if necessary, to prevent another...attack." She clamped her teeth on her lower lip, and he knew that last word had slipped out, an indication of her deepest fears, which she'd tried very hard to keep hidden from him.

"I know you will, Cece," he said gently, wishing he could reach out and take her trembling hand in his. "I'm counting on you."

The waitress came back, asking if they wanted or needed anything else. When Jeff said no, more gruffly than he intended, she blinked in surprise, then slapped the bill down on the table and flounced away in a huff.

"Now you've done it," Cece said with a tremulous smile and a look of relief in her eyes that told him more clearly than words she wasn't sorry their uncomfortable conversation had been interrupted.

"I'll leave her a great tip," he said, laying down two dollar bills and a handful of change. "Think that will get my name off her black list?" he asked with a grin.

"Yes," Cece said, preparing to slide out of the booth. "I'll think about what we've discussed. About Cecil and Juanita, even Tracie. I can't afford not to, for my patients' sakes."

"I'm not asking for anything else."

"I have to be going, Jeff. I really do have errands to run."

"Cece, don't just walk away like this." Two or three people had entered the diner in the past few minutes. Cece waved at two members of the Quilting Circle, which met at Worthington House every week, and Jeff nodded in their general direction. Dammit. By morning everyone in Tyler would know he was having phosphates with Cece Hayes in Marge's Diner in the middle of the afternoon.

"You promised," she said, beginning to move toward the door.

He stepped in front of her, blocking her escape, heedless of the interested looks they were getting. "Go out with me this evening."

"I can't." She looked scared and excited all at once. He wasn't sure how he could read two such distinct and differing emotions in her clear gray eyes, but he could.

"Not a date, no strings attached, just a drive around the lake. An hour or two to talk about old times, new times, catch up on each other's lives."

"No," she said. Her hand moved upward toward her throat, then fell back. "I mean, I already have a commitment this evening," she said with a little smile. "Have you forgotten? Tonight is one of my nights to teach the prenatal class at the clinic."

"I'm trying to forget," he said before he thought better of it. The clinic with its chronic money troubles was never very far from his thoughts. Everyone in town assumed Ronald Baron's family had plenty of money. That wasn't true, especially in Jeff's case. He didn't have a big private practice, and head of emergency medicine at Tyler General might sound like a lofty title, but the salary that came with it was much more down to earth.

"Maybe if you paid more attention to your responsibilities there, the place wouldn't be in such bad shape."

Jeff shoved his hands in the back pockets of his jeans to keep from balling them into fists. He knew she didn't mean that. She was lashing out at him because she was upset and confused by a lot of things, not the least of them the unresolved elements of their own past, but her words cut to the bone. He wanted the clinic to thrive, to be a viable and important part of the community. That was why its official name was the Ronald Baron Clinic. For the sake of his father's memory, he wanted it to succeed. Instead, it was in real danger of having to shut down. Another Baron bankruptcy to tarnish the family name.

"I do pay attention to my responsibilities to the clinic. I just wish they weren't interfering with my private life at the moment."

She sighed. "I shouldn't have said that. I shouldn't have come in here with you." She refused to lift her eyes to meet his. Instead, she stared at the top button of his shirt and he felt the warm touch of her gaze on his skin.

"That's not true."

"Yes, it is. Please, Jeff, let me go."

"I suppose I have to." He was determined not to end their meeting on such an unhappy note. "Liza will have my hide if I make you so uncomfortable you don't show up at class tonight."

She raised her eyes and smiled, accepting his peace offering. There was a light trembling at the corner of her mouth. He wanted to reach out and touch the spot, bend his head and kiss the soft skin.

"Liza's getting anxious. I can't let her down."

"So am I."

"What?"

"Getting anxious to be an uncle," he said with what he hoped was an innocent smile.

"I thought that's what you meant." She smiled again when she reached the door. "Goodbye, Dr. Baron. It's been...interesting...talking to you." Her voice was pitched loud enough for everyone in the diner to hear.

"Goodbye, Cece," he said, grinding his teeth. Even he didn't have enough nerve to say something teasing and provocative in front of the teenage waitress and two of the biggest gossips in town. "See you around."

She shrugged and walked out the door, swinging her tote bag onto her shoulder as she went. He walked out, too, without turning around. He didn't want to see the interested, speculative looks on the faces of the other patrons in the restaurant. As far as they were concerned, Dr. Jeffrey Baron, Tyler's most eligible bachelor, had just struck out with Cece Scanlon Hayes. She'd certainly put him in his place, and looked at the end as if she enjoyed doing it.

He'd forgotten that impish quality of hers. He stood a little taller as he headed back down Main Street. She hadn't been able to remain angry with him for very long at all. Her sudden mood swings, her uncertainty, proved she wasn't as sure of herself around him as she wanted to be.

Sooner or later he'd get her alone, really alone, where they could talk, work out the past and look ahead to the future. He stopped short in front of his car, key ring in hand. Did her ambivalence mean that her emotions were coming back to life, as his were after the long dormant months since his divorce?

Was she ready to fall in love again?

Was he?

CECE SHUT OFF the projector and walked across the clinic meeting room to switch on the light. Behind her the four mothers-to-be and their labor partners were unusually quiet, the impact of the film they'd just seen evident in their protracted silence. It was another way

her prenatal class in Tyler was similar to the ones she
and Steve had conducted in the little hospital in Santa
Rosita. Whenever they showed the movie of an actual
birth, everyone was awed, and very often frightened
out of their wits. Especially the first-time fathers.
Steve always had a little man-to-man joke he told at
this point. Unfortunately for Cece, it didn't sound well
translated into English, and would sound even more
ridiculous coming from a woman if it did.

"Well?" She turned around slowly, giving everyone a moment to compose themselves, being careful
not to let any of her amusement show when she looked
into their bewildered, anxious faces. "What do you
think? Any questions?"

"My God," Liza Forrester said irreverently, breaking the silence and the tension in the room. "I want
out!"

"Liza," her husband began, then broke off helplessly, shaking his head.

"Too late," Cece pointed out with a laugh.

"Me, too," the pregnant teenager, Tanya, echoed.

"It will be okay, honey." Tanya's mother was acting as her labor coach because the baby's father was
away, serving in the National Guard. "It isn't so bad,
really. Why, you were my first baby and you just came
poppin' out."

Tanya wasn't going to be lulled into complacency by
the statement. "Are you telling the truth?" she asked,
eyeing her parent sternly, one hand folded protec-
tively over her stomach. Her baby wasn't due until
around Thanksgiving, but she was taking the child-

birth classes now so they didn't interfere with her senior class activities when school started in September.

Her mother had the grace to look sheepish. "Well, I might be soft-pedaling it a little. But trust me, honey, it's going to be worth every minute when you hold your own little one in your arms."

Tanya wasn't the only person in the room soothed by the older woman's down-to-earth tone and comforting words. Out of the corner of her eye Cece saw Liza lean back into the sheltering circle of her husband's arm as he bent his dark head to whisper something in her ear. Tom and Bette Wilson, who were expecting their second child and attending the classes so that Tom could be present in the delivery room this time, held hands and smiled into each other's eyes. This exchange of love and reassurance, too, was the same as in Santa Rosita, and Cece experienced a pang of loneliness and regret when she remembered that she had no one to share such a moment with anymore.

She shook off the momentary sadness and glanced on around the room. Only Mary and Daniel Pierce remained seated and separate. A second glance showed her why. Mary's face was drawn and pale, her expression listless. She rubbed the back of her neck as though she were in pain.

"Are you feeling all right?" Cece asked, skirting the pushed-aside tables and chairs as she moved toward the young couple. "Is something wrong?"

"My head hurts," Mary complained. "I think I must be getting the flu."

"She's been feeling bad for a couple of days," her husband added. He looked very young and very worried. His wife's pregnancy was a drain on their slender financial resources. Mary hadn't felt strong enough to work more than a day or two a week for the past month or so, Cece had learned. If she was truly ill, or if there was something wrong with the baby, the consequences would be devastating to their future.

"Any signs or symptoms that something is going wrong, that there's a problem with the baby?" Cece asked quietly, dropping to her knees beside Mary's chair. Laughter and snatches of conversation were breaking out around them. Cece let the others work off their excitement, voice their fears and have their anxiety reassured by others who faced the same fate.

"No. I just feel bad." She refused to meet Cece's eyes.

"Okay." Cece reached up and touched Mary's forehead lightly. If she had a fever it was very slight. It was a warm night and the room wasn't air-conditioned; there was only a big floor fan whirring away in the corner. "When's your next appointment for a checkup at the clinic?"

"Monday," Mary said, still in the same listless tone of voice that sent warning prickles dancing up and down Cece's spine.

"Too far away. Daniel, you two stay after class and I'll check Mary over, okay?"

"We'll do that."

"I think that about wraps it up for tonight," Cece called as she stood up. "Next session is Tuesday at seven. We'll be discussing the types of pain medication available during labor and delivery, their advantages and their drawbacks, both for mothers and babies."

"I want to be out cold," Liza said decisively. "I do not intend to stay awake through that." She gestured extravagantly toward the blank movie screen standing against the far wall of the room.

"You'll do fine, Liza," Cece said with a smile. "If any of you think of any questions about what you saw tonight, write them down and we'll discuss them next week. Good night. Drive safely and have a good weekend."

"I'll make sure everything's locked up," Cliff Forrester said to Cece as he ushered his wife out of the room. "All you'll have to do is pull the door shut behind you and make sure the dead bolt goes home."

"Thanks, Cliff. I won't be more than a few minutes, but I'm worried about how bad Mary's feeling. Maybe she's only catching the flu or a bad cold, but I want to make sure."

"We'll wait," Liza interrupted. "So you don't have to leave by yourself."

"Thank you," Cece replied, secretly relieved she wouldn't have to cross the dark parking lot completely alone. The clinic was located in the roughest part of town, and while Cece wasn't scared, she didn't like wandering around in a deserted parking lot by herself any better than the next woman.

Cliff looked at his wife, then across the room at Cece. "I should have thought of that myself. We'll be out in the waiting room. C'mon, Liza."

"Take your time, Cece. We're not in any hurry." Liza smiled the high-voltage Baron smile and prepared to follow her husband out of the room.

"Okay, you two," Cece said, beckoning to Mary and Daniel. "Let's see if I can find my way around the examining room well enough to locate everything I need."

Mary remained seated.

"C'mon, sweetheart," Daniel urged his young wife.

"I can't," she whispered, tears gathering in her eyes. "I lied to you. I've been cramping all day. I think the baby is coming and it's too soon."

"Dear God," Liza wailed, eavesdropping from the doorway, her horrified blue eyes flying to meet Cece's gaze. "What are we going to do with her? Cliff," she called loudly, "Mary's going into labor! Cece, we have to do something. Now."

"Slow down, Liza," Cece ordered, grateful when Cliff arrived back in the room just moments later. Liza's scattergun approach to life had its advantages, but going off in several different directions at once during an emergency wasn't one of them.

"Would you call the hospital and tell them we're bringing in an eighth-month, first pregnancy in possible premature labor?" she asked him, choosing her words carefully, trying not to get too technical. "I'll drive her in my mother's car. It's bigger and she can lie down if she wants. Daniel can follow us in their truck. I'll have to ask you to lock up for me."

"No problem."

"I'll drive your mother's car so you can help Mary if she needs you," Liza said, altering the plan as she watched the sobbing woman with worried blue eyes. "I mean, if that will be of any help to you."

"It will. Okay, let's go." Cece walked over and put her hand on Mary's shoulder. The mother-to-be's fear and pain drove all the terror out of Cece's brain. This was what she was trained for. She knew her job. She was good at it. But she also knew she wouldn't have to stay with Mary until the baby was born, so she was safe a while longer. She wouldn't be responsible for bringing a new life into the world...without Steve's help. She wouldn't have to face again the undeniable reality of being alone. Not tonight. Not yet.

CHAPTER SEVEN

"WE'RE MAKING a habit of meeting here," Jeff said, coming through the sliding glass doors of the ER entrance into the humid August night to help Cece maneuver Mary Pierce out of the car and into a wheelchair held steady by an ER nurse.

"Sorry," Cece said, sounding a little breathless, a little nervous. "I hate to deflate your ego, Doctor, but it's not your irresistible charm that keeps me coming back."

"What is it, then?" he asked, gesturing the nurse aside in order to wheel Mary along the corridor toward the OB ward himself. It was pretty quiet this early in the evening. So far no patients were waiting for him in the examination cubicles. The ER could get along without him for fifteen minutes. Mary was a friend as well as a clinic patient. She was scared and she needed his reassurance.

"My lifelong affinity for being in the wrong place at the wrong time."

"I like your first assessment better." He grinned at the swift, fleeting rush of color his retort brought to Cece's cheeks. As long as she wasn't indifferent to him he had a chance to wear her down, make her realize their love deserved a second chance. "I've called OB and they're ready for her." He halted the chair outside the doors of the obstetrics ward and buzzed for admittance.

"Don't let anything happen to my baby, Dr. Baron," Mary said with a sniff, transferring her vise-like grip from Cece's hand to Jeff's.

"Don't worry. Dr. Merton, the hospital's obstetrician, will be taking care of you. He's the best we've got. He delivers all my patients." He jabbed the buzzer again. "Jeez, I hate summer weekends. We're way understaffed."

"They are slow." Cece frowned as she peered through the glass square set in the heavy metal door.

"This is Grand Central Station compared to what it will be Labor Day weekend," Jeff muttered under his breath. "Everyone who can get time off will be gone, trying to get in one last summer fling."

"Where's Danny?" Mary groaned as a contraction gripped her.

"Filling out the paperwork to get you checked in," Cece told her. "Now concentrate. Remember your breathing. In. Out. In. Out."

"Don't leave," Mary gasped as Jeff jabbed the buzzer again.

"I'll stick around as long as I can," he promised. "But I'm on duty in the ER. Hank Merton will be delivering the baby. And Cece's a midwife. She'll stay with you."

"No," Cece said in a kind of strangled whisper. "I can't."

"Why not?" He was surprised by the sudden distress he saw darken her gray eyes.

"How is she?" Liza demanded, coming up beside them as quickly as her increased bulk would allow.

"Who let you back here?" Jeff demanded as the door buzzed from inside, signaling them to enter.

Liza's intrusion gave Cece the perfect excuse to ignore Jeff's question. Why was she afraid to help bring this baby into the world? It was what she was trained for, after all. Now, because of Liza's rushing onto the scene, he might never learn the truth.

"I'm sorry." Liza appeared uncharacteristically cowed by his reprimand. "I—I only wanted to know if there was anything else I could do to help, that's all."

"There isn't, babe. Come home with me."

Jeff swung around to find his brother-in-law striding toward them.

"Take her home, Cliff," he said more quietly, as he prepared to wheel Mary through the doors. "She's too close to delivering, herself, to be this upset." He turned his head, looking back over his shoulder at his youngest sister. "Take Cece with you. She's had a long day."

"We'll stay until the baby's born," Liza said stubbornly. Cece didn't say anything.

"It might take the rest of the night. It might not happen at all." He didn't think Hank Merton would be able to arrest Mary's labor, but he didn't say so out loud.

"We'll stay."

"No, we won't," Cliff said with quiet force. He reached out and took Liza by the shoulders, turning her to face him with strong, gentle hands. "You've got a family, a baby of your own to think about now."

Jeff glanced at Cece. She was watching Cliff and Liza with a look of great sadness on her face. Her gray eyes were raincloud dark with unshed tears and he thought he'd never seen her look more beautiful. He also knew instinctively that she was afraid to be with Mary when the baby was born because she had no babies of her own. And she had lost the man she loved, the man who would have given her those babies if he had lived.

"Go home," he commanded gently. "Cece, too."

"I'm okay," Liza insisted, making one last stubborn attempt to assert her considerable will. "I won't be able to sleep a wink. There's got to be some way to get more money for the clinic so things like this don't happen. Mary hasn't been feeling well for days. She tried to wait till clinic day to see you and look what happened."

"If there's a way to get more money, we'll find it. But not tonight. Take her home, Cliff." He agreed with every word his sister said, but the hard truth was there were no funds to open the clinic for any additional hours. He was truly his father's son where money matters were concerned. He was a pretty damn good doctor but a lousy businessman.

"But, Jeff—"

"Go home, Liza." He looked at Cece, saw she was once more in control, shutting him out. He felt the pain of her continued withdrawal at the core of his soul. "Go home, Cece," he said, looking away, looking at Cliff, the only other male. "Take them home. I've got work to do."

GO HOME, CECE. Funny how three little words like that could cause you so much pain. She hadn't been able to sleep all night thinking about them, seeing again in her mind's eye the tired, defeated look on Jeff's face. Knowing it was her fault that it was there.

She needed to get out of doors, walk off the nervous energy, or she'd never get through the day at Worthington House without blowing up at someone. The nighttime hours had been warm but now there was a dawn chill in the air. Cece opened the bottom drawer of her dresser and pulled out a lightweight blue sweatshirt from a stack of clothing her mother had stored there. Underneath the clothing was a cardboard box of high school mementos she'd placed there herself after her marriage.

For a long moment she remained on her knees on the floor before the drawer, hesitant to open the box because among the photographs of her and Britt in their drill team uniforms, the football programs and pressed flower corsages from homecomings and proms, there was something that didn't belong to her. She lifted the cardboard lid and there it was.

Jeff's class ring.

She'd never returned it to him. Because he had never returned hers. Or at least that had been the justification she'd used ten years ago.

She lifted the ring, felt its weight in her hand and looked down at the still-familiar dark blue stone in its setting of dull gold. At first, in her pain and anger at his desertion, she'd felt justified in keeping it. Ransom for her own missing ring, she'd rationalized then. Or one last desperate tie to the boy she loved? she wondered now.

Later she'd been too embarrassed and too full of righteous anger to try to give it back on visits home when their paths might have crossed but didn't. Then she'd met Steve and forgotten all about the ring until she was packing her things for her mother to store when they left for Nicaragua.

Cece pushed the drawer shut. She stood and laid the ring on the dresser. The blue stone gleamed darkly in the early-morning light. Someday, when the timing was right, she'd bring up the subject to Jeff, casually, with just the right level of tolerant amusement for the folly of their youth, and ask him if he wanted it back.

And ask if he had kept hers safe, too, all these years.

"Sentimental and silly," Cece berated herself under her breath. "Get out of this house and start walking it off."

She threw the sweatshirt over her shoulders and tied the sleeves in a knot as she tiptoed quietly past her mother's room and down the stairs. Annabelle was still asleep. It wasn't quite six o'clock yet, barely dawn. Cece pulled her hair back as she went, securing it with a wide elastic band of neon pink.

The birds were awake to keep her company as she walked along the sidewalk past the houses where her

friends had grown up and where she'd played as a
child. She hadn't gone far, only a block or two, but
already she felt better, more herself. A car turned onto
the street ahead of her. Her heartbeat quickened.

She didn't have to look twice to recognize Jeff's car.
He was obviously just leaving the hospital, which was
out of sight down the street along which he'd come.
Cece kept walking, but she wasn't certain she was
ready to face him at six o'clock in the morning, wearing a T-shirt and running shorts and her hair in a
ponytail.

He saw her almost at once and pulled the car over
to the curb beside her. He rolled down the window and
said, "Hi. You're out and about very early." He
looked tired and sleepy and elated, the same way Steve
had looked after a safe delivery that ended a long
night's labor. But when she looked closer, she saw
sadness and defeat in his eyes, and her heart demanded to know why.

"I couldn't sleep. How is Mary? And the baby?" It
was hard to ask that question.

"Mary's fine. And I think the baby will be, too. It's
a little too early to tell. He's very small. But his condition is stable."

"A boy?"

He nodded and smiled, and Cece couldn't help it,
she smiled, too.

"Danny will be very pleased."

"They wanted to name him Henry Jeffrey, after
both of us doctors, but we talked them out of it." He
shrugged and chuckled again. "Poor kid."

She laughed, too, feeling light and a little silly with relief—and with the pleasure of seeing him again.

"I was heading out to the boathouse to tell Liza and Cliff the good news, but it's been one hell of a long night. I know it's only a five-mile drive but right now it might as well be the moon." It was back, that shadow of defeat that darkened his eyes and bowed his shoulders. He folded his arms across the steering wheel and propped his chin on his hands. He closed his eyes, and the simple gesture was her undoing.

She could never be indifferent to this man, she realized. She might hate him, she might love him as she had so long ago, but he would never be just a man. She was a very different person than she'd been ten years ago. Then she'd sat in her dorm room and cried her eyes out when Jeff hadn't returned, but she'd never found out why he hadn't. Today she would.

Cece rested her hands on the doorframe and leaned forward. "Scoot over," she said, ignoring the automatic warning signals her brain set off to brighten her heart.

"What?" Jeff's eyes flew open. He straightened, still gripping the steering wheel with both hands. "What did you say?"

"I said, scoot over. I'll drive you out to the boathouse."

He stared at her for a long, breath-stopping moment. "I'm not up to arguing with you, Cece."

"No arguments," she promised.

"Okay." He slid across the bench seat and Cece slipped behind the wheel. Automatically her hand went to the ignition. There was no key.

"Hey, is this thing hot-wired?" she asked in a bantering tone to cover the unexpected awkwardness of the moment.

"Yeah. It's a trick I learned in college. I left my keys on the desk in my office. I was just too damned bushed to go back for them."

"I never knew you had a criminal turn of mind."

"It runs in the family," he said grimly, leaning his head back against the seat and closing his eyes.

They drove in silence for several minutes because Cece couldn't think of anything else to say after Jeff's last remark. He slept, or pretended to be asleep. She glanced at him from the corner of her eye. His hair was too long, shaggy around the edges, but still that glorious shade of chestnut brown that had half the girls at Tyler High chasing him relentlessly when they were young, and that still turned most women's heads today.

The extra length did nothing to detract from his good looks. He had matured into a very handsome man. His face was angular, his jaw stubborn, his nose straight and commanding. He had broad shoulders and his waist was as narrow as it had been in high school. They passed Britt's farm, and on an impulse she didn't care to put a name to, Cece turned down an unpaved road that she knew ended in a small grassy turnout, with one or two weathered picnic tables and

a boat ramp with a great view of the lake and Timberlake Lodge on the far shore.

She tried to tell herself Jeff was really asleep and
wouldn't even notice the short detour. She tried to tell
herself she only wanted to see the lodge and the im-
provements the Addison Hotel Corporation had made
to it from a distance first. It had nothing to do with
this being "their place," she rationalized as they
bounced along the shady, unpaved road bordered by
a field of wheat stubble and fencerow of scraggly willow trees.

"I didn't think you needed directions to the boathouse," he said as she pulled into the little park, "but
obviously I was wrong. We're on the opposite side of
the lake, in case you haven't noticed." He rolled his
head toward her, his blue eyes questioning, though he
was very much aware of their surroundings.

She reached for the ignition again automatically,
then realized there was no way to shut off the engine.
She lowered the window instead, giving herself a moment to collect her thoughts. Birdsong filled the air,
and across the water, barely audible above the idling
car engine, drifted the putt-putt of an outboard motor, as some early-morning fisherman set out across
the lake to try his luck.

"I . . . I wanted to see Timberlake Lodge," she said
at last.

"It is a good spot to stop and take a look at the
place." Jeff settled back against the seat. He lifted one
sneakered foot to rest against the dash, the soft faded
denim of his jeans pulling tight across his thighs. Cece

looked away, back out over the blue-gray water, her pulse beat annoyingly quick.

"You aren't going to make this easy for me, are you?" she heard herself asking.

"What do you mean by easy?" He turned his head just enough to look at her from the corner of his eye. "Do you mean am I going to kiss you when you don't want to be kissed and give you the perfect excuse never to see me again? Forget it." He looked out the front window at the sky turning from dawn gray to blue as the sun rose higher behind them.

"No, that's not what I mean. We're going to talk about you. We're going to talk about . . . us."

"There isn't any 'us,' Cece. You've made that point to me more than once."

Cece gritted her teeth. He'd always been stubborn; but so was she.

"I want to know why you walked out on me ten years ago. I'm not getting out of this car until I have it."

"That's ancient history." He still wouldn't look at her. Cece curled her hands around the steering wheel. She wished she hadn't said anything. He wasn't going to tell her what she wanted to hear. And who was she to insist? She had too many things inside her she didn't want revealed to ask him to bare his soul to her.

"Please, Jeff. I've always wondered if it was something I said or did. I . . . need to know."

"Forget it, Cece. It's been a hell of a night. We nearly lost Mary's baby twice. I'm beat. The last thing

I want to do is rehash a love affair that's been history for ten years."

"The baby almost died?" Cece had trouble getting the words past the sudden constriction in her throat.

"I told you he's stable now," he said more gently. A few moments of silence passed. "You were scared to death you'd have to go into that delivery room last night. Why, Cece?"

"That's not true," she said too quickly, too forcefully.

"Yes, you were." He twisted in his seat so that they were almost facing each other.

He wasn't touching her but she felt as if he was. His voice was low and rough and it affected her like a caress. She lifted her hand and rubbed the skin above her wrist, smoothing, caressing. He'd turned the tables on her yet again. She felt trapped, driven into a corner, and very much aware of the man beside her.

"You're so scared you took a job at Worthington House. That's as far from delivering babies as you can get. You're scared to death," he repeated quietly.

The distance between them was so small that if he moved his hand even a few inches along the seat it would touch her thigh. She forced back a cowardly need to move away. She might as well tell him the truth. She'd always been able to talk to Jeff, tell him things that perplexed and mystified her. She wished he would do the same with her.

"I haven't delivered a baby in almost eighteen months." She couldn't stop the wavering tone of disbelief that filtered into the words. "I was nervous.

That's not unusual. You looked a little gun-shy your-self last night." That quickly, that easily, she was back under his spell, falling into the familiar, comfortable routine of telling him her innermost thoughts.

"Babies are out of my league. Hank Merton is the OB man in Tyler, not me. I haven't delivered a baby since med school. That's a good enough excuse, as far as I'm concerned. But yours isn't. I don't buy the notion that your professional skills are too rusty to trust. What's the real reason?"

"Damn it, Jeff. I don't want to talk about it." She saw her hand was bunched into a fist on the steering wheel and deliberately relaxed her clenched fingers. He reached forward and captured her hand between his own.

"It's because of something that happened in Nicaragua, isn't it? Something to do with your husband's death."

"Yes," she whispered and nearly choked on unshed tears. She'd cried enough over Steve's senseless death. For a while after he died she was afraid she'd never be able to stop. She didn't want to start again.

"Tell me, Cece." He made no move to pull her into his arms, although her heart and body were at war with conflicting emotions if he should. Part of her wanted to be held in his arms, safe and secure. The rest of her knew she would find no sanctuary there, only need and passion and the reawakening of old, insistent desires.

"We always worked as a team," she began haltingly, then the words just came pouring out. "But that last night, the night of the earthquake, I was tired and a little angry and I stayed home."

"Why were you angry?" He didn't release her hand but shifted toward her, lifting his free hand to brush a stray wisp of hair away from her cheek.

"Because I wanted to make love and he didn't." She gave a watery little giggle and to her horror felt two tears spill over and glide down her cheeks. "We wanted a baby very much, you see. And it was just the right time of the month. I wanted him to stay with me, make love, start a baby of our own, but he said he needed to check out the two little ones we had in the nursery one more time before we went to bed." She looked past him, seeing Steve's face, or trying to. Sometimes now, it was hard to remember what he looked like, without seeing a photograph. "He wanted me to come along but I said no. I wanted to stay home, take a cool bath, find my prettiest nightie. Make everything just perfect for when he came back. Only he never made it home."

"Cece, you don't have to tell me the rest." Very gently he reached out and wiped a tear away with his thumb. "Don't hurt yourself by telling me."

She shook her head. "I want to. Steve got out of the hospital okay. But when he found out the two newborns were still in the nursery, he went back in. The little ones were still alive—a beam had fallen across their cots, holding the roof up. He got to them, handed them out. And then the roof caved in on him. We were very isolated in Santa Rosita, you know." She closed her eyes against the horror of the memory, but surprisingly, tears no longer clogged her throat. The words came more easily than they ever had before. "It took two days to get equipment there to dig him out. He died an hour before the bulldozer arrived."

"God, Cece, I'm sorry. Sorry as hell." This time he wasn't gentle. He hauled her across the seat into his arms and held her close.

"The babies lived but Steve didn't. He died before he could give me a baby of our own to love, to remember him by. I can't forgive him for that." She didn't fight him when he pushed her head down on his shoulder. It felt good. It felt right, and she couldn't seem to resist, to conjure up the guilt and the grief that had kept her insulated from life and living—from loving—for the past eighteen months.

"It's harder to forgive yourself, isn't it, Cece, love?" He tipped up her chin, kissed her lightly, sweetly. "You've always carried the weight of the world on your shoulders. You've even decided my walking out on you when my dad . . . died . . . was your fault."

"Sometimes," she admitted. "You still haven't told me why you did."

"Shh, love." She didn't close her eyes but watched him until he bent forward and the dear, familiar angles of his face blurred before her tear-washed gaze.

"Don't call me love," she murmured when his lips left hers again, when she found she could draw enough breath into her lungs to keep her brain functioning. They hadn't settled anything, not really. She couldn't let him keep doing what he was doing; at least until they'd straightened things out between them. "Please, Jeff. Not yet."

"I won't promise anything, Cece. Not while I have you in my arms. I don't want to think, or talk. All I want to do is hold you." He kissed her again, harder at first, then gentling, caressing, their breath mingling, their lips clinging.

"I'm not ready for this," she said, dredging up her last reserves of resistance. "*We* aren't ready for this."

"I won't ask you to do anything you're not ready for. I never did in the past."

"Yes, you did," she whispered. "You wanted me to leave Ann Arbor. Come back here with you. You knew I couldn't. My scholarship wasn't transferable."

He pressed his fingers to her lips. "No more, Cece. I don't want to talk about the end. I want to talk about the beginning. Do you remember the first time we made love?" He leaned his forehead against hers for a moment, then moved slightly away. "Do you remember? Here on this spot?"

"I remember." She had wanted him as much that first time, every time, as he had wanted her... dear heaven, still wanted her, she was sure. She didn't open her eyes, couldn't look at him and know he was recalling the taste and touch, the scent and feel of her skin beneath his hands—as she was his.

"I'll wait for you to come back and join the living, Cece," he whispered against her hair, his voice thick with passion and restraint. "I'll wait, but God, it's going to be hard."

I'll do the same, she promised in her heart. *I'll do the same.*

CHAPTER EIGHT

"FREDDIE, have you finished filling the water pitchers at the patients' bedsides?" Cece asked as she came out of the medication room. She wiggled the handle of the door to make sure it was locked and then walked along the corridor toward Freddie Houser.

"My cart's cleaned up and put away and everything," Freddie answered, thrusting her hands into the pockets of her shapeless smock. "I didn't give Mr. Bremer any, though. I feel bad about that." She turned her head to look back into the sunlight-filled ward.

"Mr. Bremer is very ill. He isn't able to drink by himself just yet," Cece reminded her as gently and patiently as she could. It was a busy Sunday morning and she didn't feel up to trying to explain Jacob Bremer's condition to Freddie in terms she could understand.

"Mrs. Pelsten told me he had a stroke."

"Yes. It's very difficult for him to swallow right now. That's why he can't have water at his bedside just yet."

"He might choke and die," Freddie agreed, nodding importantly. "That would hurt a lot."

"We'll take good care of him," Cece promised with a smile. "Now you'd better hurry and change or you'll be late for church." She motioned toward the stairs. Freddie, she knew, would prefer to use the elevator, but she needed the exercise. "Now hurry, it's almost ten o'clock. And you'll want to be on time to help set up chairs."

Freddie clamped her hand to her mouth. "I forgot." She clattered on down the steps, one hand on the smooth oak handrail, the other still in her smock pocket, which was bulging as always with the miscellaneous objects she collected each day.

"Be careful. Don't fall," Cece cautioned automatically. She wished Dr. Phelps were back in town. He understood Freddie better than anyone. He'd treated her most of her life. The tension and heightened atmosphere of suspicion among the staff at Worthington House was affecting Freddie, even if they were successful in hiding their worries from most of the other residents. It had been a week since Violet's attack. She was doing well, as was Wilhelm Badenhop, who would soon be returning to his own home. But still the fear was there, and the questions. Who had administered the morphine? And why?

"I wish it was you reading Bible stories today," Freddie called, coming to a halt halfway down the steps. "I do. You're my friend."

"I'm glad you feel that way." Cece was touched but also slightly overwhelmed by the admission. Everything about Worthington House had overwhelmed her these past days. She was a good nurse. She was a good administrator. But she was a lousy detective, and she lived in dread of what the tests Jeff had ordered on their narcotics supply would reveal. "Now scoot, Freddie. You'll be late," Cece said as they both went down the stairs.

"I'll hurry!"

"Good morning, Freddie. Good morning, Cecelia. It's a lovely Sabbath day, isn't it?"

Cece halted at the bottom of the staircase as Freddie hurried on toward her room. Very few people called her Cecelia. One of them was Jeff's mother. She smiled and returned Alyssa Baron's greeting.

"It is a very lovely morning, Mrs. Baron."

"Please. I was Mrs. Baron when you and Jeff were in high school. Now I'd much prefer it if you called me Alyssa."

"Thank you," Cece said with a smile that she hoped didn't betray her nervousness at the meeting. "If you'll promise to call me Cece."

"Cecelia is a lovely name." Alyssa returned her smile with one so genuine that Cece felt her nervousness slip away. She didn't know if her reluctance to speak to Jeff's mother was a residue of embarrassment from the past, from the times she'd caught them kissing in her living room all those years ago, or because she could have caught them kissing in Jeff's car just yesterday.

"It's also very old-fashioned. It was my great-grandmother's name. I'm not ready to identify with her yet."

"I understand," Alyssa said with a laugh that sounded like wind chimes in a meadow. Perhaps it was the dress she wore that strengthened that illusion, all soft and floating, the colors of summer, with sheer elbow-length sleeves and a stand-up collar. "Cece it will be."

"Will you be helping with the Sunday service?" Cece asked, moving into the foyer/reception area between the dining room, where the Protestant worship service was held, and the dayroom.

"Yes," Alyssa said. "I'm a little early but I wanted to prepare the Sunday School lesson. Jacob Bremer usually helps me, you know. How is he?"

"As well as can be expected."

"We'll pray for him today."

"I'm sure that will help."

Alyssa's concern for the residents of Worthington House was more than just lip service. She did care about them as individuals.

"Alyssa, would you—could you spend a little extra time with Freddie Houser today? She's upset about Mr. Bremer...and other things. She needs some TLC and I'm afraid we've been extra busy here. It's hard to find as much time to spend with her as she would like."

"Certainly," Alyssa said without hesitation. "I'd be happy to. I have no plans at all today. Perhaps we could go for a drive...or something."

"Freddie loves ice cream," Cece offered.

"That settles it. I'll drive her down to Lake Geneva and we'll window-shop and eat our way from one end of town to the other. How does that sound?"

"Wonderful. I was hoping to take her for an outing myself, but we're short-staffed and I'm stuck here all day."

"I'm more than happy to help. And I won't keep you standing here talking any longer, either. Goodbye, Cece."

"Goodbye, Alyssa," Cece responded, surprised the name and a smile came so naturally to her lips. "And thank you."

"My pleasure." Alyssa turned away and walked into the dining room with long graceful strides, her dress floating around her knees.

"I'll say one thing for Alyssa Baron," Juanita Pelsten said, coming up beside Cece with a chart for her to initial, "she treats everyone with class."

"Yes, she does."

"All the Barons have charm. They get it naturally, I guess. Ronald was quite a ladies' man, so it's said."

"I don't remember," Cece replied in a tone of voice meant to discourage further speculation. She felt disloyal talking about Jeff's father and didn't care to analyze why.

"Here comes another bundle of charm," Juanita remarked with a frankly admiring glance as Edward Wocheck entered the front door. "Boy, what they say is sure true. Women just get older but men get better."

"He is a very good-looking man," Cece agreed, scribbling her initials on the chart. She saw no harm in agreeing with Juanita's opinion. It was a true statement, after all.

"Ronald Baron really looked his age before he died," the middle-aged nurse said in a confidential, reminiscent voice. "But Edward...wow! I'd have dated him myself in high school if I'd known he was going to turn out like this. I'll bet Alyssa wishes she'd run off and married him thirty years ago when she had the chance, instead of hitching herself up to good old Ronald."

Alyssa Baron had been in love with Edward Wocheck? Cece hadn't known that. So they had something in common. Alyssa, too, had had a first love, a young love that she'd lost before finding another.

"Uh-oh. Looks like they're going to meet again. I wonder if they'll be discussing the grand jury hearing. It's coming up soon." Alyssa was coming out of the dining room with her hands full of songbooks. She stopped dead in her tracks when she spotted Edward. It didn't take an expert on human relationships to see she was flustered by his appearance. "Too bad I can't stick around and see what happens," Juanita whispered in Cece's ear, "but I have ten o'clock medications to pass. Do you suppose he'll say anything about his father being called to testify about the night Margaret Ingalls was murdered?"

"Phil Wocheck? Testify?"

"Cece, have you been living in a cave the past two days?"

"I—I guess so." She'd been more concerned with her own problems at Worthington House than with the Ingalls case. Even now she found it almost impossible to consider Juanita a possible suspect as she listened to the older woman's harmless gossip.

"Edward was the gardener and handyman at Timberlake Lodge when Margaret died. Rumor has it Phil knows a lot more about her death than he's telling. Just rumor, of course," Juanita said, sneaking one last peek at Edward and Alyssa as she pretended to study Cece's initials on the chart.

"I didn't know," Cece admitted.

"Ask your mother, girl," Juanita said with a grin and a wink. "She knows." She glanced at her watch. "Good Lord! I'm late. But look at the two of them. That must be what they're talking about. From the looks on their faces, I'd say he isn't asking her to the American Legion ice cream social Labor Day weekend. Gotta run."

"I'll be in my office if anyone needs me." Cece turned her back on Edward and Alyssa, but not before she'd seen enough in the tight set of Edward's jaw, in the stricken look on Alyssa's face, to make her think Juanita's assessment of their conversation was right on the mark.

"I KNOW YOUR FATHER has been called to testify before the grand jury, Edward," Alyssa said, trying hard to keep the fear tightening her chest from creeping into her voice. "Amanda has obtained a list of witnesses subpoenaed by the prosecution. Why? What does

your father know about the night my mother...died?"
After all these weeks she still couldn't bring herself to
say "my mother was murdered." She doubted she ever
would.

"I don't know, Lyssa," he said gently, but with steel
in his voice. Perhaps that was what she found most
changed about him—his voice. The physical changes
she could accept. After all, three decades had passed
since he'd left Tyler to explore the world and make his
fortune. Time and circumstances had altered his ex-
ternal appearance; that was to be expected. But when
he called her Lyssa, as he always had, she somehow
thought his voice should be the same. But it wasn't. It
was deep and assured, with just a hint now and then
of Continental phrasing and British intonation from
having spent so many years abroad. Talking to him
like this, without the benefit of others to provide a
buffer, made her feel very young and very gauche.

"What can he remember after all this time?" she
asked, trying to keep her voice pitched low. She didn't
want anyone to overhear their conversation.

He put his arm under her elbow and steered her into
the deserted activity room, where the baby quilt she'd
commissioned for Liza was set up in its frame. She
studied the design of interlocking blocks and the ap-
pliquéd border of bunnies and chicks in a riot of rain-
bow colors far more intently than necessary, trying to
hide her distress...and her doubts. "Almost forty
years have passed since that night. Your father's health
has suffered. His memory may be faulty as well."

Edward's dark brows drew together in a slight frown. Alyssa realized too late that she sounded angry and defensive, and she hated herself for letting the fear show. Her emotions always lay close to the surface. She worked hard to keep them hidden, but sometimes the armor slipped, as it had just now.

"He was the caretaker of the lodge for years, Lyssa. That might be all they want to question him about."

"Do you think so?"

Two of the residents stopped in the doorway a moment before crossing the hallway into the dining room. The pianist arrived and started practicing hymns. Someone began to sing along.

"I don't know." Edward watched her closely.

"*I* don't remember." She clutched the songbooks to her breast, unaware how clearly her distress showed in her voice, in her eyes.

"You were just a child." He bent his head, lifted his hand as though to touch her hair, caress her cheek, but dropped it again.

Alyssa barely noticed. Her thoughts were turned inward, back to that terrible night. Her dreams lately had been more clear, the men in them less shadowy, more defined. Her father she recognized, always telling her in a sad, weary voice that her mother had gone away, wasn't coming back, and that they would have to make a family together, just the two of them.

But it wasn't her father who had carried her away from Margaret, crying heartbrokenly. It was a man who looked very much like the one standing before her, very much as Phil Wocheck had looked at that age. Edward's return to Tyler had triggered that particular memory, she was sure of it now. But Phil wasn't the man who had made her mother cry, who had hurt her mother, of that she was almost certain. In her dreams there was another man. One she didn't know and couldn't place.

At least, she thought there was another man. Or was it only her own mind playing tricks on her to keep her from remembering the truth? Sometimes the horror rose up to choke off her breath. Perhaps she had killed her mother. Why else did she keep dreaming of herself, so little and afraid, holding a gun? And pulling the trigger? She wanted to reach out and touch the quilt in its frame, be reassured by its warmth and softness, but her hands were full of songbooks. She stood quietly, aching with anxiety.

"Lyssa, are you all right?" Edward's voice brought her back from the cold darkness of nightmare.

"Yes," she said, deliberately relaxing her grip on the songbooks, lowering them to her waist. Alyssa smiled down at the quilt, proof of hope for the future, a symbol of her love for Liza's unborn child, her grandchild. "I'm fine. It's just..." She let the sentence trail off into silence. "We probably shouldn't even be talking about this. Amanda told me not to speak to anyone until the grand jury has finished hearing the evidence against my father."

"How's he holding up?" Edward's voice held concern, with none of the hatred he'd felt for her father years ago evident in his words.

"I'm worried about him. His health is suffering. He's not a young man."

"I wouldn't worry too much, Lyssa. He's a tough old bastard." He smiled then, and it was as if the years fell away before her eyes. This was the Eddie she'd known and thought she loved so long ago.

She smiled back; she couldn't help herself. "He is very strong. And determined to see his name cleared."

"The word around town is that Amanda is going to represent him."

Alyssa nodded. "My father insists on it." She lifted her head proudly. "I know she'll do an excellent job."

"The state will assign their best people to this case," he cautioned. "If Amanda needs any help, let me know. Addison Corporation has a fistful of topflight lawyers on retainer."

"Thank you for the offer, Edward," she said stiffly, formally. There were just too many people milling around the lobby, glancing into the dayroom, walking in and out of the dining room as they waited for the service to start. She couldn't be at ease around him. He was too often in her thoughts these days anyway, in her daydreams. When he was with her, close to her, it made her nervous. She hadn't felt like this—so alive, so much a woman—in many years. Her feelings for him, both old and new, confused her and undermined her hard-won serenity. "I have to go. I'll see you again, I hope."

Did she really want to see him again? *No*, her brain told her, but the sudden acceleration of her heartbeat made a lie of the thought.

"Of course we'll see each other, Lyssa." Was it only her imagination or did he intend to make her name sound like a caress, like love words? "Soon."

ALYSSA TURNED and hurried across the hall, as if she couldn't get away from him fast enough. She couldn't seem to make up her mind how to treat him—as an old friend or a new enemy.

He watched the sway of her hips beneath the soft folds of her dress. She was a very attractive woman. And though he might not love her anymore, she was still important to him, there was no use lying to himself about that. When he first returned to Tyler, he'd thought she was still the same old Alyssa, her father's little girl in a woman's body, soft, pliable, easily led. Now he wasn't so sure. She was under a hell of a lot of pressure, but she hadn't broken under the strain.

He'd learned to trust his hunches over the years and he had one now. Whatever was frightening Alyssa Baron came from within, something that she had seen or heard the night Margaret Ingalls died.

Something that concerned his father, as well.

That was why he was here so early on a Sunday morning—to visit Phil. He hadn't expected to meet Alyssa at Worthington House, but the chance encounter wasn't going to stop him from trying to find out everything his dad knew about Margaret's death.

Alyssa was convinced her father was innocent of any crime. That conviction shone from her summer blue eyes, sounded in the sweet cadences of her voice. She truly believed Judson had not killed his wife.

Edward wasn't so sure about Phil.

He started down the hall and saw his father sitting in his wheelchair, watching him from the doorway of his room. The old man was frowning, his expression dour.

"Good morning, Dad."

Phil only grunted in reply and backed his chair into the room so that Edward could enter. "Shut the door," he said, maneuvering himself close to the window. "What brings you here so early in the morning? Why aren't you at Mass?"

"I haven't gone to Mass in twenty years, you know that."

"Humph," Phil growled, looking out the window, not at his son. "Your immortal soul is in danger. You should go."

"I'll think about it, Dad. That's not why I'm here." Edward closed the door and walked across the small sunny room, placing himself between his father and the window, forcing the old man to look at him.

Phil frowned harder, his bushy white eyebrows effectively hiding the expression in his faded gray eyes. "You came to see Alyssa Ingalls," he said slyly, trying to draw him into an argument.

Edward loved his father, but their relationship had never been a particularly friendly one. He wasn't about to be sidetracked. He ignored the gambit and Phil's use of Alyssa's maiden name. "I had no idea she would be here," he said tersely. "That's not why I came."

"Why then?" the old man asked, folding his gnarled hands in his lap, looking down, away from the bright light coming into the room through the window behind Edward's back.

Edward moved to the bed, sat down on the high, hard mattress. "I came about you appearing before the grand jury when it convenes. I came to hear from your own mouth what happened at Timberlake Lodge the night Margaret Ingalls died."

Phil stared hard, looking him straight in the eye. "I don't remember what happened."

"That's a lie, Dad. I think you do remember." Edward felt his heart thud against the wall of his chest. "Do you know who killed Margaret Ingalls?"

"No." Phil spit the word into the air between them. "No."

"You're lying to me, Dad. I was there when Brick found the gun in your room at the Kelseys'." He stood up, shoved his hands into the pockets of his slacks, leaned forward. He hated intimidating his own father but he didn't see any other way to make the stubborn old man tell him the truth. "Did you kill Margaret Ingalls?"

"No." Phil rose shakily to his feet, gripping the arms of his chair for balance, his face white with pain and the strain of bearing his weight on his healing hip. "I did not kill that whore."

"Sit down, Dad. Sit down before you fall." Edward put both hands under his father's arms. Phil grasped his forearms, leaned against him and lowered himself back into the chair. "I did not kill her."

Edward squatted, bringing his face level with the stooped old man's. "Then why did you have the gun? Why did you keep it all those years? There's been no love lost between you and Judson Ingalls. Why did you hide Margaret's suitcase in the potting shed? That was you, wasn't it?" The old man nodded once. "Why were you shielding Judson Ingalls at the risk of being implicated in the murder yourself?"

"Don't ask me any more questions, Edward. You do not want to know the answers."

"Dad, you're going to have to talk to the grand jury. They can put you in jail. If you don't cooperate, the district attorney will think you have something to hide. You could end up in the same boat that Judson Ingalls is in."

Phil shrugged, grinning vaguely. He lifted gnarled, shaking hands. His shoulders drooped, his mouth dropped open. He looked frail and vague, helpless. The transformation sent a cold chill down Edward's spine. "What can they do? I am an old man. I'm crippled. I forget things. Many things. More things every day. Margaret Ingalls—may her whoring soul burn in hell for eternity—died forty years ago. I—" he spread his hands pathetically "—I cannot even remember what I had for breakfast today."

Edward jerked to his feet. "Damn it, Dad. Stop that. Your mind's as good as it ever was. You do remember what happened that night out at Timberlake. But why in hell are you protecting Judson Ingalls? It's not up to you to play judge and jury. All you have to do is tell them what happened. What you know to be true."

"The truth is not always so simply told." Phil straightened in his chair. "Do not push this matter, son. You may not like to hear what I say. It is true I have no love for Judson Ingalls. But no man deserves to be made to dance to a woman's tune as he was. There were always parties, and dances, drink. And other men. She had no shame."

"Or maybe she wanted everyone to think as much," Edward interjected thoughtfully. "Maybe she only wanted Judson to think there were other men so that he would pay more attention to her."

Phil shrugged again. He looked down at his hands, clasped together in his lap. "Possibly, but I do not think so. That night, the night she died, she was running away from Judson. And her child."

"Leaving Alyssa? She must have been very vain and selfish. Or very unhappy."

"A woman does not leave her child," Phil said, without a hint of compassion for the long-dead Margaret. "There is no excuse good enough. I'd been working by the lake, getting ready to plant a tree the next morning. I heard a shot and ran to the lodge to see what had happened."

"How was it that you heard a gun fired and no one else did?"

Phil lifted his hands in a helpless gesture. "I was walking across the yard. The guests, Margaret's guests, were dancing and drinking and making much noise, the way Americans do, in the main room of the lodge.

Margaret's bedroom was on the other side of the building, facing the lake.'' He looked toward the window, but Edward knew his eyes were seeing inward, into the past. "It was almost dark. There were loud voices coming from the room—an argument, a bad one. Then there was a shot, and I saw a man run from Margaret's room, around the building. It was dark. I could not tell if it was Judson Ingalls or another.''

"Did you hear a car go down the driveway? Or see one leave?''

"There was always much coming and going at Timberlake during one of Margaret's parties....'' Phil's voice trailed off. He sat silently, staring out the window.

"What happened next, Dad?'' Edward prompted, more gently than before. His father looked very old and frail. He felt like a bastard, making him relive the past this way.

"I looked into the room. There were clothes on the bed, a suitcase half-full of her things. Dresses, lacy things, a hat with feathers. The safe in the wall was open, and Margaret was lying on the floor by the bed.''

"Was she dead?'' Edward couldn't stop the prickle of fear that raised the hair at the back of his neck.

"Yes. But I didn't know that at the time. I only saw her lying on the floor, a little under the bed. And there was blood. Much blood.'' He spoke the words simply, without embellishment, but the effect was dramatic.

"Go on, Dad." Edward leaned forward, hands between his knees, his forearms braced on his thighs. "Did you check to see if she was still alive?"

Phil shook his head. "So much blood, on her face, in her hair. I didn't think she could be alive. And she was not alone."

"Alyssa?"

"Yes. The child. She was crying, almost hysterical. She kept calling for her mommy. She could not see Margaret from where she was standing. I picked her up in my arms. Carried her to her bedroom, shutting the door to Margaret's room behind me. We met no one in the halls. I laid her in bed. She was dressed in a little pink-and-white-striped nightgown with lace. Here and here." He pointed to his throat and to his wrists. "So small and pretty. She was a little princess. But so sad and so frightened. I stayed with her, talked to her. All the time I was afraid someone would find Margaret. Find the gun, which was lying on her bed."

"But no one did," Edward interjected.

"No one had been in the room. When I went back I touched her body. There was no pulse, as I knew there would not be. Margaret was dead. Murdered. I made myself look around the room. I thought there might be something to tell me who the man I saw running away could be. He was her lover, I think."

"Or her husband."

Phil lifted his shoulders, thin and bony beneath his short-sleeved, white Sunday shirt. "I do not know. But I do know she was running away. There was a note on the mantelpiece. It was her paper, the color of lilacs in May and smelling of her scent. I read it. She was running away from her husband, abandoning her child. So I helped her to go from Timberlake. I packed her clothes and put her suitcase in the potting shed where no one ever went but me. I wrapped her in a shawl and buried her body in the hole I had already dug for the tree I was planting. If the lawyers and the juries want to say I killed her, that is fine. I do not care. I'm an old man. I do not have many years left. I will spend them in prison if I have to, but I will not say more.''

"Why, Dad?" Edward did reach out this time, taking his father's cold, twisted hands between his own. "There's no love lost between you and Judson Ingalls. If he's the man you saw leaving Margaret's room, then he should have to pay for what he did to her."

Phil twisted his hands from Edward's grasp and clamped his gnarled fingers around his son's wrists. His grip was surprisingly strong. "I care nothing for Ingalls. Let them think he was the man who ran from the room. I will tell that much of my story if they make me. But I will not tell the rest."

"You can tell me, Dad."

"Yes," Phil said, relaxing back against his chair. "Because you still love her, whether you know it or not. Whether she knows it or not."

"Lyssa? She was just a child, a little girl."

"She was holding the gun when I stepped through the French doors," Phil said. "She was standing on the other side of the bed with the gun in her hands, still warm from the shot." He released Edward's hands, slumped back in his chair. "Alyssa, the child, was holding the gun. I think, God help me, that she shot her mother, and I will take that knowledge with me to my grave."

CHAPTER NINE

"CECE? Cece, are you home?"

"Coming, Liza," she called, recognizing her visitor's voice and frowning slightly at the strident tone. "What's wrong?" She pushed her hair behind her ears and ran her hands down the front of her cotton shorts before opening the front door and letting in a blast of humid, early-September heat.

"I need your help." Liza was panting slightly, as if she'd run all the way up the walk from the street. A battered old pickup was parked at the curb. "At the clinic."

"What's the problem?"

"Come on, I'll explain it in the truck," Jeff's sister urged, tugging at Cece's hand. "We've got work to do. And not a man in sight. They're never around when we need them, are they?"

"Liza, what in heaven's name is going on?" Cece demanded, setting her feet on the top step, refusing to be dragged off her mother's front porch until she knew exactly what she was needed to do.

"You've got to help me clear the supplies and equipment out of the clinic. The landlord's foreclosing. We've got twenty-four hours to come up with the back rent or he's changing the locks on the doors."

"The clinic is being evicted? I didn't think the money problems were that bad."

"Believe me, they are," Liza insisted.

"Surely if you talk to the man... Who is the landlord, anyway?"

"Some car dealer from Chicago. The clinic might be on the wrong side of the tracks, but the property is worth a lot of money. I'm sure he's trying to break the lease. Cliff's in Madison, picking up replacement parts for the air-conditioning unit at Timberlake. I tried to get Byron and Nora to help but I forgot. They're out of town on sort of a belated honeymoon," she continued breathlessly. "Jeff's working a double shift in the ER tonight because it's the holiday weekend and everyone else is off. There's no one to get the stuff out but us."

"Surely the clinic directors could try reasoning with the man...."

Liza gave her a scathing look. "Cece, haven't you figured it out by now? There are no clinic directors. It's Jeff. Just Jeff. It's always been his project. Didn't the name give it away to you?"

"I—I've never heard the name. You've always just called it the free clinic."

"Well, it's the Ronald Baron Clinic. Named after my dad. Jeff runs it. Staffs it most of the time. And pays most of the bills."

Cece didn't know whom to be more angry at—Jeff, for never telling her the truth, or herself, for not figuring out the obvious without having to be told. He had loved his father, mourned his death and what he felt was his dishonor. She should have known he would try to restore Ronald's place in Tyler's esteem.

Liza was tugging at her hand again. "Come on. It's going to get dark early tonight. It's clouding up to rain. We've got to hurry."

"I've got some money in the bank. I could lend it to Jeff. Wouldn't that be easier?"

"Do you have five thousand dollars?" Liza asked, turning to start down the steps. She grabbed the wrought-iron railing to steady herself, her unwieldy stomach throwing her off balance.

"Five...thousand dollars?"

"It is a lot," Liza agreed, her incredible blue eyes narrowed thoughtfully. "A whole year's rent, actually. I guess the guy that owns the building isn't such a rat after all. But that's beside the point." She waved the observation aside as she half walked, half ran down the sidewalk. "Are you going to help me or not?" she called over her shoulder.

"Liza, slow down. You'll slip and fall, hurt yourself or the baby." Cece had noticed last night at their final prenatal class that Liza's baby had dropped, but she hadn't said anything. With a first baby, it could mean that birth was still a week or two away. Liza's due date was a week from Sunday.

"I'm fine." She stopped and looked back as she rounded the front fender of the old pickup. "Please, Cece. I don't think I can do it alone. Jeff's already paid for most of the stuff in there. Maybe we can use it someplace else. Keep the clinic going, if we can get it out."

"I'll come," Cece said, bowing to the inevitable. "But I'll drive."

THE NEXT FOUR HOURS were hectic. Liza had keys to the building and they drove around to the back door, backing the truck to within a few feet of the entrance. Liza wanted to take everything she could lay her hands on, but Cece suggested they pack the clinic records and all the smaller portable equipment and supplies first.

Then, as rain clouds rolled across the setting sun, they were faced with the problem of where to store what they had taken. Liza decided on her grandfather's house, and they rattled into the driveway just as Alyssa was also returning home. She took one look at Liza's flushed face and excited eyes as her daughter explained their predicament and insisted on being included in the move.

They'd taken most of the lightweight and portable equipment and supplies the first time around. Now, as afternoon faded into evening, they were faced with moving unwieldy carts and cabinets and heavy furniture. Cece and Alyssa managed with much pushing and shoving to get the rest of the filing cabinets and medicine lockers onto the back of the pickup, but Cece felt like a rag doll by the time they were finished. She sank onto the lowered tailgate of the pickup, breathing hard.

"We should never have attempted this without more help and the proper equipment," Alyssa said candidly.

"Probably not," Cece agreed, resting her left shoulder against the fender as she shifted to face Alyssa. "But it's hard to say no to Liza when she's in full sail."

Alyssa laughed. "Yes, it is." She rested her elbows on the sides of the truck and lowered her chin to the back of her crossed hands. "I just hope we're doing the right thing. Jeff may not appreciate our taking the initiative this way. He may have had other plans. He seldom loses his temper, but when he does..." She lifted her head. "I, for one, don't care to be nearby."

"Someone should have told me this was Jeff's clinic," Cece said, sounding miserable and not caring.

"Yes, *he* should have," Alyssa replied. Their eyes met for a long, telling moment.

Cece looked down at her hands. "He's very good at avoiding conversations about himself."

"Jeff doesn't wear his heart on his sleeve. He's very like his father in that respect. The kind of man who keeps his troubles to himself."

"He never asked for my help," Cece said, looking inward, looking into the past. "He always seemed so sure of himself, so in control." She stopped talking before she said anything else that was too revealing of her confused feelings.

"It's hard sometimes, to love someone so strong and self-sufficient." Jeff's mother looked out across the scraggly, weed-filled lot behind the clinic. "You can't always tell what is strength and what is silent desperation." She was quiet a moment, as if listening to the evening sounds, hearing the distant whistle of a train and children arguing over a baseball game in the backyard of the house next door. "He took his father's death, his suicide, very hard. Then, finding out Tyler Elevator was bankrupt made it harder to bear. None of us had realized my husband's financial problems were so severe."

"And Jeff blamed himself."

"He loved his father. He felt guilty for not being there for him, though heaven knows what a nineteen-year-old boy could have done to make things different."

"He could have told me. He should have told me."

"Yes," Alyssa agreed. "But he didn't. And we can't go back and make things right in the past, no matter how badly we want to."

Cece remained silent.

"We'd better get back to work," Alyssa said gently but firmly. She pushed herself away from the truck in one graceful motion. "It's clouding up quickly. It will probably rain before dark, just as my son-in-law predicted."

Her observations on the weather gave Cece a moment to pull herself together, just as Alyssa no doubt had intended it should.

"Back to work," Cece agreed. But, in light of what Alyssa had said about Jeff, she couldn't help analyzing his behavior ten years ago from a different perspective—from the view of a woman who had loved a man and lost him, not with the narrow, selfish vision of an idealistic heartbroken girl.

"Where's Liza?" Alyssa asked, looking around. She'd tied her hair back with the celadon-and-blue silk scarf that had been draped across her shoulders hours before. There was a grease stain on her dark green linen slacks. Cece had never seen Jeff's mother looking so tired or disheveled, or so very much alive.

"Inside, resting on the couch. I hope," Cece added under her breath. Sliding off the tailgate, she brushed dust and cobwebs off her yellow shorts.

"We'd better check on her." Alyssa didn't sound worried about her daughter, or seem that way, either. Unless you looked into her eyes. Her eyes were scared. "She's very close to her time," she said, as though she couldn't keep herself from talking. "And if she's anything like me... Well, by the time Liza came along I was camping on the hospital doorstep weeks before my due date."

"First babies always take longer," Cece replied automatically, finding obscure comfort herself in the old truism. She wasn't worried about Liza going into labor, she told herself sternly. She wasn't worried at all.

But she wasn't surprised when they found her that way. She was sitting on the floor outside the doorway of the first exam cubicle, knees drawn up, white-faced and trembling.

"Liza!" Alyssa dropped to her knees beside her daughter. "Liza, honey, did you hurt yourself? Or is it the baby?" Cece's eyes followed Alyssa's as she glanced into the cubicle, saw the heavy, old-fashioned examination table lodged firmly in the doorway.

"I couldn't get it out," Liza said breathlessly. "I don't know about the baby. I thought I twisted my back. Now—ouch!—it's both, I think. For the past hour or so I've had cramps, then this incredible contraction...and I think...my water broke." She clutched the doorframe as another contraction caught her. "You lied to me." She glared at Cece. "You said there'd be time to get used to it...to get ready for it."

"There usually is," Cece said grimly. "But I don't think this is going to be one of them."

"Cliff," Liza said, drawing a sobbing breath as the contraction eased. "I want Cliff."

"I'll call the lodge and tell them to send him in to town the moment he returns from Madison," Alyssa promised, helping Cece get Liza to her feet.

"He won't get here in time. I know it," she moaned.

"Of course he will," Cece said bracingly, as much for her own sake as for Liza's. "First babies always take awhile. Remember, Mary was in labor all night."

"I won't be." She clutched her stomach. "Cece! Mom, I think you'd better call Jeff first and tell him we're on our way."

Alyssa looked anxious, glancing at Cece for guidance.

"Maybe I'd better check her over before we leave for the hospital." Cece's pulse was racing. She was scared, certain she couldn't handle this alone. "Liza, lie down here on the couch." They were passing through the meeting room. Liza sank gratefully onto the wide old leather couch.

"I'll get Jeff on the line," Alyssa said, spotting the phone on the wall.

Cece conducted the examination quickly but thoroughly, the actions familiar and natural, but forced, the way she'd feared they would be after so many months. She didn't want to be alone. She needed help...she needed Jeff. Liza's labor was indeed proceeding at breakneck speed, but there was still time to get her to the hospital, turn her over to the staff at Tyler General.

She heard Alyssa speaking quietly into the phone. So did Liza, who looked across the room at her mother. "Is that Jeff? Tell him to clear the halls. I'm on my way." A contraction rippled across her swollen stomach. Cece glanced at her watch. Three minutes. Closer and harder than ever.

"Breathe, Liza," she commanded, suiting action to words, leading Jeff's sister through the exercise automatically, scared to death inside. Liza obeyed, settling back against the high arm of the couch, her knees drawn up in a more comfortable position. "Tell Jeff she's progressing very rapidly," she directed Alyssa, holding Liza's hand as the contraction strengthened, then tapered off. Ten minutes at the most and they'd be at the hospital. She wouldn't be alone.

"He wants to talk to you, Cece." Alyssa held out the receiver. "Hurry, please," she said more quietly, catching and holding Cece's gaze over the top of Liza's head. "I'll sit with her," she added, as Cece advanced toward the phone. The worry in Alyssa's eyes faded away, by a sheer act of will, Cece suspected, as she moved toward the couch where her daughter lay.

"Cece? Is that you?"

She hadn't heard Jeff's voice in almost a week. She hadn't realized how much she missed him until she did. For a long heartbeat or two she didn't answer. "Yes, Jeff, it's me." In the background the sounds of controlled, directed chaos came echoing through the receiver. Her pulse jumped and accelerated once again. Something was very wrong.

"We've got a real situation here," he said, raising his voice to carry over the noise around him. "Two pickup trucks loaded with teenagers were racing each other out on the lake road. One of them sideswiped the other. In about fifteen minutes we're going to have every ambulance from two counties in here. I'm drafting every doctor in house to help me out. That includes Hank Merton." He sounded as calm as if they were merely discussing the approaching storm, whose thunder and lightning were playing havoc with the connection. "Tell me my baby sister is going to hang around long enough to get these kids stabilized and evacuated to Madison and Milwaukee."

"I can't," Cece replied, hoping, for Alyssa's and Liza's sakes, she sounded equally in control of her small emergency. "You're going to be an uncle very soon." In her heart, she wanted him to hear the fear she was hiding from the others; hear and take the fear away.

"Dammit, that's what I was afraid you'd say. Leave it to Liza to do it in record time." A siren wailed in the distant background. "Cece, are you still there?"

"I'm here."

"You'll do fine." There was no special emphasis on the words. He made it a fact, a given.

"I can't do it, Jeff."

"Yes, you can. You haven't been in the trenches for a while, that's all. You'll be fine as soon as the shootin' starts, soldier."

"Jeff, it isn't funny."

The siren grew louder. "Listen, Cece, I have to go. They're bringing in the first load of kids." This time she heard a faint surge of adrenaline in his voice. "I'm trusting my sister and her baby's life to you. Don't let me down." His voice held her, buoyed her, gave her strength.

"We'll do fine," she said, and suddenly, incredibly, she meant it.

"Where are you, anyway?" His voice was muffled, as if he'd turned away from the phone.

Cece felt a jolt of guilt. Jeff truly didn't know what they were up to. Liza *had* taken on the rescue of the clinic assets entirely on her own.

"We're at the clinic."

"The clinic? Damn that interfering little sister of mine." The words were harsh, but there was no censure in his tone.

"You should have told me, Jeff."

"I know. No more soul-searching now, Cece. There's no time. At least you should be able to find everything you need. And Mom's a brick—don't let anyone tell you she's not. Jesus," he said reverently, under his breath. The siren was very loud. "Here we go." The connection was broken abruptly.

"Cece!" It was Liza, calling urgently.

Cece steepled her fingers before her lips. She took a long, deep breath, a second, a third. She could do it. She had to believe that, have faith in herself. She could deliver Liza's baby. She didn't need Jeff, although she wished desperately that he could be at her side.

Jeff, not Steve.

She couldn't stop to consider the significance of that momentous admission. She didn't have time. She had a baby to deliver—by herself.

"Coming, Liza," she called, already running through a list of items she'd need that Alyssa was going to have to find in the chaos of boxes standing on the floor around them. "It's just you and me and the little one—and Grandma. And we're all going to be just fine. Ready?"

Liza nodded, reaching out to grasp Cece's outstretched hand.

"Here we go."

"GRANDDAD, what are you doing here?" Jeff got out of the car and walked toward Judson, turning up the collar of his jacket against the lightly falling rain that lingered after the recent thunderstorms.

"What does it look like I'm doing?" the old man responded sharply. "I'm checking the cover on this load of your clinic equipment to see that it's tied down properly and nothing got soaked by the rain. Looks like your mother and the Scanlon girl did a good job," he added, his voice muffled as he looked under the lightweight plastic tarp. "Everything's right and tight under there."

"Where is Mom? And Cece? And Liza?" Jeff added, looking around the parking lot, spotting his sister Amanda's car and the Timberlake Lodge pickup that Cliff sometimes drove when doing work for the hotel. "Is everyone inside?"

"Yep," Judson said with a nod toward the clinic door. "They're in there with your sister and my new great-granddaughter."

"The baby's been born already?" Jeff asked, not all that surprised by the news. He grinned. "Liza's always in such a damned hurry."

"Since she was a little girl," Judson agreed.

"I'm an uncle," Jeff said with a grin. "It's a girl?"

"That's what I said."

"I'd better go inside."

"They're waiting for you," Judson informed him. "You look damned near as thunderstruck as Forrester did when he got here and found out Mary Elizabeth was ready to deliver."

"Poor Cliff." Jeff grinned again. He wanted to see Liza and the baby. He also wanted to be with Cece. How had she handled the birth? What were her thoughts about it? How was she feeling? *Did she want to be with him?*

"She's a pretty baby, if I do say so myself." Judson retied the corner of the tarp he'd loosened. "I'm go-

ing to drive this stuff out to the plant and store it there.
The night watchman can help me unload it. Your
mother and Liza got the garage at the house full up to
the rafters already." He leaned one arm on the side of
the truck. "Taking this stuff out of here is probably
illegal."

"Probably," Jeff agreed, meeting his grandfather's eyes. "I owe the guy who owns this building
damn near a whole year's rent."

"We'll get it straightened out," the old man said
gruffly, looking away. "In the meantime, I don't see
any need for all this gear to be locked up here doing no
one any good. I may not have agreed with you opening this clinic. I've always believed people should help
themselves, not depend on the government or others
for everything. But I'm not so blind stubborn I can't
see now there's a need for it to go on functioning."

"No landlord is going to take me on without a lot
of earnest money up front. And I just don't have it."
Jeff stared out across the parking lot, unable to look
his grandfather in the eye.

Judson chuckled gruffly. "Boy, you may well be the
only poor doctor I ever heard of."

"I may be one of a kind," Jeff agreed with a rueful
grin.

"I'll tell you what I'm going to do," Judson said,
twirling his flashlight between his big, square-fingered
hands. "I'm going to let you set up shop out at the
plant. There's four offices sitting empty since I had to
let those two assistant managers and their secretaries
go. I have to heat them in the winter and cool them in

the summer whether anyone's using them or not. We can work out something about the electricity, if you insist, but no rent. What do you say, Jeff?"

"Are you sure you want to do that?"

Judson reached out and put his arm around Jeff's shoulders. "I'm sure. If there's one thing I've learned from this whole terrible business of your grandmother's death, it's that you can't always be in control of what happens to you. You can't always get out of a jam on your own, either—you need family and friends. Some people don't have family to lean on. They need help, someone to reach out to. Like you and the work you do at the clinic. I may be old and set in my ways, but I'm not a fool. I can still learn, and change a little even at my age."

Jeff knew how hard it was for his grandfather to talk about Margaret's murder even so obliquely. He also knew Judson meant what he said. He might have been against the idea of the clinic before, but from now on he'd back it to the limit.

"You've got a deal, Granddad," Jeff said, holding out his hand. Judson clasped it firmly between his own.

"Good. We won't speak of it again." This disclaimer, too, was in character for the older man. Once he made up his mind, considered you worthy of the authority he'd delegated to you, he backed off, let you operate on your own. "You do what you have to do out at the plant to get this clinic open again as quick as you can. I'd say spare no expense, but I'm not feeling quite that sentimental or reckless." He chuckled and clapped Jeff on the shoulder once more. "Just do what you have to and I'll sign the checks."

"Thanks, Granddad." Jeff could have said more but he didn't. Words weren't necessary between them at the moment.

"Let's go inside," Judson suggested. "I want to see that new little one again. She's pretty as a picture, looks just like Mary Elizabeth and your mother."

Jeff opened the clinic door. Liza's voice carried clearly down the hall. It was filled with excitement and satisfaction, mingled with her usual stubborn determination to have her own way. She was half sitting, half lying on the meeting room couch holding her daughter in her arms, her legs covered by a thin cotton blanket. Cliff was perched on the back of the sofa, looking dazed and proud as he gazed lovingly at his wife and daughter. He kept reaching out a finger, tentatively, to touch the baby's downy blond hair.

"I'm going to name her Margaret," Liza said defiantly, obviously not for the first time. "Margaret Alyssa," she elaborated, glancing at her mother, who was sitting on the couch also, Cece and Amanda standing by her side. "I've been looking at all those old pictures we found out at the lodge. Remember the package of them I told you about? She looks just like you did when you were a baby. And she looks just like Grandmother, too. Granddad—" she held out her hand when she realized Judson had entered the room "—say it's all right. It's time we Ingallses stood up together, did something to show this whole town that we know what they're saying about you . . . and about Margaret . . . isn't true.''

"It's all right with me, honey." His strong face twisted with emotion, Judson leaned down, kissed Liza on top of her head. "I've made my peace with your grandmother's ghost, even though it took getting thrown in jail to do it. I should have forgiven her a long time ago. I hope she forgave me . . . before she died.''

Judson touched the baby's waving, upraised fist and turned away, walking across the room to stare out the window at nothing. Alyssa looked stricken by her father's grief and remorse, but seemed unable to act on the impulse to comfort him. Jeff stepped forward to admire his niece and to give his mother and Judson a few moments to come to grips with their feelings. He didn't seem able to do much to solve his family's troubles, but he could at least give them a little privacy by returning everyone's attention to the baby in his sister's arms.

"She's a beauty, sis," he said, leaning forward to give his sister a quick kiss on the cheek. She looked exhausted, but flushed with success and pride at her accomplishment.

"Jeff! You're here. Is everything all right at the hospital? What about those kids in the accident?" She lifted the baby for him to take in his arms.

"They're all pretty well banged up—cuts, bruises, broken bones. Three of them we're transferring to Sugar Creek, but they're all going to make it. It's a miracle. Just like this little princess. Hello, Margaret Alyssa. I'm your Uncle Jeff.''

He glanced up to find Cece watching him with the same proud fierceness in her expression that Liza had, only her eyes were different—softer, sadder. Their gazes met and held for a long heartbeat before Cece looked away, back at Liza and Cliff, shutting him out. But Jeff read the emotions behind the barrier of her thick dark lashes as easily as he'd been able to read the needs and desires of a younger, less complicated Cece a decade before. She was mourning what she had lost: the man, the children he would have given her.

Jeff was consumed with a sudden overwhelming urge to wipe that sadness from her eyes and from her heart. He didn't begrudge her her memories of a dead husband, but he didn't want her to mourn at Steve Hayes's grave for the rest of her life. She was his. She belonged to him now, even if she didn't know it yet. He wanted to be the man in her thoughts and in her dreams. He wanted to be the father of her children.

He looked down at his niece, her red baby face screwed into a frown, her tiny fists curled against her cheek, and his body tightened with a need more intense than anything he had ever known. Together he and Cece could produce a child as marvelous as this one. Together they could create a family and a future of their own, strong enough to blot out the sadness of the past.

But that resolution was more easily made than kept. There were greater obstacles to overcome than the memories of Cece's lost love and his own unresolved feelings about his father's suicide. There was the very real and troubling series of events that had occurred at Worthington House over the past couple of weeks. The results of the tests he'd had done on the retirement center's stock of narcotics by an independent laboratory had arrived by express mail. And Cece wasn't going to want to hear what he had to tell her about those results.

He frowned, and the baby, in her own way, sensed his confusion and unrest. She opened her tiny red mouth and let out a wail of protest. Automatically Liza reached out her hands for her daughter, frowning, too, at his ineptness, and Jeff relinquished his niece with a grin.

"Did you pinch her?" Liza asked facetiously, bending over her daughter to make certain no harm had come to the infant.

"No." Jeff laughed, all of a sudden not knowing what to do with his hands. The baby had felt right and good in his arms and he missed holding her. "Listen, why don't you let me drive you out to the hospital and have Hank Merton check you over?"

"Not tonight," Liza said, lifting her free hand to her mouth to stifle a yawn. "I'm beat. I want to sleep in my own bed. And anyway, Cece said I'm fine. She says it was the easiest delivery she's ever seen," she boasted. "I'll make an appointment tomorrow to get a checkup for Margaret Alyssa and me. Okay?" she added to placate him. "But tonight the Forrester family is going back to the boathouse. Besides, I want to track down Nora and Byron, wherever they are, and tell them the good news. And Cliff's mother as well."

"She really is doing fine, Jeff," Cece put in. "There's no need to go to the hospital tonight."

"You're the boss," Jeff said, making her look at him once again, feeling his gut tighten with desire, his heart hammer against his chest when she smiled at him.

"No, Doctor," she replied with a great deal of satisfaction in her voice. "I'm only the midwife."

CHAPTER TEN

"CECE, WAIT."

She turned around, the keys to Liza's Thunderbird still in her hand. She'd assumed she had made good her escape from the boathouse where Liza and Cliff lived now that the lodge was open to the public, and where Liza had chosen to return with her newborn daughter. Jeff was still inside, busy congratulating his sister and brother-in-law, admiring his new niece, or so she'd thought. She'd been wrong.

"I'll drive you home in my car." He reached out his hand for the keys.

"Liza trusts me with her car." She smiled. "Don't you?" She curled her fingers around the keys, but couldn't deny the pleasure she felt inside that he hadn't let her leave alone.

"If you ride with me, it'll save Cliff having to come in to town with someone to get it in the morning."

In the morning. She wanted very much to still be with Jeff in the morning. A shiver of desire whispered across her skin. She wanted him, wanted him as her lover and her life partner, and she couldn't hide from the knowledge any longer.

Did he want the same? Did he dream of holding her in his arms, making love to her over and over again until dawn lightened the eastern sky? Timberlake Lodge rose behind them on the hillside, hiding the moon that had come out from behind the clouds. Half in darkness, half in moonlight, the old fishing lodge seemed suspended between its past and its future, casting its shadow almost to their feet. It was too dark where they stood in the parking lot to read Jeff's expression—and she was too afraid to ask.

"I should be getting home," she heard herself say. "My mother will be worried." It had been a long day, but it was hard to keep the exhilaration she felt over Liza's successful delivery out of her voice. She didn't want to come down from her high, be reminded of the problems that awaited her at Worthington House, face her own overwhelming feelings for the man standing beside her. Not yet.

"You've been avoiding me all week. I'm not going to let you get away from me tonight."

"I haven't been avoiding you." She still held the car keys, but she made no further move to open the door.

Jeff came a step closer. "What have you been doing?" He reached out one long arm and leaned against the car. He was wearing a short-sleeved summer shirt. The hair on his arm was golden in the light of the moon. She wanted to run her fingers along the hard muscles and tendons of his forearm, his wrist, the back of his hand. She corralled her runaway imagination, making herself think sensibly.

What had she been doing? She took her courage in both hands. "I've been waiting for you."

"Waiting for me?" He leaned closer. She stood her ground. There was nowhere else for her to go. No matter how much she had loved her husband, and mourned his death, some part of her had always been waiting for Jeff Baron.

"Waiting for you to tell me the truth about the clinic, the truth about why you didn't come back to me after your father's death. The truth about what you feel for me now."

"You don't want much from a man, do you?"

His lips were only inches from hers. Her heart beat fast and loud in her ears. "Honesty," she said, a whisper only. "Is that too much to ask?"

"No." He brushed her lips with his. "Not for you."

"Then tell me why... you left me."

"Because we had too many dreams, Cece." He cupped the back of her head in the palm of his hand. "Too many dreams to save the world, while my dad couldn't even save himself."

"His suicide affected you very deeply." She could see the pain, old and familiar, in his eyes, where the moonlight fell in a streak across his face.

"I loved my dad. I told him over and over again how you and I were going to go off together someplace halfway around the world and save lives because people there needed help. At the same time, right here in Tyler, right under our noses, my dad lost nearly everything he had and never told a soul. I'd come home talking about saving mankind, spending his money while I was doing it, and he never once asked me for help. And I never once offered, never even noticed he was having any problems.''

"We were idealistic and in love, and very, very young. A lot of farmers and the people they did business with went bankrupt then. You can't blame yourself for your father's death.''

"I know that now,'' he said, "but ten years ago I didn't. After his suicide I needed time to catch up. And there wasn't any money. That meant a lot more to me then than it does now.'' He chuckled ruefully, pressing her back against the car, resting his weight, heavy and arousing, against her. "And then there was you.''

"Me?'' What if he told her he loved her? What would she say?

"Yes, you. You were always so sure of yourself, so damned obstinate about the right way of doing things, always taking on the burdens of the world, with me tagging along behind you.''

"You make me sound like a zealot,'' she said miserably as he brushed the corners of her mouth with his thumbs, his eyes fixed on hers, making it impossible for her to look away.

"You were,'' he said with a smile that looked back into the past and saw the good times, not the pain. "But so earnest and so sure of yourself. After my dad . . . killed himself . . . I wasn't so sure about me. I needed time to sort things out, find my own best way of helping people. The trouble was we were both too young to realize that.''

"So you didn't come back for me. And I couldn't afford to come home. Not having enough money wasn't your problem alone."

"I felt as if it was. My whole world had been knocked off its foundation. I was suddenly faced with having to find money to continue school and to live on. My granddad did what he could, but it was still a shock. By the time I had my head screwed back on straight, you'd already found your Steve and married him."

"I loved him," she said, feeling the prick of tears behind her eyes, healing tears that washed away some more of her sadness and left only sweet, fading memories in its place.

"I'm glad. I wasn't that lucky. I made a few more mistakes in those years. The last and the biggest was my marriage. She regretted it almost as quickly as I did. We stuck it out for a while but it just got worse. She called it quits and I let her go. Then I came back to Tyler and found out this was where I belonged all the time."

"It's home," she said, and that was all. He kissed her then, long and tenderly.

"It's home," he repeated as he lifted his mouth from hers. He watched her closely for a long moment. His blue eyes, dark as indigo in the moonlight, narrowed in speculation. "I think we need to talk," he said, reaching down to ensnare her wrist so quickly she couldn't pull her hand away. "Give me the keys. We'll take my car." Her fingers opened at the slight pressure of his hand, almost as if they had a mind and will of their own. He opened the car door and pushed the keys under the seat. "The car will be safe here." He shut the door, firmly but quietly. "Come on."

"Where are we going? We can continue talking right here," she insisted, or tried to. Her voice broke infuriatingly in the middle of the sentence.

"Okay, Cece. I'll spell it out for you," he said with a look that heated her blood. "I don't want to talk. I want you someplace we can be alone, just the two of us." He gave her hand a tug. "Where do you want to go? Your place or mine?"

"I live with my mother," she reminded him, dragging her feet, uncertain now of what she did want.

"Come to think of it, so do I." He pretended to consider their options. "We could always go to that seedy motel out on the highway. I never had enough nerve to take you there when we were kids."

"Jeff." She stopped short, not because of what he had said, but because of what she had seen. He'd pulled his car keys out of his pants pocket. Something round and smooth caught the light. There was a spark of cool fire as a moonbeam reflected off polished stone. "Let me see," she said, holding out her hand. "Let me see."

He held up the key ring.

"It's my high school class ring," she said, feeling the last of her doubts slip away. Such an absurd little thing to tip the scales of your life. "You've kept it all these years."

"Yes," he said, looking down at the ring. "I have."

"Didn't your wife object?" She wished she had the strength of character not to ask him that question, but she didn't.

He looked directly into her eyes. "No," he said. "But I told you she decided pretty soon after we were married that she wasn't interested in my present or my future, let alone my past." He opened the car door. "Get in."

Cece did as she was told. She wanted to be alone with him, even if it meant in the dubious privacy of his car. Jeff climbed in on the driver's side and pulled her into his arms.

"I want to make love to you."

"That's sexist phrasing," she said, teasing a little, trying to make light of his words and the potent images they evoked until she had her racing heartbeat under control.

"I don't give a damn if it is," he said, his voice low and rough and intensely exciting. "I want you, all of you, here, tonight, even if it's in the back seat of this car."

Jeff..." To her chagrin tears stung her eyes. His passion, his need frightened her. She didn't know what to say, what to feel. She was falling in love again and scared to death. He knew she hadn't changed; making love was not something she did just because it felt right. It was a form of commitment, as binding as a vow. "I won't have an affair with you, Jeff." One tear escaped and slipped down her cheek.

Jeff wiped away the drop of moisture with the pad of his thumb. "Dammit, Cece. Don't cry. Don't make me feel like a clumsy, awkward boy again, like I'm trying to score on our first date. I want this to be right, to be special."

Suddenly she saw his pain and uncertainty as clearly as her own. He wasn't asking her only for physical love, but for her heart. Even if he hadn't yet spoken the words aloud, she knew he loved her. A smile trembled on her lips. She reached up, cupped his face in her hands, felt the stubble of his beard and the hard line of his jaw beneath her fingertips.

"With you it was always special."

"God, Cece." He pulled her close, kissed her hard and long, his hands roaming hungrily over the light cotton fabric of her blouse, the curve of her hip, her thigh. He groaned, shifting his weight on the seat, cursing the steering wheel, the gearshift, the seat belt posts that dug into his thigh.

Cece giggled. She couldn't help herself. She felt giddy with relief, with the wonder of bringing a new life into the world . . . with love? "Maybe it wasn't always so special," she said, laughing up into his face as he scowled down at her. For a moment she thought he was going to be angry. Then he smiled, wickedly, a pirate's smile as he eyed his prize.

"You're going to pay for that," he said ominously, pulling her upright into his arms, into his embrace, one hand boldly caressing the soft fullness of her breast, making her gasp with pleasure and need. "C'mon," he said, getting out of the car, pulling her across the seat with him.

"Where are we going?" Cece whispered, breathless, but not from the pace he set.

"Inside," he hissed, striding along the path toward the boathouse.

"We can't." Cece hung back. "Liza and Cliff are sleeping upstairs. They'll hear us. Come down to investigate."

Jeff shook his head, stray beams of moonlight glinting in his hair. "They won't notice a thing. They're in a world of their own tonight. Trust me."

"We'll get caught," she whispered back, following him through the small door at the back of the two-story building. "Where did you get a key?" she demanded.

"Everything the family wanted to save when Granddad sold the lodge to Edward Wocheck and the Addison Hotel people is stored in here. He kept the strip of land from the road to the lake for the family. We all have keys."

They stepped inside. The smell of dust and motor oil tickled Cece's nose. The sound of the lake was very near, just beyond the far wall. Jeff reached around her, flipped a switch, and a low-wattage bulb created a wan circle of light. Objects sprang out from the shadows all around them. The center of the high-ceilinged room was dominated by a small sailboat supported in a wooden cradle, her mast dismantled, her paint gray and peeling. The rest of the space was crowded with upended rowboats and outboard motors on racks along the wall, fishing equipment, shroud-covered lawn furniture and a stuffed moose head with a huge rack of antlers, sitting majestically in a fan-backed wicker chair against the wall.

"Goodness," Cece said, eyeing the moose head.

"Quite a collection," Jeff agreed, stepping forward to run his hand over the sleek bow of the little sailboat. "Looks like a giant flea market in here."

"She's a beauty." Cece, too, reached out to touch the sailboat.

"I asked Granddad to keep her. I'd like to restore her . . . someday, when I've got the time."

The boat was not new. Even Cece, who didn't know that much about sailboats, could see the craftsmanship was excellent, although the fine wood decks were dulled by dust and time. The boat was a classic, in need of lots of hard work and elbow grease to bring her back to her original glory.

"She belonged to my grandmother," Jeff said, his jaw hardening. "She's been locked up in here for forty years. It's time she saw the sunlight and felt the waves against her bow."

He stood quietly for a moment, his hand clenched into a fist as he struggled with his emotions. Cece didn't believe Judson Ingalls had killed his wife. She didn't have any proof, only a certainty in her heart. She wanted to pass that certainty on to Jeff, let him know how she felt. To do that, she'd have to make the first move to comfort him, and she knew if she stepped back into his embrace, her comforting would turn to need and need to desire.

"It's time for all of your grandmother's things to be brought back into the sunlight . . . including her mem-

ory. It will all work out right in the end, I know it will.
Just like the problems at Worthington House." She
lifted her arms and clasped her hands behind his neck.
She pressed against him, surprised and gratified by his
immediate response as his hands circled her waist and
pulled her more firmly into the cradle of his hips. He
lowered his head to kiss her.

"No more talk about Worthington House. No more
talk about my grandmother's death. Tonight it's just
us, Cece. You and me. Man and woman." He teased
her lips apart, let her feel his tongue, bold and strong
in her mouth, made her remember that she was a
woman, not a girl. And that he was a man, full-grown
and needy, not a boy.

"Jeff..." His hands roamed over her body, his
mouth teased and coaxed, demanded her response. "I
don't know..."

Was she ready for this? Was she ready to face life
head-on again, let go of the past completely? She had
loved her husband, would always love him, but he was
dead and gone and Jeff was very much alive. Once
again she was confused, off balance, uncertain of
what to say or do.

"Don't say anything else, Cece. Don't think about
anything else." He led her to a chaise longue beneath
the boathouse's single uncovered window, pulled off
the dusty linen sheet that covered its flowered cushion
and dropped it on the floor. He started undressing her,
then himself, then he lay down on the cushioned
wooden chaise, which protested his weight. "Just love
me. I know you're ready for love, physical love, be-

cause you're ready to come back to living. I saw it in your eyes tonight when you looked at Liza's baby. The baby you delivered.''

"I did," she said, her voice filled with wonder. "Liza and I did it together." The words came out thick and jumbled as he settled her beside him, smoothed his palm over her breast and down lower until his hand rested heavily at the juncture of her thighs. "I was scared to death at first, but I just kept going. One step at a time." She knew she wasn't making sense, but Jeff would understand. He had always understood her. "Liza was great. And Margaret Alyssa is the most beautiful baby in the world."

"I know, Cece. Welcome back." He parted her legs, settled his weight on top of her. "We'll talk about it later. Now let me love you."

She felt him then, at the soft, moist entrance to her body and her heart. She stiffened involuntarily, momentarily afraid to let him go farther, not because she didn't want to have him make love to her, but because she was afraid he would ask her to love him in return.

He read her mind as he had so often in the past.

"Don't worry, Cece. I'm not going to tell you I love you. I'm not going to ask you to tell me you love me." He pressed forward, entering her smoothly, slowly, making her gasp and close her eyes in pleasure. "I'm not going to say it first this time. You are. But when you're ready, not a moment before."

"Jeff?" Her head was spinning. All her senses seemed concentrated on their joining and nowhere else.

"Shh, no more words." He pressed into her, strong and sure. She lifted her hips, answering each thrust with one of her own.

Did she love him?

She thought she did. It had snuck up on her somehow, the old feelings that had lain dormant in her soul for all these years. She loved him, but she was afraid to say the words out loud. He quickened the tempo of his thrusts and her body responded to his, took up the rhythm, urging him on. Words no longer held much importance; only sighs and caresses were needed to communicate. She exploded beneath him in a shower of fire and heat. He followed her over the edge into oblivion and moments later she was asleep in his arms.

JEFF REACHED OVER the side of the chaise and picked up the dusty cover sheet, drew it over them both, stifling a sneeze. Cece was asleep in his arms where she belonged. He lay quietly a moment, savoring the scent of her hair in his nostrils, the warmth of her body curled trustingly against him. He listened for sounds of movement above them in the top-floor apartment. All was quiet. Liza and Cliff were probably asleep, or marveling over their newborn daughter, lost in a world of their own.

It was very late—after two, according to his watch. The moon had almost set, its light coming in directly through the window above their heads. He brushed his lips across her hair in the lightest of kisses, and settled down to wait for dawn.

What was growing between them again was as tenuous and fragile as a new life. He had to go slowly, bind her to him again with love and caring so tightly she could never slip away. They had laid much of the past to rest tonight, but the present still held more than enough pitfalls to undermine their growing love for each other. The problem at Worthington House could still come between them. Even now, he had information in his possession that might do just that.

Cece stirred against him. She hugged him tight in her sleep, her arm slipping down to his waist. He felt himself become aroused and kissed her tousled hair, hoping to wake her gently, to make love to her once more before reality intervened and they became what amounted to professional adversaries once more.

He raised himself against the chaise cushions, tipped up her chin and kissed her awake. Later. Later he'd tell her that someone on staff at Worthington House was responsible for the attacks on the residents. But not now...not yet. Cece's eyelids trembled, then fluttered open. She smiled up at him, lifted her hand to his cheek and threaded her fingers through his hair. She pulled his head down, taking control of the kiss, thrusting her tongue boldly into his mouth, letting him know she desired him just as much as he wanted her.

Jeff pulled her across his chest. "Just once more, Cece," he said, unaware of the rough edge passion had given his voice. "Just once more."

"Yes," she said dreamily, straddling him, lifting herself just enough so that her breasts brushed against his chest, silken skin against his roughness. She bent her head to kiss him again and shivered with desire, and with the chill of the predawn temperature. The dust sheet had slipped down to tangle around their hips. He pulled it up but it slipped again as Cece moved provocatively above him. Her movements were incendiary, but her skin was cold to the touch. With a muffled curse Jeff leaned over and grabbed his shirt off the floor, holding it as she slipped her arms in the sleeves.

"Feel better?" he asked as she stretched out on top of him.

"Mmm," Cece agreed, resting her weight fully against him, frowning slightly as paper rustled and the sharp edges of the lab report in the pocket of his shirt pushed against her breast.

"Give me that," he said, almost holding his breath, afraid the moment would be broken.

"Okay," Cece agreed, pulling the papers out of the pocket, her dreamy smile turning to a frown as she studied the offending documents in the diffuse moonlight streaming down around them. "Jeff, what are these? The lab reports on the Worthington House drugs you sent to Madison?"

He made an attempt to snatch them away but it was too late. The mood was broken, shattered beyond repair. Reality snapped back into focus around them.

"Yes, they are."

"Why didn't you tell me you had them?"

"I was going to. There just hasn't been time." He sounded defensive and wished to hell he didn't.

"Everything checks out okay, doesn't it?" she asked, slipping off him to perch gingerly on the edge of the chaise, already putting distance between them.

Jeff bit the inside of his lip to keep from cursing out loud. He didn't want to have this conversation now. The timing was as lousy as it could be.

"Everything checks out. The medications hadn't been tampered with."

He could see her turning over the implications of that disclosure in her mind. Her eyes narrowed. "So there's no problem, right? My staff is off the hook as far as being under suspicion goes?"

Jeff couldn't lie to her. "*Someone* injected Violet Orthwein with morphine, Cece. It just didn't come from the Worthington House stock."

"You're telling me none of the incidents could have been accidents, aren't you?" she said at last, her voice cool and composed. She moved a fraction of an inch farther away from him, but she might as well have gotten up and walked across the room.

He reached for her, but she stood up, evading his hands. "Dammit, Cece. I didn't want to get into this tonight." He sat up, reached down and grabbed his pants.

Cece pulled his shirt tight around her, hiding herself from him, when only moments before she'd gloried in her nakedness. "You think they were deliberate attempts on my patients' lives. That someone I know and work with every day is responsible.... That Luetta Peterson was murdered?"

"It looks like it," Jeff said between clenched teeth. He dragged up the zipper on his jeans and stood, towering over her.

She was watching him closely, trying to read his expression in the near-darkness. He could see the dawning apprehension and disbelief on her face, knew that by the time they left the boathouse, they'd be back at square one.

"You really believe the guilty party is someone working at Worthington House," she said very softly.

"I don't see any other possibility. All the attacks took place early in the morning, when there aren't many outsiders in the building—no visitors and no delivery people."

"I don't believe it." Cece was pulling on her own clothes, as though frantic to get out of his sight. She didn't look at him again, but she didn't have to. He'd seen her eyes; they'd told him louder than words that she felt he'd betrayed her trust in their love a second time. "I don't believe any of my nurses would do such a thing."

"Nurses are people. Very occasionally one of them kills, Cece," he said as gently as he could.

She didn't say anything, just turned her back and finished dressing. When she was done she faced him once more.

"Cece, we have to discuss this." He was losing her because of something over which he had no control. He raked his hand through his hair, frustrated, angry and terrified she'd walk out of his life forever.

"Not now," she said, and he heard the desperation in her voice. "It's late. I have to think about this."

He reached out his hand to stop her. She flinched. "Please, Jeff. No. I want to go home."

CHAPTER ELEVEN

THE UPPER CORRIDOR of Worthington House was deserted, the building quiet. It was four o'clock in the morning, the hour of deepest sleep for most of the residents, time for the night-shift nurses to catch up on their record keeping or to take a break, sit down in the lounge, put their feet up and gather their energy for the last busy hours of duty.

Cece walked soundlessly along the hallway, listening, alert for anything unusual, a cough or a sigh. Or a cry for help? She shivered, wrapping her arms around her waist. She shouldn't have done this, come in so early, not after the emotional day and night just passed. But she couldn't sleep, her churning, contradictory thoughts wouldn't let her rest, so after Jeff had driven her to her mother's house and left her, she'd showered and changed into her uniform, walking the few blocks to Worthington House through the muggy darkness.

Now she was watching over the extended care patients for the short-staffed night nurses, and they were too grateful for the extra help to question why she was there.

But that didn't stop her from questioning herself. Why was she there? Did she really need these extra quiet hours to prepare herself for the confrontation she'd face later in the morning when Jeff arrived to discuss his findings with Cecil Kellaway? Did she agree with Jeff that Cecil was as likely a suspect in the attacks as any other member of the staff? Or did she think her presence in the building might prevent another attack no matter who the culprit was?

Cece had opened a cupboard behind the nurse's desk and was staring blankly at its contents when the silence was shattered by the sound of glass breaking, in the men's ward at the far end of the hall near the staircase. The sudden noise made Cece jump and her heart hammered in her chest. She hesitated just a moment, then rushed along the corridor. The stairwell on her right was in darkness, illuminated only by track lights installed just above the risers; the lower hall was in shadows. She hurried into the room and snapped on the overhead light.

Three of the male patients in the small ward were asleep. Jacob Bremer was awake, lying half in, half out of his bed, kept from falling to the floor only by the restraining rail. His water glass lay broken on the floor, along with several small personal possessions that had been on top of his nightstand. His face was flushed, his eyes frightened. He tried to speak as Cece helped him back onto the high mattress, but she couldn't understand his garbled utterances. She only knew he was frightened, very frightened, although he appeared to be unharmed.

As she straightened his stroke-withered right arm and leg, he held up his good left hand and dropped a filled, disposable hypodermic syringe, the needle still covered by its plastic sheath, into Cece's outstretched hand. Gooseflesh rose on her arms, and prickles of fear made the hair at the back of her neck stand on end. She knew what was in the syringe without tasting, smelling or running laboratory tests. It was morphine. Jacob Bremer, unable to speak or help himself, was the latest victim of the unknown assailant who stalked Worthington House. Only this time, because the old man had somehow found the strength to fight for his life, the murderer had failed once more.

"I'll be back, Jacob," Cece said, straightening his covers automatically. "You're safe. I'll be back." His assailant might still be in the building, was most likely one of the staff on duty then. She rushed down the stairs to find the downstairs nurses' station deserted. She hurried along the lower corridor, refusing to imagine other victims behind the closed doors. She pushed open the door to the solarium to find both duty nurses and their two nursing assistants still enjoying their break.

Cece stared at the four, surprised faces staring back at her. "Has anyone left this room in the past ten minutes?" she asked.

"We've all been here for at least that long," the extended care duty nurse replied, pushing back her coffee cup as she stood up. "Is something wrong?"

"So you saw no one run by your station?" she asked, turning to the second nurse.

"No," she stammered, caught off guard. "Everything was quiet so I came down here for a cup of coffee."

"Has there been another attack?" the first nurse asked.

There was no use trying to hide what had been happening any longer. Nor should Cece have been surprised the grim situation was by now common knowledge among her staff, even though Cecil, Jeff and she had agreed to keep it quiet. The two nursing assistants were staring at the nurses, hearing confirmation for the first time of the rumors that must have been sweeping Worthington House for the past several days.

"Yes." Cece held out her hand. She was still holding the filled syringe. She realized with a sinking feeling that she'd made a terrible mistake, that she should never have picked it up in the first place. It was evidence in a crime. She'd compromised the integrity of that evidence.

Protocol demanded she call the administrator first. Common sense told her a criminal was at large, possibly still in the building. "I'm going to call the police," she said. "Someone just tried to kill Jacob Bremer. While we're waiting for the police to arrive, I want all the other patients checked to make sure they're okay. And don't do it alone. Go in pairs."

"But Mrs. Hayes—" the duty nurse objected.

Cece wasn't about to waste any more time talking. There would be plenty of opportunity for that later. "No buts," she ordered, already starting down the hall to the apartmentlike rooms on the lower floor. "Just do as I say. Now!"

Cece paused a moment at the nurse's desk to set off the silent alarm that connected Worthington House to the Tyler police dispatcher. Then she wrapped the syringe in a tissue, slipped it into her pocket and kept walking. Quietly she opened the door to Phil Wocheck's room. He was snoring peacefully, sleeping undisturbed. So were the other two residents on his side of the hall. Cece's heartbeat slowed a little. She opened the door to Freddie Houser's room and found her sitting in a reclining chair, illuminated only by the feeble glow of a table lamp in the shape of a doll dressed in ruffles and lace, which Cece knew had stood at her bedside since she was a little girl. She was wearing her quilted slippers and terry-cloth housecoat, belted tightly around her.

"Freddie, why are you awake so early?" Cece asked softly as she entered the room.

"I heard noise and talking," she said, smiling at Cece. "I thought it was time to get up. But it's still dark outside. I was wrong. Should I go back to bed?"

"If you want to," Cece said, returning the smile. "Or you can sit here in your chair, but it's very early. Breakfast isn't for almost three hours."

"I'll go back to bed," Freddie decided with a vigorous nod.

"I have some more work to do," Cece explained, patting Freddie's hand. "I'll stop back a little later and tuck you in."

"Okay." Freddie stood up and began to work at the knot in her belt. She bent her head to the task, ignoring Cece, as if she were no longer in the room.

"Can you manage the knot, Freddie?"

Another vigorous nod. "Yes."

"Good. Sleep tight."

"Don't forget to come back," Freddie said anxiously, abandoning for a moment her effort to untie the knot.

"As soon as I can," Cece promised. She closed the door quietly behind her, stopped once again at the nurses' station to call Cecil Kellaway and was relieved to find him at home. Had she believed he wouldn't be? He lived close enough to Worthington House to have returned to his home in the several minutes since the attack, so that was no guarantee he wasn't the assailant.

Cece hung up the phone and walked to the front entrance to wait for the police. A few moments later a squad car pulled up, and Police Lieutenant Brick Bauer headed up the sidewalk.

Cece swung open the front door. You needed a key to get into Worthington House at night, although all the doors opened from the inside at the slightest touch, allowing easy exit from the building. Before Brick was three steps inside the door, Cecil Kellaway stopped his car behind the squad car and hurried up the sidewalk, looking sleepy and disheveled, alarmed and, when he spotted Brick standing beside Cece, very, very angry.

"What's going on here, Cece?" Brick asked, looking around him, his hands relaxed at his side, yet only inches from his holstered gun.

"Someone tried to harm one of the patients," Cece explained. "Jacob Bremer."

"Are you sure?" Cecil Kellaway demanded. He was glaring at her as he tucked his shirttail into his pants.

"Yes." Cece gave him back look for look. He didn't appear any more guilty than she did. She wouldn't accuse him herself, that was up to Jeff, but she was tired of being discreet, of trying to solve the series of attacks from within Worthington House's power structure. They needed professional help, and Brick would provide it. "I heard a glass fall and break in the men's ward. I found Jacob Bremer half in, half out of his bed. He was very frightened and agitated. He was clutching this in his hand," Cece said, taking the syringe from her pocket and unwrapping the tissue covering.

Brick picked it up by the very tip of the plunger and examined it closely. "Do you want to hazard a guess as to what this contains?" he asked.

"Morphine," Cece responded before Cecil could silence her. "And it's not a guess. I'm sure that's what the syringe contains."

"You're jumping to conclusions, Mrs. Hayes," Cecil said darkly, but his denial lacked real conviction.

Cece chose her words carefully. Inside she was trembling like a leaf, but she didn't let her nervousness show. "I won't stand by and let anyone else be harmed. We can't keep these attacks quiet any longer. It's gone far beyond a staff matter. Jeff Baron has the lab results from the medications he had tested for us in Madison. He planned to inform you of the findings this morning."

Cecil's eyes widened. "How do you know that?"

"He told me." Cece didn't care any longer if the whole town knew she was involved with Jeff. "Our supplies hadn't been tampered with. That means the person doing this has access not only to Worthington House but also to an outside supply of narcotics. We're in over our heads, Mr. Kellaway."

"She's right, Kellaway. And I don't want anything held back because you're protecting your job," Brick said gruffly. "I've been up all night and I'm too tired to play games. Tell me everything that's been going on here."

The look he gave Cece was as hard and assessing as the one he turned on Kellaway, even though Cece had known him since grade school. His scrutiny didn't bother Cece, though. He was a good cop, doing his job; she hadn't expected anything else.

"I want to hear the whole story," Brick added firmly, "And I want to hear it now."

JEFF TOOK the front steps to Worthington House two at a time. He ran his hand over the stubble of beard on his chin. He'd taken a quick shower before he fell into bed less than an hour ago, but he hadn't taken time to shave. His stomach growled from neglect and he needed a cup of coffee so badly he'd consider committing a crime himself to get one. He pushed open the door of the retirement center just as the first rays of sunlight broke over the horizon and reflected off the glass. He narrowed his eyes against the sudden brightness.

"Lieutenant Bauer and the others are waiting for you in Mr. Kellaway's office," the nurse behind the main-floor desk told him as he approached.

"Thanks," Jeff mumbled, pushing his hand through his hair. He couldn't remember combing it, but hoped he had.

"Hi," Freddie Houser said. She was wearing her pajamas and bathrobe. Her hair looked as if it had been combed with a rake.

"Hi," Jeff said. "Did all the excitement wake you up?"

"Yes."

Jeff switched his attention to the nurse. He gave her his best smile. "Is there a chance you can get me a cup of coffee anytime soon?"

"Of course, Dr. Jeff."

"I'll get it," Freddie volunteered, jumping up from her chair.

"Well . . ." The nurse frowned slightly.

"Please."

"Okay. But walk slowly so you don't spill any on yourself and get burned," she cautioned.

"I will. Do you want cream and sugar?" Freddie asked.

"Black, please."

"I'll get it."

"I'll be in Mr. Kellaway's office," Jeff told her. "Just bring it to me there."

"I'll knock," Freddie promised. "That's good manners." She hurried off, faster than Jeff had ever seen her move.

"All the commotion woke her up. She's too nervous to stay in her room, so I had her come and sit with me," the nurse explained. "I'll keep an eye out so she doesn't forget to bring you your coffee. She has a short attention span when she's excited."

"Thanks." Jeff headed off in the same direction Freddie had taken, but with far less enthusiasm. He wasn't looking forward to another confrontation with Cecil Kellaway. Or Cece, for that matter.

"Baron, you took your time getting here," Kellaway announced as Jeff entered his crowded office. He was seated behind his desk and didn't rise.

Brick Bauer was standing with one shoulder propped against the wall. He nodded to Jeff, friendly but all-business. His presence altered the situation slightly. Jeff knew as well as Cece did that he had no real evidence against Kellaway or Juanita Pelsten, or anyone else at Worthington House, for that matter. He decided to keep his suspicions to himself for a little longer. Cece was seated in one of the two chairs in front of the desk. Jeff took the other. He didn't close the door to the hall. He didn't want Freddie to forget about his coffee.

"Why didn't you call me yesterday about the results of the lab tests you ordered?" Kellaway continued in the same belligerent tone.

"I never got the time. There was one hell of an accident out on the lake road. Nine teenagers in two pickup trucks."

"I heard as much," Cecil admitted, sounding only slightly mollified.

"You did a damned good job patching those kids back together," Brick said, still lounging against the wall.

"Thanks. You were no slouch yourself in triage."

Brick shrugged off the praise. "My sources tell me family congratulations are in order. You're an uncle now, right?"

Jeff grinned. "Right. Cece delivered a beautiful little baby girl for Liza and Cliff."

One dark eyebrow rose. Brick directed his next comment to Cece. "Delivering babies is a long step from working in a nursing home."

"It's what I'm trained for," she said with a smile that jolted Jeff's heartbeat as strongly as his longed-for caffeine fix would. "I haven't had much opportunity to practice midwifery since I returned to Tyler."

"Not much call for that in this job, I'll agree," Brick said, deadpan. Cece smiled at his joke.

"No, there isn't."

"Let's get on with this," Cecil interrupted. "I want Bauer out of here before the first-shift workers arrive."

"I'll leave when I've completed my investigation, not before."

"Here's your coffee, Dr. Jeff," Freddie said from the doorway. She stood hesitantly, balancing a half-filled cup of coffee carefully in her hands. "It's black, just like you said."

"Thanks. You saved my life." Jeff took a swallow of the coffee. It wasn't very hot but it was strong enough to cut through his exhaustion.

"What are you doing up so early?" Kellaway was still impatient, but gentler when dealing with the retarded woman.

"I can't sleep." Freddie looked confused and unhappy, as she often did when her routine was disrupted.

"It's all right." Cece smiled at her as if there was nothing wrong in the world. "Go back to the nurses' station. I'll come and talk to you later, okay?"

Freddie bobbed her head. "Okay."

No one spoke until she was gone. Brick straightened up and walked across the room to shut the door. "Cece and Kellaway filled me in on what's been happening here the past couple of weeks, Jeff," he said, consulting a small notebook he took from his shirt pocket. "Two attacks, the first on Wilhelm Badenhop and then Violet Orthwein. Both appear to have been overdoses of a narcotic drug, apparently morphine."

"Their symptoms bear that out," Jeff agreed, "and in Violet Orthwein's case, blood tests showed she had been given morphine."

"Cece says there's some question about Luetta Peterson's death last month, also."

"Pure speculation, nothing more," Kellaway insisted.

"He's right, there's no proof. We'll have to wait until Doc Phelps returns for more information. He signed her death certificate."

"Then tonight, someone, possibly an employee—certainly someone familiar with the building and the routine—attempted to inject Jacob Bremer with the liquid contained in this syringe." Brick pointed to the plastic-encased syringe lying on Kellaway's desk.

"That's right," Cece said, turning her head to Jeff. "Jacob must have wakened and struggled with the person. He knocked his water glass off the stand. I heard it shatter when it hit the floor and started toward the ward. I didn't see anyone leave the room. When I entered the ward I found Jacob half out of his bed. He was clutching that syringe in his hand. By the time I got him settled and went downstairs, there was no one in sight. His speech has been so severely affected by the stroke that he couldn't tell me what had happened, of course. I had to guess."

"Where were all the night nurses?" Jeff asked, keeping his face carefully neutral. He owed Kellaway the professional courtesy of revealing his suspicions in private.

"They were all in the staff lounge."

"I'll talk to them later." Brick picked up the syringe. "Why didn't you people contact the police after the first attack?"

"There's been no proof of any attacks," Kellaway said, glaring at Cece and Jeff with equal venom. "Just what these two have cooked up between them."

"We didn't cook up anything between us," Jeff said, refusing to be goaded. Cece's fingers tightened on the arm of her chair but she remained silent. "I have documentation in the Orthwein case," he went on, "and I'll bet my diploma morphine caused Wilhelm Badenhop's episode of respiratory arrest, as well."

"What about the drugs Kellaway says you had tested?"

Jeff fished the lab reports out of his pocket and handed them to Brick. "The narcotics in possession of the nursing staff at Worthington House, as well as their record keeping, all check out, just as Cece predicted they would."

"There," Kellaway said in triumph. "I told you."

"But that doesn't rule out that someone working here is still the culprit," Brick said, glancing up from the report, pinning Jeff with his eyes. "Someone with access to a locked medication room."

"Correct."

"And all of these incidents, with the exception of Luetta Peterson's death, occurred since Cece became director of nursing, isn't that also correct?"

Cece had been looking at the syringe on the desk. Now her head shot up. Brick switched his gaze to her face. She watched him as he spoke, surprise and apprehension widening her gray eyes, darkening the irises to smoke. Jeff should have known Brick couldn't dismiss Cece as a suspect, he realized, any more than he could any of the rest of Worthington House's employees. This was not the boy they'd known since grade school. He was a policeman, a professional law enforcement officer, and she had knowledge of a crime.

"Yes," she said. "I had only visited Worthington House once or twice before Miss Peterson died. I didn't officially begin my employment until several days after her funeral." Cece's voice was steady, with only a tiny quaver of distress audible in her tone.

Jeff wrapped both hands around his coffee cup. He wanted more than anything to reach out and take her in his arms, protect her from Brick's badgering, but that would be the worst thing he could do.

"You've been present when all the attacks have occurred?"

"Yes," Cece said again.

"Surely you're not accusing Mrs. Hayes of any wrongdoing?" Kellaway spluttered, rising from behind his desk.

"Hell, no," Brick said, ignoring Kellaway's bombast, one corner of his mouth lifting in the same ornery grin Jeff remembered from sixth grade. "I don't have enough to go on here to accuse anyone of anything. But I'll need your fingerprints, Cece. And Mr. Bremer's, to compare with any others I might find on the syringe." He looked at the syringe and shook his head. "But it's a long shot we'll come up with one we can use."

"Of course," Cece replied.

"In the meantime, I'll put someone on guard in both hallways at night. I suggest you have your staff do their work in pairs, if possible, until we can interview the workers and eliminate suspects. It might be a good idea to start screening visitors, as well."

"Good Lord, this will be all over town by noon," Kellaway said with what sounded very much like a groan. Jeff could picture the man inundated with phone calls and visits from irate relatives of residents. The mental image gave him some satisfaction.

"Can't be helped." Brick glanced at his watch. "I know you must be beat, buddy. But I need you to interpret the mumbo jumbo on these lab reports. Can you meet me back at the station house in, say, forty-five minutes?"

"Sure thing," Jeff said. "That will give me time to order breakfast at Marge's."

"See you at seven." Brick's tone dismissed Jeff as he nodded his head toward Cece. "If Kellaway here agrees, I'd like you to be present when I interview the night nurses. Medical jargon makes me nervous."

"I'll be needing Mrs. Hayes's assistance in making all these duty changes you've recommended," Kellaway pointed out.

"You'll have to muddle on by yourself until I'm finished with her," Brick said, and turned his back on the angry administrator without another word. "Where's the best place to do this?" he asked Cece, as though Kellaway were no longer in the room.

"The staff lounge," she said, with an apologetic smile for Kellaway. "It's in the old solarium." She didn't look at Jeff again, so he knew that nothing had changed between them in the few hours they'd been apart. She was still angry with him for not telling her about the lab tests earlier, and it might take her a while to remember, instead, how sweet and wonderful their lovemaking had been.

"I'll meet you there in fifteen minutes," Brick said.

Fifteen minutes wasn't long, but Jeff figured it would have to do. As Brick turned back to Kellaway, Jeff made his move. "C'mon, Cece." He took her hand in his, although she struggled briefly to be free of his grip. "I need to speak to you a moment. And I need another cup of coffee."

"I don't want you talking to my staff, Baron," Kellaway snapped.

"This is personal, Cecil old man, not professional. She'll be in the solarium when you need her, Brick," he threw over his shoulder as he led Cece down the hall.

The solarium was deserted. The early sun was blocked by leafy maples, so only pale light filtered through the windows, dim but sufficient to see her face. He didn't touch her except for where his fingers were locked around her wrist. He set his empty coffee cup down on a table with a thump that made Cece jump.

"I can't stay in here with you. You know as well as I do it's a conflict of interest."

"Screw that," he said angrily. Fear twisted his gut. They were working through their past, but the present was even more dangerous to his plans to make

Cece Scanlon Hayes his wife. "What's going on here at Worthington House has nothing to do with what I want to talk to you about."

"Making love with you was a mistake," she said softly. It was too dark to know for sure, but he thought he saw tears in her eyes, eyes the same shade of gray as the dawn.

"How do you know that was the personal subject I meant to bring up?" He smiled down at her, letting her see that he hadn't forgotten she'd lain naked in his arms such a short time ago.

"I—I..." She was flustered and showed it.

He smiled again. "Making love with you wasn't a mistake. Not telling you I had the lab results before we did was a mistake. Leaving the boathouse before we'd straightened it out was a mistake, too. But surely you can give me the benefit of the doubt." He shook his head. "It's been one hell of a day, Cece." He glanced out the window. "It's been one hell of a night. Doctors don't always make the right judgment calls, just like the rest of the world. Don't you think patching those nine teenagers back together and the birth of my niece might give me an excuse for letting the lab reports slip my mind?"

"Yes," she said softly. She was wary but not unresponsive. He could feel her tremble beneath the light touch of his hand; he could see a pulse beat high and fast in her throat. "But it doesn't make it any easier for me to decide about us."

"Cece, don't blame yourself." He wanted to kiss her so badly he was shaking inside. He could smell her scent, soft and flowery, feel the warmth of her skin beneath his fingers. The taste of her lips was fresh in his memory. "We'll figure out who's doing this in time."

"That's not good enough." She covered his hand with her own. "The patients here don't have time. The attack tonight proves that. I can't trust anyone here anymore, and I can't let anything distract me from my duty until they're safe." She lifted her free hand tentatively, reluctant to touch his cheek. "You distract me, Jeff. You make me want to forget everything and everybody else in the world."

"Because if something happened to one of your patients and you weren't here, you'd never forgive yourself, am I right, Cece?"

"Yes," she said quietly. He pulled her into his arms, gently, lightly, and held her close. She moved restlessly in his embrace. "It would be my fault."

"No." Jeff tightened his grip, afraid she would try to leave rather than face the truth. "Someone might die because you were being selfish, doing something for yourself instead of for another."

"Yes," she said again, still so softly he had to strain to hear the word. He felt the dampness of a tear wet his shirt as she rested her cheek against his chest. She had made him speak the truth about the pain of his father's death. Now he was doing the same for her.

"Like Steve died."

She looked up at him and her eyes filled with shining tears. "Yes."

"It wasn't your fault, Cece," he said gently, his hands making small circles on her back, soothing, arousing.

"I know that in my head," she said, letting the tears fall—healing tears, Jeff hoped. "But not always with my heart."

"You care—that's why it's hard to let go. I wouldn't want you any other way." He lifted his hand to the back of her head, pressured her lightly to kiss him, to burn away the past in the heat of the present and the promise of the future. He pressed her closer, felt her breasts against his chest, her soft stomach against his manhood, her thighs between his. He remembered their lovemaking in the boathouse and wanted her again with a fierce, primitive need that he ignored for his sake as well as hers. "I love you, Cece."

She lifted her fingers to his lips. "Don't Jeff. Don't say you love me tonight. Not here, not now."

"I won't say it again." She had to come to him. She had to make the decisions for her future. She had to say goodbye to a lost love and old hurts. Forever. "I'll wait for you to be ready, but it's going to be the hardest thing I've ever done."

"I'll be in the solarium with Cece," he heard Brick say, his raised voice carrying down the hall to where they stood.

Jeff kissed her again, lightly, swiftly.

"You have to go," she said, still looking dazed with desire and uncertainty. He thought he'd never seen her so beautiful. "Brick will want to start the interviews right away."

"I'll go. But I'll be back. We've got to find some time and some place for ourselves."

She managed a smile. "It is just like being back in high school again, isn't it?"

"One of us has to get a place of our own," Jeff agreed, his voice a low, frustrated growl.

"Baron, you still here?" Brick asked as he filled the doorway of the solarium with his broad shoulders.

"Just leaving, Lieutenant."

Brick looked past him to where Cece was standing, pretending to study a fern sitting on the table at the end of the wicker couch. "I took a minute to look in on my grandmother, just to make sure she was okay."

"We checked all the residents and patients right away, Brick, and everyone but Jacob Bremer was fine."

"I knew you would have, but..." Brick put sentiment aside and went on, "Ready for the interviews?"

"Yes." She nodded, looking at Brick, not at Jeff. She smiled. "I'm ready."

"Good. Let's go. Is that a coffeepot over there against the wall?" Brick asked, gesturing toward the insulated pitcher and stack of foam cups on a metal tray.

"Lukewarm but strong enough to fell an ox," Jeff observed as he started out of the room.

"I could use a cup," Brick said, making a beeline for the pot, missing, or pretending to miss, the atmosphere of strain and desire between his two old high school classmates. "And some breakfast. What time does the kitchen open in this place?"

CHAPTER TWELVE

"WELL, IF YOU WANT my opinion," Tisha Olsen said in her usual, shoot-from-the-hip manner, "this business of someone trying to bump off all the old fogies at Worthington House has at least moved your father's case off center stage."

Jeff winced, then looked up from the cabinet he was bolting to the wall with Johnny Kelsey's help. He glanced past the Ingalls F and M foreman to where his mother was painting another cupboard along the far wall. She turned her head and caught his eye and the tail end of his frown, but said nothing.

"There are rumors flying all over town," Tisha continued, as she swirled her cloth across the windowpane she'd volunteered to clean. "Is it one of the nurses, maybe? Or Cecil Kellaway? He's a pretty rare bird by Tyler's standards, with that phony limey accent and all. Or maybe it's Annabelle Scanlon's daughter, the one who came back a widow from South America, or some such place."

"Cece's husband died in an earthquake in Nicaragua," Liza said from a comfortable chair by the door, where she was holding court for Ingalls F and M employees who wanted to stop by and pay their respects to Margaret Alyssa. "And I'd watch what I said about Cece. Jeff's sweet on her. He always has been."

"Thanks, sis," Jeff muttered, refusing to meet Johnny Kelsey's interested gaze.

"If it weren't for Cece," Liza continued, as if she hadn't heard his disgruntled reply, "they'd have never figured out anything was wrong at Worthington House. And Jeff, of course. He helped, too."

"Thanks again, sis." This time Jeff grinned, bowing to the inevitable. He loved Cece, and the sooner the whole town knew about it, the better. It was harder than hell to swim against the current of public opinion in Tyler if the town approved of a romance. He was going to make very sure they approved of his. "Maybe I should start moonlighting as a detective. Earn a few extra bucks to pay for keeping this place going." He maneuvered the subject way from the Worthington House attacks and his love life as smoothly as he could. Tisha Olsen was a magnet for gossip. He didn't want any more rumors racing through town than there already were.

"We'll find a way to get this place solvent." Tisha went on washing windows as she talked, polishing the glass energetically, her red hair covered by a bright green scarf, her head bobbing up and down to emphasize her point. "I may not be good at organizing fancy fund-raising dinners like your mother, but I know some people who can cough up a few bucks to help a good cause, and without the overhead of a dinner dance out at the lake." She stepped back from the window, hands on hips, to survey her work. Satis-

fied, she turned to face the room at large. "Your
grandfather's going to help me, whether he knows it
yet or not. I want to get his mind off the grand jury
proceedings. Any objections?" She didn't single out
Alyssa, but everyone in the room knew the challenge
had been directed at her.

Alyssa laid her paintbrush very carefully on the edge
of the can. She had a smudge of white paint on her
cheek, but it did nothing to detract from her beauty or
her dignity. She turned to face Tisha, wiping her hands
on one of the shop rags Johnny had brought with him
from the plant floor. Outside the office, the muted
rumble of the assembly lines underscored their conversation. "That's a good idea," she said politely, but
with little enthusiasm. "I'll do what I can, also—that
goes without saying."

Jeff wished his mother could lighten up, accept that
his grandfather and Tisha were attracted to each other.
But perhaps, with all the other stress in her life, that
was too much to ask of her at the moment. He wondered idly what it would be like to have Tisha Olsen
for a grandmother. It certainly wouldn't be dull.

"Great!" Tisha replied with a grin, seeming oblivious of Alyssa's cool tone. She turned back to her
window. "I'm going to start with Eddie Wocheck.
He's rolling in dough."

She looked back over her shoulder to see if Jeff's
mother was still watching her. Alyssa hadn't moved a
muscle. Only the widening of her eyes showed her
surprise at Tisha's last remarks. Tisha saw the surprise, too, and laughed again. "You weren't the only

one of us girls sweet on Eddie in high school, Alyssa.
We all had crushes on him. But I had my sights set on
excitement and the big city. I never saw the potential
in him—my mistake. But now he's got millions and he
can spend some of them on this clinic. I'm going to
ask him to make a big donation...for old times' sake.''

Alyssa picked up her paintbrush. To Jeff's amaze-
ment, and that of everyone else in the room, she
smiled. "You do that, Tisha," she said, touching the
tip of the paintbrush to a spot on the shelf that caught
her eye. "You just go ahead and do that."

ALYSSA LOOKED into Phil Wocheck's room from the
doorway. It was empty. Timberlake's old gardener and
handyman was testifying before the grand jury today,
telling what he remembered of the night her mother
died. Alyssa lifted her fingers to her temples. If only
she could be there, listening to what he had to say, to
compare his recollections with her own fragmented
memories. Would she then be able to answer the
ceaseless questions that plagued her sleep with rest-
less dreams?

But there was no way she could learn what Phil
would say. Even Amanda could not be present during
the hearing. These proceedings were completely in the
control, and for the benefit of, the prosecution, her
daughter had explained. They wouldn't know what
was said until they were over, and then only if she
could show proof that she needed the testimony to
prepare Judson's defense, if he was bound over for
trial.

"Lyssa, I didn't expect to find you here this afternoon."

She turned slowly to face Edward. She had recognized his voice instantly and schooled her expression to one of pleased recognition, nothing more. "I'm here to lead the Wednesday afternoon Scripture group. I volunteered to do it until they could find someone to take Jacob Bremer's place." She wrapped her right hand around her left elbow. It had turned cool the past day or so, and her long-sleeved cotton blouse felt good against her skin. She wondered if Edward would mention the series of attacks that had happened here recently, but he said nothing about them.

"You're a very giving person, Lyssa."

"I have too much time on my hands."

He didn't reply, letting his compliment stand by ignoring her attempt to brush it aside.

"Did you leave your father alone at the courthouse?" she asked, changing the subject abruptly.

He watched her closely. A pulse point beat high and fast in her throat. The corners of her mouth were tight with strain. She was disturbed about something but doing her best to hide her unease.

"Yes," he answered. "I came here to get him a sweater. The air conditioner in the courthouse had been running all morning. It's too chilly for an old man."

"Has your father given his testimony?" The words came reluctantly, born of her worry for her father.

"Not yet. Possibly after lunch."

But this morning Edward had given his own brief account of finding Judson's gun in his father's room at the Kelseys'. It was one more thing they would question Phil about that his son had no control over. He didn't like not being in control of a situation. It went against his nature.

"I see." She smiled, a lifting of the corners of her mouth, nothing more. "I'm probably out of line asking you these questions."

"You might be," he said, smiling in return. "I'm not a lawyer, and honestly I haven't a clue what's going on over there."

"When I was a little girl, I used to wish I was invisible and could walk through walls and go anywhere I chose. I feel that way today." She wrapped both arms beneath her breasts, as though to comfort herself. "I've never paid much attention to criminal proceedings before this." She tried to smile again and failed. "I never knew a grand jury hearing was carried out behind closed doors. That even the defense attorneys were barred from attending."

"Alyssa, don't let yourself become too upset by this." He felt torn in his soul. He wanted to take her in his arms, hold her close and protect her from her fears. But at the same time his anxiety for his father's welfare jabbed at him like a sharp, pointed stick. What did Alyssa know of the night her mother died? What did she remember? Had she somehow seen the man who had killed Margaret? Was that man her father? Or his? The nagging worry would not be totally dismissed.

And hardest of all to believe was the possibility that the child, Alyssa, had shot Margaret herself. Surely, on that point at least, his father's memory had served him false. Or was the old man lying to protect himself?

"Edward?"

Alyssa was speaking to him. He brought his attention back to her with the discipline learned in dozens of boardrooms on three continents over the past thirty years.

"Yes? I'm sorry, I didn't hear what you just said. My age is creeping up on me."

She laughed this time, and he thought back to warm afternoons on a screened porch and a summer garden. He smiled at her, seeing more than a little of the girl he'd loved so long ago in the mature and lovely woman standing before him. But he also saw the shadows, the ghosts of the past, behind her smile, and wondered again if what his father had told him was true. For her sake as well as his own, he needed to learn what had actually happened the night of Margaret Ingalls's death.

"You look remarkably well preserved to me," she said, unaware of the tenor of his thoughts.

"I might say the same about you." He fell to the temptation of touching her hair. She let him, but made no move to touch him back.

"Shall we call a staff member to find your father's sweater or do you think we can locate it ourselves?" Only the faintest tremor in her voice alerted him to the fact that she wasn't unmoved by his brief caress.

"No need to call anyone. He told me where to find it."

She walked into the room ahead of him, her skirt swaying gracefully around her knees, her breasts outlined gently by the soft white cotton of her blouse. He'd become very aware of her body over the months he'd been in Tyler, an awareness born of a single awkward kiss under the mistletoe last Christmas. Or more accurately, an awareness resurrected from the ashes of the hunger he'd felt for her in his youth.

He stepped past her, opened the closet door and found the old wool cardigan just where his father had said it would be.

"Edward, what does your father remember of the night my mother died?"

He should have expected this, but the question surprised him anyway. He hesitated for several seconds, smoothing his hands over the sweater before he raised his eyes to look at her again. "I don't know what he's going to say, Alyssa. He wouldn't confide in me."

He was telling the truth as far as it went. Phil hadn't confided in him; Edward had had to drag the information out of him. Shrewd businessman though he was, it made him feel decidedly uncomfortable, being less than honest with Alyssa.

"Does he remember my being there? In her room that night?" she asked, so softly he had to tip his head forward to hear her. She wasn't looking at him directly. Her eyes were focused somewhere near the knot of his tie. She wrapped her arms around herself again, as though hugging her courage close to her heart.

"Don't force it, Lyssa."

"I think I was there," she whispered, raising her eyes. The irises were huge and indigo, the color of the twilight sky. "In my dreams I remember being there."

"Do you really remember, Lyssa? Or was it only a dream?"

He felt disloyal asking the questions, but if he had to choose between people he cared for, then his first loyalty must be to his father, to his blood. It was not inconceivable that the grand jury might believe Phil was an accessory to the murder. There was nothing to prove that he was not.

"Bits and pieces." Alyssa turned to the window. "I remember bits and pieces, all jumbled up. Nothing makes sense. I remember being in my mother's room that night, although my father has told me that I wasn't—that he came to me in my room after he found her note . . . after he destroyed her things . . . to tell me she had gone. I was asleep in my bed."

"But your memories tell you differently?" he inquired gently, wondering how long they could be private in such a place, wondering how much longer he should leave his father unattended at the courthouse.

She shrugged, still facing the window, not allowing him to see her face, to attempt to decipher the emotions hidden behind her expression.

"I remember a gunshot, loud and frightening." She did turn to face him then, and there was stark terror in her eyes. "My mother falling by the bed. And then someone carried me away. Your father, I think." She frowned and lifted her fingers to her temple. "He called me *malushka*. It's a Polish word, isn't it?"

"Yes. It means little girl. But he called you that often. I remember."

"Yes," she said. "That's why I can't trust my dreams. And because I see another man. A stranger? My father?" The last was barely audible. She shook her head. "I don't know."

"Have you considered professional help? Hypnosis, perhaps?" He wasn't sure that was the answer. What if the results were more upsetting than her partial memories? How accurate were hypnotic recollections? Could the findings even be trusted?

"No." She closed her eyes for a heartbeat. Her question echoed his own. "What if the truth is even more terrible than my dreams?"

"I don't know how to answer that, Lyssa," he said gently, his voice low and soothing, the same voice he'd used to comfort his stepson, Devon, when he was a child. "I wish I could help you make your decision but I can't." He used words instead of his embrace. He made them a comforting touch because he had no right to take her in his arms and hold her close. She made him feel like a boy again. The rawboned, awkward boy from the wrong side of the tracks who wanted to be her knight in shining armor, who wanted to carry her off with him to live happily ever after in a castle in the sky.

It hadn't happened that way thirty years ago. It wasn't going to happen that way now. Too many problems, problems with no easy solutions, stood between them, now and for the foreseeable future.

"DAD, YOU OUGHT TO BE in bed. It's late." Alyssa stepped onto the screened porch at the back of the house. Crickets chirped loudly along the foundation. Cicadas shrilled in the maple tree beside the steps, but their hearts were no longer in their song. September had gotten a good hold on the land and summer would soon be only a memory.

"Can't sleep," Judson said, not rising from his chair as she approached. "Have a seat." He motioned to the empty rocking chair beside him.

"Do you need a jacket?" Alyssa asked, leaning over the tall back of the empty rocker, resting her hand on the smooth wood. The matching walnut rocking chairs had stood on the porch as long as she could remember, hand carved from native wood, old when her father had been a toddler, playing with his blocks on long-ago summer days.

"No, Alyssa. I'm fine. Sit down," he invited again.

Alyssa obeyed. They sat in silent companionship for a few minutes. Alyssa listened to the crickets and the locusts, watched the moon play hide-and-seek behind the maple leaves and thought of all the questions she needed answers to.

She glanced over at her father's profile, saw the frown that pulled down the corners of his mouth, the worry that bowed his shoulders like a physical weight, and held her tongue. What could she ask him, after all? *Did you kill my mother and bury her body by a*

*willow tree? Did I see you do it? Or did I somehow get
the gun and pull the trigger myself?* She could no more
ask the first question than find an answer to the third.

"How did the work go on the clinic this morning?" Judson inquired after the silence had length-
ened between them.

"We're almost finished. The county inspector gave
us the final okay this afternoon. Jeff will be able to
begin seeing patients in a day or two," Alyssa answered with a smile, pushing her dark thoughts and
unanswerable questions back along the edges of her
mind, confining them there until they once again
broke free in the small hours of the night to ruin her
sleep.

"Liza stopped by with Margaret Alyssa this afternoon while you were gone," Judson said, concealing
his pride with difficulty. "That's a fine looking baby
she's got there."

"Does it bother you that she named the baby after
Mother?" Alyssa bit her lip, wondering if she should
have brought the matter up at all.

Judson was silent a moment. "No," he said finally. "I meant what I said when Mary Elizabeth
asked me the same question. I don't hate your mother
anymore. Maybe I never did." He didn't turn his head
but kept looking out over the flower beds, fading in
the September heat, at the garden he'd tended faith-
fully for almost fifty years.

Alyssa lost her courage. She changed the subject,
hating herself for doing so. "I think Jeff is falling in
love with Cece Scanlon all over again." She didn't

know why she'd said the words, they just tumbled out. She clasped her hands together in her lap. She wanted desperately to be able to speak of something happy and hopeful with her father—small talk, family talk, nothing of murder, or haunted memories or grand jury indictments. That didn't seem too much to ask of life.

"They make a good pair. I thought so even when they were in high school. Guess twenty more years of living improved my judgment on picking mates for my offspring."

"What do you mean, Dad?" she asked, but she thought she knew. Her heart beat a little more quickly just as it always did when Edward was mentioned in conversation—or even alluded to. She felt her face flush with heat and was glad the shadows on the porch hid her reaction.

"I mean, I knew the Scanlon girl would amount to something. That she'd make a good wife for Jeff. I was right. Haven't heard enough about that trouble over there in the old folks' home to figure out who's responsible, but the girl's got brains and heart. She'll get to the bottom of it before any out-of-town police investigators. Or even Brick Bauer, unless I miss my guess."

No more mention of Edward Wocheck or that Judson had misjudged his potential in life. She hadn't expected him to say he was sorry he'd opposed their marriage all those years ago. Perhaps he wasn't sorry. He'd avoided spending any more time than necessary with Edward since he'd returned to Tyler. Knowing

Judson's stubborn streak, she thought it was very likely he still didn't like the man.

Alyssa sighed softly. So many things were different, so many things remained the same. She dismissed Edward from her thoughts with only a small battle of mind over heart. She'd done it so often over the past months it was becoming second nature to her.

"Jeff and Cece do make a good team. They'll solve this mystery and soon. Before anyone else is put at risk. I'm sure of it."

"Maybe," Judson said, sitting very still in his rocker, "I should hire them to get me out of this god-awful mess I'm in." He didn't turn his head to look at her, but Alyssa felt him reach out to her just the same. "I didn't kill your mother, Alyssa. I swear to you. Remember that. No matter what happens from now on, remember I'm telling you the truth."

"I believe you, Dad," she said, but not quickly enough.

He rose stiffly, slowly from his chair, like a man much older than his years. "For all my faults, Alyssa, I've never lied to you."

"Dad. I didn't mean it that way." How could she tell him what was in her heart when she was so confused by her own feelings that she couldn't sort them into any kind of order?

"I know you didn't. But if my own daughter has doubts, how can I expect anything different from the rest of the town? Good night, Alyssa. I'm going to bed."

He walked into the house. The wooden screen door closed behind him with a bang. Alyssa stayed where she was, hating herself for that betraying moment of indecision that had hurt him so. He had said he didn't hate her mother anymore. Alyssa had never hated Margaret, but for a moment she almost did. Beautiful, vain, spoiled Margaret. Dead for forty years, she was still causing her family heartache and pain.

Somehow, Alyssa had to learn the truth behind her mother's death. For Judson's sake, for her own sake, for her children's futures. So they could all be free of Margaret's ghost—and the past.

CHAPTER THIRTEEN

JEFF WALKED through the front door of Worthington House and hesitated in the shadows of the activity room. A quilt frame sat proudly in the middle of the big, airy room. The Quilting Circle ladies were starting a new project, he noticed, another beautiful heirloom-quality coverlet to be auctioned off at some charity function or another for a large amount of money. Those ladies were the eyes and ears of Worthington House, and of Tyler. He bet it wouldn't take them a day to find out who was trying to kill the people upstairs. Kellaway would be better off enlisting their help than trying to keep everything hushed up. Jeff chuckled, but not with humor; the sound was more of a frustrated snort. Stopping the flow of information in Tyler was like trying to empty Lake Michigan with a spoon. It couldn't be done. But neither had it helped them catch the person responsible for the attacks.

He was due to go on duty at the hospital in a little more than an hour, at midnight. He hadn't seen Cece for three days and he didn't intend to stretch that number to four. He wondered if she'd even left this pile of bricks in that time. He doubted it. Cece would feel it was her responsibility alone to see that no one else was harmed. That was why he hadn't even taken the time to stop at her mother's house. She was here. He'd bet his last dime on it.

"Cece."

She was standing at the foot of the stairs, talking to Freddie Houser. Freddie was wearing her usual green smock and white pants. She looked rumpled and her hair needed combing, but she smiled at him.

"Hi, Dr. Jeff. I'm going upstairs with snacks for the nurses.

"I wouldn't mind a bowl of popcorn myself," Jeff said, resting one hand on the newel post, watching Cece from the corner of his eye as he talked to Freddie. She was dressed simply in a swingy cotton skirt and blouse the color of a ripe peach, beneath a long white lab coat. There were dark circles under her eyes, and fatigue pulled at the corners of her mouth. "Maybe I'll just come upstairs with you."

"Dr. Jeff, don't be silly." Freddie giggled, slapping at his hand. "You don't live here."

"I'll take a rain check on the popcorn." When Freddie looked puzzled, he added, "That means I'll come back and have some on another evening."

"Okay," she said, and headed up the stairs. "Goodbye," she added from several steps up. Her face wrinkled into a frown. "Should I give some popcorn to the policeman, too?" she asked Cece.

"That would be nice, Freddie. I'm sure he'd enjoy some."

"I will, then." She smiled again and kept on climbing.

Jeff watched her go, then turned his attention back to Cece. "I had a hunch I might find you here."

"It isn't hard. She's here day and night." Juanita Pelsten, who appeared to be working a double shift herself, called out from the desk at the nurses' station, as if he'd spoken to her and not Cece.

Jeff looked over his shoulder at the older woman. "I figured as much. That's why I'm bustin' her out of this dump," he growled in a terrible Cagney imitation.

"I shouldn't leave," Cece began, and Jeff knew she was as reluctant to be alone with him as she was to be away from Worthington House.

"No buts," he said, giving up on the Cagney, but making his words an order. "You look like hell."

"I do not," she responded, stung by his bluntness.

"I hate to agree with somebody who's so rude," Juanita said from behind the desk, "but he's right. Go with the man. Get something to eat. Watch the moon rise over the lake. Brick Bauer's upstairs. I'm down here and I promise no one's going to get by me. Go!"

"I couldn't have said it better myself," Jeff agreed, wondering how he could possibly continue to suspect a woman as stable and down-to-earth as Juanita appeared to be. He pulled the papers Cece was carrying out of her hand. "Here." He slapped them onto the countertop. "If I can't get her to go home and go to bed, I'll have her back here before midnight."

"Or she'll turn into a pumpkin?" Juanita asked, entering into the spirit of things, even if Cece wasn't.

"No, I'll turn into an unemployed M.D."

"We can't have that."

"No, we can't. Let's go, Cece."

"I don't want to go," she insisted, but her words lacked conviction.

"Doctor's orders." Juanita laughed, waving them away as she went back to her charting.

He took Cece by the hand before she could protest some more and pulled her into the darkened activity room and into his arms. "Kiss me," he commanded, and lowered his mouth to hers. He didn't feel like arguing with her at the moment, and if he asked permission for a kiss, she would surely say no. So he didn't ask. He just kissed her.

And she kissed him back.

But not all at once. She stiffened her spine and pushed at his chest with both hands, but he only held her tighter and kept on kissing her until she stopped struggling. When she softened in his embrace and slipped her arms around his waist, he teased her lips with the tip of his tongue until her mouth flowered open beneath his.

"I've missed you, Cece." His voice was rough around the edges with the strength of his need for her. He was tired of being a nice guy, of being patient and giving her time to learn to love him again. He was too afraid of losing her to the outside forces that seemed to be ruling their lives. But dragging her into the deserted activity room to steal a kiss was as far as he was prepared to go with the caveman approach. Wooing and winning Cece was a job he didn't intend to botch by letting his hormones get out of line. "I've missed you," he said, making himself hold her lightly, just barely within the circle of his arms.

"I've missed you, too." Her voice was soft, breathless. "But I've been so very busy here."

He lifted his fingers and touched her lips, silencing her. "You don't have to say anything. I told you I'd wait for you. I'm not going back on my word." He released her, letting her step out of his arms, but not letting her move far enough away to regain her equilibrium. "C'mon. We're leaving." He took her hand, leading her down the steps and along the walk at a trot.

"What's wrong?" Cece asked, getting into the car.

At least she didn't seem bent on escape. Jeff took that as a good sign. "Now that I've got you," he admitted ruefully, "I don't know what to do with you."

She laughed lightly, sweetly, and his stomach did somersaults. "You seemed to know pretty well what you wanted two minutes ago."

"I still want you," he said with a teasing leer. "I just don't know where the hell to take you."

"I'm too old to neck in cars." Cece folded her hands in her lap, suddenly prim. She giggled, seeing the absurdity of the situation and making the best of it, just as he was trying to do.

"We'll do something else," he improvised. "We'll eat. Food's always been a great substitute for sex. How about pie and coffee at Marge's Diner?"

She bit her lip, turning her head to look back at Worthington House.

"Today's special is blueberry à la mode." He laid his arm across her shoulder, skimmed her hair behind her ear with his other hand and drew her close to nuzzle her neck. "You can't be with the residents every moment."

Cece turned her head to let his lips brush her cheek and the corner of her mouth. "I know. It's just that since we've learned for certain it's one of us, someone they all trust to care for and protect them, I can't stay away."

"I'm only asking for an hour. You need a break. And I need to be with you."

She lifted her hand to his cheek, turned more fully toward him and deepened the kiss. "I'll stay with you as long as I can."

Jeff groaned. "I want you for the rest of time, but I'll settle for the next half hour."

"It's a deal." Cece settled back against the seat. "If we hurry, there just might still be two pieces of blueberry pie left at Marge's."

THERE WAS a small knot of people milling around the counter at Marge's Diner when they walked in, even though it was after eleven o'clock. The group split and dispersed as they approached, to reveal George Phelps and his bride. George swiveled his stool and waved in their direction.

"Jeff. Good to see you. I planned to get in touch with you in the morning. Let you know you wouldn't be needed to oversee my practice anymore." He grinned and held out his hand. His teeth were very white in his tanned face, and he looked fit and healthy and rested. "How's it going?"

The two men shook hands, then George turned to smile at his wife. "Sweetheart, why don't we take one of the tables? Since Jeff is here we might as well catch up on how things are going at the office."

"What would you two like?" Marge asked, smiling as she rose.

"Black coffee," Jeff replied.

"The same for me." Cece smiled back at Marge. "Congratulations on your marriage."

"Thank you, Cece. I've never done anything so impulsive, or so romantic, in my life."

"Where have you been?" Jeff asked, signaling the waitress for two pieces of the blueberry pie displayed in the glass case on the counter.

"We went island hopping," George said, reaching for Marge's hand as they sat down around a table near the back of the room.

"We've been all over the Caribbean—the Bahamas, Jamaica, the Cayman Islands. It was lovely. Paradise," Marge said and blushed.

"We chartered a boat and just went where the spirit moved us. The weather was great. Kind of unusual for this time of year, I understand, but we're not complaining."

"Glad you had a good time," Jeff said, inspecting his piece of pie with the tip of his fork.

One or two customers came into the diner and wandered over to the table to greet the newlyweds. George Phelps had a large practice and everyone knew who he was. Marge had friends all over town. When the newcomers left, George went back to the subject at hand.

"I appreciate your taking my practice like that at a moment's notice, Jeff. I never planned to stay away as long as we did. But—" he glanced at Marge "—well, I've never been in love like this before."

"Maybe someday you can do the same for me," Jeff said and left it at that.

George studied Jeff as he ate his pie. "I've been feeling guilty ever since you walked in here, leaving you with my practice so long, what with your grandfather's troubles and all."

"It's been hectic."

Cece sensed Jeff's reluctance to talk about his grandfather's problems, but George Phelps felt no such restraint. "I understand Phil Wocheck's being called on to testify in front of the grand jury. That doesn't sound good. Phil's resented Judson ever since he found out how Judson felt about young Eddie having the brass to want to marry your mother all those years ago."

"That's ancient history, George," Marge said, gently nudging her husband away from the subject as she refilled their coffee cups.

"This whole business of Margaret's death is ancient history, but that hasn't kept the D.A. from going ahead full throttle. I say let bygones be bygones and let the dead rest in peace."

"It's too late for that," Jeff said roughly. "My grandfather's innocent and we intend to prove it."

"Of course, my boy," George said, nodding his head. "Never believed for an instant Judson killed Margaret, although from what I remember of the woman, there were times when he might have felt driven to it."

"George, don't speak ill of the dead."

"We have other problems to deal with." Jeff pushed his plate aside with half a piece of pie still on it. Cece felt her throat tighten with apprehension. Worthington House. It had actually slipped her mind for a few minutes. Now the anxiety was back full force. She moved restlessly in her seat. George Phelps needed to know what had happened there in his absence. It might as well be now.

"What other problems?" George curled his hands around his coffee cup and furrowed his brow. He looked more annoyed than worried or concerned.

"There's trouble at Worthington House. We probably shouldn't be talking about it here, but there are rumors all over town. I'm surprised you haven't heard about it already."

"We've only been back in town a few hours. We read about your grandfather's indictment in the paper when I went through the mail," George explained. "But what's this about Worthington House?"

"Someone's been trying to do away with the patients there," Jeff said bluntly. "We suspect it might be one of the staff, but we haven't got any proof."

"What the hell do you mean by that?"

"After you left town, Wilhelm Badenhop nearly died of respiratory arrest. A few days later Cece brought Violet Orthwein out to Tyler General in almost the same condition. Examining her in the ER, I found a needle puncture that shouldn't have been there."

"Jeff ran some tests," Cece interrupted, "because he suspected a drug overdose."

"What did you find?" George looked as if they had his complete attention at last.

"Morphine sulfate."

"My Lord, a mercy killer? Here in Tyler?" Marge said out loud the words no one else had spoken.

Mercy killer. The bald definition made Cece's blood run cold.

George ignored his wife and continued to watch Jeff. "Don't be silly, Marge," he said, licking his lips nervously. "Go on, Jeff. What was it—a nursing error, mislabeled medications?" He patted his shirt pocket, searching for his pipe. He took it out but made no move to fill or light it.

Jeff glanced at Cece.

"No." Cece looked down at her hands. She still had trouble believing what was happening. "There were no charting errors. All our meds check out okay." She raised her eyes to meet George Phelps's disbelieving gaze. "But Marge is right. Someone's deliberately harming patients. A few days ago, very late at night, I heard someone in the men's ward. They ran off before I could see who it was, but left a loaded syringe behind. It contained morphine."

"Was anyone harmed?" Marge asked, her voice thready with shock.

Cece shook her head, but it was Jeff who answered.

"No, thank God. Not that time. Jacob Bremer was the target. He put up a fight and scared the assailant off."

"Didn't he see who it was?"

"He wasn't able to tell the police much. Unfortunately, it was dark in the men's ward, and he'd been sound asleep moments before. As Wilhelm and Violet were, apparently."

"What about fingerprints on the syringe?" George asked, looking down at the pipe he was twisting between his fingers.

"Cece's, of course. Jacob handed it to her after he wrestled it away from his assailant, and the other prints were too smudged to be useful."

"You're sure of this?"

"Yes."

"I can't believe it."

"George, it's not impossible that Luetta Peterson was also a victim," Jeff said quietly, but without softening his tone. "I'm sorry, Marge."

"Cousin Luetta was very sick," Marge said. "She died very suddenly, I know, but it was a blessing."

"Jeez!" George shook his head, unbelieving. "This whole scenario sounds impossible. Things like this happen in big city hospitals where they can't or don't screen their staff like they should, not in Tyler."

"After the attack on Jacob I couldn't keep the police out of it any longer. Kellaway wants my hide, but he can't do anything about it. For a while I thought he might even be responsible for the attacks. Now I'm not so sure. There aren't any clear-cut suspects. For the moment all we can do is keep on our toes. Brick Bauer's got a guard posted on each floor. He's there himself tonight. He's sent out police bulletins to all the pharmacies in the area. Since Worthington House's narcotics inventory checked out clean, the killer has to be getting it from somewhere else."

"Somewhere else?" George looked down at his hands.

"Brick's got a list of all Worthington House employees," Jeff continued. "He's asking all the county pharmacies to match it up with their controlled-substance prescriptions. It's a long shot and so far nothing's turned up. We'll have to widen the circle in a few days toward Madison, Beloit, Milwaukee. Start notifying doctors, as well. Once morphine is prescribed into a home environment, it's pretty hard to trace."

"Home environment?" George's head snapped up. His pipe dropped from nerveless fingers, clattering onto the Formica tabletop. "What makes you say that?"

Jeff shrugged, his eyes narrowing as he studied George's face, now pale beneath his tan. "It makes sense. A health care professional with a badly injured or terminally ill family member. Morphine is prescribed. The patient dies. A whole vial is left—doesn't have to be accounted for, returned to the pharmacy or destroyed in front of witnesses."

Jeff was just improvising, talking through possibilities off the top of his head, Cece realized. She'd done it a hundred times herself, but not in exactly the same configuration that Jeff had just laid out for them. It made sense. As much sense as anything else about this frightening affair.

"It could have happened that way." George was looking at Jeff but not seeing him. "It could have happened that way."

"George, what in hell are you talking about?" Jeff's voice was still low, controlled, but it demanded a response all the same.

"Phyllis Houser. I prescribed morphine for her at the end."

"She died at home, I remember." Marge reached out, laid her hand on top of George's, which was again wrapped tightly around the bowl of his pipe.

George nodded. "Freddie watched the nurse give her injections every day."

"Nurse." Jeff leaned forward. "Who was the nurse?"

"A woman from out of town," George said, dismissing Jeff's query. But his eyes came back to meet the young doctor's. "Freddie kept asking about the morphine," he recalled, frowning as he sifted through his memories. "I told her it would make her mother feel better, take her pain away, let her sleep. And when she didn't wake up from that sleep she would be in heaven."

Cece gripped the edge of the table so hard her fingers hurt. "Freddie always wants to help," she said, hearing the tremor in her own voice. "She wants everyone to feel better, to be happy... in heaven."

"Freddie isn't capable of giving someone an injection, is she?" Marge asked.

"I don't know." Jeff turned to Cece.

"I don't know, either. She's a very talented mimic." Her heart was beating high and hard in her throat. She'd considered every member of her nursing staff as a possible suspect at one time or another, but never once had she suspected a resident or patient. Her intellect scoffed at the possibility, but her instinct told her it might be true. "Freddie has free run of Worthington House. She wanders all over the place, day and night."

Jeff was already halfway out of his chair when George Phelps spoke again.

"I don't know what happened to the morphine I prescribed for Phyllis Houser after her death," he said, turning paler still. "But I do remember I wrote the last prescription only one day before she died."

CHAPTER FOURTEEN

CECE FELT as if she were moving underwater. She clutched the door handle of Jeff's car as if it were a lifeline. She wanted to jump out of the car and run ahead, cut across yards and down alleys, avoiding what traffic there was this late at night. "Hurry, Jeff."

She couldn't get the picture of Freddie in her rumpled smock and white slacks, her flyaway hair and childish smile, out of her mind. Was she capable of such acts? If Cece had been able to catch a glimpse of Jacob Bremer's attacker, she could now believe George Phelps's theory or dismiss it completely from her mind. But she couldn't do either. Freddie, sweet, childlike Freddie, was suddenly the prime suspect.

"We'll make it," Jeff said, sliding through a stop sign on Main Street, Marge and George Phelps right behind them in George's Lincoln. "If it is Freddie, there's no cause to think she's going to try again tonight."

"We can't be sure of that, Jeff." Cece sucked in her breath as Jeff passed a car with only inches to spare at the intersection of Main and Elm. Even in Tyler it was dangerous to drive so fast. He skidded across Main and accelerated.

Two blocks later they pulled to a halt in front of Worthington House. George's Lincoln turned the corner behind them, but Cece and Jeff didn't wait for the older doctor and his new wife. They were already up the steps of the retirement center and through the door before George switched off his engine.

"Juanita, have you seen Freddie Houser lately?" Cece asked the duty nurse.

"She's upstairs with the snack cart," Juanita replied, her eyes widening at their whirlwind entrance and Cece's breathless tone of voice. Her eyes widened further when George Phelps and Marge came through the front door almost as fast.

"Upstairs," Jeff called over his shoulder, taking the steps two at a time, Cece right on his heels.

In the extended care wing, Brick Bauer was leaning his elbow on the nurses' station, talking quietly to the young woman sitting behind it.

They walked swiftly toward the desk. Brick watched them come, alert but not alarmed. His gaze moved past Jeff and Cece as George and Marge came into view at the top of the stairs. His eyes narrowed. "What's up?" he asked.

"Where's Freddie Houser?" Jeff asked.

Cece was already moving down the hall. She'd spotted Freddie's snack cart. It was parked outside the men's ward. *Jacob Bremer's room.* Where none of the patients was able to eat popcorn or drink juice and soft drinks on his own.

She made herself slow down, breathe deeply, still the thudding of her heart in her ears and walk into the room as though nothing were wrong. But something was wrong. Very, very wrong. Freddie was standing on the far side of Jacob's bed. In her hand was a syringe. She was bending over the old man, holding him down with her other hand, anchoring his good arm to the bed as he struggled weakly to free himself. Cece didn't know what to do next, but she had to do something.

"Freddie," she said, softly but commandingly, "give me the syringe. You aren't allowed to give medications to the patients here." She advanced into the room, moving slowly, smoothly, each step a separate physical order from her brain to her bones and muscles. Her hand was trembling so badly that for a moment she was afraid to hold it out to take the syringe.

"No." Freddie shook her head emphatically. "I'm going to help him. I know how. He's tired and sick. He hurts. He can't even talk to tell us what he wants. He can't even eat popcorn!" She looked down at the old man, patting his hand, oblivious of his terror. When she loosened her hold on his arm, Jacob made a grab for the syringe. Freddie stepped back a little from the bed, moving more quickly than Cece had ever seen her move before.

"Give me the syringe," Cece repeated in the same authoritative tone. "You aren't supposed to have it. The medication inside is very dangerous."

"It's good. It's what Dr. George gave my mom." Tears filled Freddie's eyes. "It helped her to sleep. It helped her go to heaven. *I* helped her go to heaven. I don't like to stick people," she said confidingly, with a little smile for Cece. "But it's the way you have to do it. My mom showed me how. I helped her go to heaven,'' she repeated, a talisman of comfort.

From the corner of her eye, Cece saw Jeff's outline in the doorway, then Brick's hand and the dark material of his uniform sleeve as he prevented him from entering the room. Should she call George Phelps into the ward? Let him try to reason with Freddie? The retarded woman was very fond of the older doctor.

Cece knew she couldn't stand there doing nothing much longer. Jacob was still struggling to free himself from Freddie's grasp. Cece saw the terror in his eyes, saw the confusion and frightening determination to complete her task in his assailant's eyes, as well.

''Dr. George is right outside,'' Cece explained gently. ''Let me call him in.''

''I don't want to talk to Dr. George,'' Freddie said, shaking her head emphatically. ''He'll be angry at me.''

''No, he won't. He's your friend.''

''My good friend. But I don't want to talk to him. I have to help Jacob.''

She could talk until she was blue in the face, Cece realized, but Freddie wouldn't change her mind. She wasn't capable of understanding that what she was doing, what she'd already done, was wrong. She was a child inside, a very small child with a small child's incomplete view of right and wrong. She thought she was helping Jacob to go to heaven, as her mother had told her she was helping her when Phyllis used her unwitting, uncomprehending daughter to help her commit suicide—for that was surely what had happened. The childlike woman had known no different when she injected Wilhelm and Violet and, most likely, Luetta Peterson. Nothing any of them said now would make a difference, either.

Somehow she must get the syringe and its lethal contents away from Freddie. And she would have to act quickly before Freddie became frightened and plunged the needle willy-nilly into the old man's arm.

"Jacob isn't ready to go to heaven," Cece said, her throat raw with the effort to speak slowly, normally, when all she wanted to do was scream for Jeff to come and help her, for Freddie to put down the syringe and walk away.

"Let Cece do it." Brick's voice was a low growl, barely reaching into the room, as he tightened his grip on Jeff's shoulder. But Freddie had excellent hearing and her eyes flickered toward the men in the doorway. Cece took two quick steps around the end of the bed.

Freddie was holding the syringe only a few inches from Jacob's arm. Cece knew if Freddie plunged the needle into his skin she could injure him severely, regardless of whether she injected the full dose of narcotic. She pushed aside visions of the needle breaking off in a vein, of air bubbles released into his bloodstream and finding their way to his heart or lungs to cause death as surely as the morphine.

"Freddie, I've never lied to you," Cece said, holding out her hand. "Jacob doesn't want to go to sleep. He doesn't want to go to heaven. He's going to get better. Don't you want to help him get better?"

"He can't talk. He can't walk. He can't even eat popcorn," the childlike woman repeated. "He needs to go to heaven. He could have gone to heaven the other night but he knocked over his water glass. I was scared it would be my fault it broke. I ran down the stairs so fast no one saw me."

Cece was so close she could reach out and grab the syringe, but she did not. She wanted Freddie to hand it to her. She wanted her to make the decision, if she could.

Tears stung the back of Cece's throat. Poor Freddie, what would happen to her after tonight? Where could she go that she would be cared for—and watched over so closely that nothing like this could ever happen again—and still be loved? "Only Jesus can take people to heaven," Cece told her gently. "It's wrong for you to try and do it for them."

"But my mom?" Freddie looked bewildered. Tears welled up in her eyes and spilled onto her cheeks. "My mom said I was a good girl to help her."

"But she never told you to try to help others go to heaven, did she?"

"No...," Freddie agreed, her voice wobbling. "But the medicine and shot needles were still there. Dr. George didn't take them away. The nurse didn't take them away. I put them in my suitcase when I came here. I saved them. Then Miss Peterson got sick and she talked to me about how nice it would be for her to see my mom again in heaven. I remembered this stuff."

Freddie let go of Jacob's arm, forgetting him completely, and reached into the pocket of her smock. She produced a glass vial, almost empty. "I went to her room one night. I gave her a shot. She went to sleep and in the morning the nurses told me she went to heaven." She stopped crying as quickly as she'd started. She smiled, fully, innocently, and Cece's heart clenched with pity and fear. "I did it. I sent her to heaven."

"But it was wrong. It was very bad."

"Bad?" Freddie's face crumpled. "I want to help. I'm not bad."

Cece held out her hand. "Give me the syringe. Please."

Freddie looked down at Cece's hand, hesitated. "Do you think I'm bad, Cece? You're my friend. I don't want you to think I'm bad." She was crying openly now, great hiccuping sobs of misery and loneliness.

There was a stir of motion at the door, but Cece paid no attention. "I won't think you're bad if you give me the needle," she promised.

"Do as she says, Freddie." George Phelps appeared at Jacob's bedside. "Be a good girl. Do as Cece says."

"Dr. George!" Freddie smiled happily through her tears. "You're back. I've missed you." She took a step toward him.

The syringe clattered to the floor. Before Cece could react, Freddie dropped to her knees to pick it up.

Cece lowered herself to the floor beside her. "Give it to me," she said gently, with a smile that held back her tears.

Freddie picked up the instrument and looked up at George Phelps. "Do as she says, Freddie," he told her.

She passed the syringe to Cece along with the vial, then buried her face in her hands. "I'm not bad," she wailed over and over. "I'm not bad. Don't stop being my friend. I'm not bad."

Cece gathered Freddie into her arms, rocked her to and fro, as though she were a baby. "I'll always be your friend. I promise."

"Always?" Freddie asked, patting Cece's hand, still crying, but smiling, too, the events of the past hour already beginning to blur in her mind.

"Always."

"You, too, Dr. George?"

"Me, too."

Jeff was beside them. Cece sensed his warmth and strength even before she lifted her head to smile at him through her tears. She handed him the syringe and the vial of morphine. He touched her cheek, then turned to Jacob. Brick stood guard at the door, keeping the rest of the staff at bay as George and Jeff examined the sick old man, to make sure he hadn't been harmed by his ordeal, and to reassure him of his safety now.

For Cece, the room narrowed down to just two: the sobbing child-woman in her arms—and Jeff.

"CECE?" JEFF SHIFTED his position on the creaking wicker couch. He thought she had fallen asleep in his arms, she was so still, her breathing so quiet. "Are you asleep?"

"No." She moved her head slightly in the negative. "I can't sleep. I can't stop thinking about Freddie."

Jeff thought of a way he could help her to sleep, help both of them to forget what had happened over the past couple of hours, but as usual it seemed they were in the wrong place at the wrong time. Although when you thought about it, in its heyday the Worthington House solarium at midnight would have been a great place to make love to a woman. Moonlight filtered down through the partially drawn blinds, traced patterns on the floor through the fern fronds hanging from their baskets. If he narrowed his eyes, he could almost see what it had been like in this room ninety years ago. The air would be heavy and moist with the scent of growing things. Cece would walk toward him, her hair piled high on her head. She would be wearing a high-necked white dress that swept the floor and buttoned with a row of tiny pearl buttons all down the back. He would unfasten them impatiently, one by one, until she lay naked in his arms....

A tear dropped onto his hand.

"Don't cry, Cece." He pulled her closer into his embrace. The wicker couch protested again.

"She's so alone. And so lonely. I should have paid more attention to her, spent more time with her, and this might never have happened."

"No." He couldn't let her take all the blame on herself. She did that too often. She always felt responsible; she wanted to mother the world. "It's not your fault. I can see it's going to be my job in life to keep you from trying to take responsibility for the actions of every other human being on this planet.''

"I promised to protect and care for Freddie and the others. I failed.'' She sniffed into the handkerchief he pulled out of his pocket and pressed into her hand.

"The system failed,'' he said, stroking her arm. She laid her head against his shoulder. She relaxed a little, but awareness fizzed and sparked between them beneath the sorrow and regret. "How could anyone know that Freddie Houser was in possession of nearly a complete vial of morphine? That she'd have thought to hide it and the syringes among her things for almost a year?''

"We never went through her treasure box,'' Cece said, looking up at him through tear-sparkled lashes. "She deserved her privacy, her dignity. But if someone had only looked, just once... If I'd only been a few seconds quicker the other night, seen her running down the stairs—''

"No more if onlys. We're all responsible to some extent for what happened. Maybe George Phelps most of all, even if his ex-wife was making his life hell just then. He prescribed the narcotic into a home environment. He pronounced Phyllis Houser dead. He should have made sure the morphine was destroyed or returned to the pharmacy. Or the nurse he'd hired to take care of Phyllis and Freddie should have. I don't remember the woman, but George says she left town for another case the next day. She did nothing to secure the medication, either. And here at Worthington house, too—someone should have checked through Freddie's things, but they didn't. The blame stretches back over a year and catches a lot of people in its net.''

''What's going to happen to Freddie?'' Cece had stopped crying. She traced his fingers with the tips of hers as their hands lay entwined on her lap. ''She's so childlike, alone and lonely.''

Jeff knew Cece would still be at Freddie's bedside if George hadn't given her a sedative that ensured she would sleep until morning and hadn't promised to stay for a while himself. Even then Jeff hadn't been able to coax Cece into the solarium until long after Brick had finished taking statements and Worthington House had settled back to normal. In another hour it would be dawn. The day shift would be coming in, the solarium would lose its memory of magic and revert to being the staff lounge. Reality and routine would intrude on their solitude.

''She can't stay here, Cece, you know that,'' he said gently. Freddie surely had a guardian. George Phelps? He didn't know who, but they'd have to find out.

''She needs someplace more structured, more equipped to handle a person with her mental handicaps.''

''We'll help to find a place like that,'' he promised her, resigning himself to the search, and to Cece making herself responsible, legally and morally, for Freddie's future contentment. He had no doubt at all that that was what would happen. He smiled and kissed the top of her head. He expected nothing less from her.

Jeff wanted Cece to sleep in his arms, but not here on a rickety wicker couch. In a bed somewhere, with clean sheets and soft music, and where no one knew the telephone number. He'd gotten Hank Merton to cover for him in the ER this shift. He wasn't due back on duty until midnight. He wondered what Cece would say if he told her he was taking her to Lake Geneva and keeping her with him until then. He wondered what her mother would say. He wondered what his own mother would say. Alyssa would look shocked, then smile and give them her blessing. Annabelle Scanlon would start planning their wedding. Fair enough—that was what he wanted, too.

"What's going to happen to Worthington House?" Cece asked, although sleepily.

"I don't know. There are no witnesses to the attacks on Wilhelm or Violet. Fortunately, Jacob wasn't harmed."

"Thank God," Cece said quietly, reverently. She snuggled closer. He looked down and saw her eyelids flicker shut.

"Thank God," he repeated.

"What about Luetta Peterson?" She was almost asleep, but still worried about Worthington House and its staff. Actually, he hoped Cecil Kellaway got the boot for this whole mess. But if he didn't, he sure as hell was going to have to run a tighter ship.

"I can't see the Peterson family wanting to have her remains disturbed. Even if Freddie did... help her to heaven...she had very little time left anyway. And she was suffering a great deal. Still, it will be up to them.

Don't worry about it." He gave her a hug, pulled her nearer. "Close your eyes," he said with a chuckle that bordered on the lascivious.

"Are you going to abduct me?" she asked, lifting heavy eyelids, smiling up at him with a teasing smile that told him she had read his lustful thoughts and shared them.

"Yes. For a day of illicit napping," he said, grinning more broadly.

Cece pretended to pout, the worry and regret retreating from her gray eyes, leaving them tear-bright and smoky. Jeff felt himself relax a little more. She wasn't going to martyr herself this time. She didn't feel she had to stay at Worthington House forever to atone for her perceived failure of duty, the way she'd cut herself off from her midwifery because of her unfounded guilt over her husband's death. "Is that all you want?"

"No." He wasn't smiling now as he lowered his head to kiss her and end her bantering questions. "I want much more than that. I want all of you. And I want you today and tomorrow and for the next fifty years. Any objections?"

"None," she said and lifted her hand to the back of his neck to bring him even closer. "None at all."

She hadn't said she loved him. Jeff tried not to panic. He couldn't force a declaration from her. He'd have to be patient a little longer. He'd have to wait.

"I need you, Cece," he said, lifting her chin with his finger so that she had to look at him, see the need and the love in his eyes, in his heart. "I need to lie down beside you at night and to wake up beside you in the morning.''

"Is that a proposal? Or are you only trying to plan my life for me?'' she asked, trying to look stern and affronted. But a tiny smile lurked at the corner of her mouth. The tears of regret and sadness dried up, leaving her eyes rain-washed gray and sparkling.

"I want to have a say in your future,'' he admitted, his voice husky with desire. "So I can plan my own.''

"I need you,'' she whispered, as though repeating a vow. "I need you to lie down beside me at night. I need to wake up beside you in the morning. Together we're stronger than apart.''

"Does that mean you're ready to forget the past?''

"All of it,'' she said, twining her fingers with his. "All the bad parts.''

"Maybe you'll come to work for me at the clinic?'' He knew no other way to ask her if she had forgiven herself for her husband's death. "Or maybe you want to work for Hank Merton. I know he's been after you since you delivered Liza's baby.''

"Yes,'' she replied after a moment's hesitation. "I'll decide when things are settled here. I owe them that much. Being director of nurses at Worthington House has been a challenge, but it isn't the kind of nursing I want to do. I spend too much time with paperwork and not with my patients. I want to be a midwife again. I'm a good one.''

"But you'd still rather work for Hank Merton than for me?'' he teased. If he kissed her again things might get out of control. As usual, they were in too public a place to give vent to their passion.

"You're too bossy," she said with a wicked answering smile. "And I think Hank will pay me more."

"But I can give you fringe benefits that Hank could never match."

She snuggled against him. "I know. But I think I'll take Hank's money and moonlight at the clinic. That ought to qualify me for those fringe benefits."

"Starting immediately," he said, lifting his hand to the back of her neck, pulling her to him until their lips met and fused. The kiss was one of passion and commitment. It sealed their vows as surely as if they were standing before a minister in a church.

"I'm not going to be able to give you all the things most people expect a doctor's wife to have," he said, remembering the anger and recrimination in his first marriage. "I might never be able to afford a country club membership, or trips to Europe every year. I haven't even got my student loans paid off. And then there's the clinic debt."

Cece raised her fingers to his lips, silencing him. "When have I ever said I wanted European vacations, or country club memberships, or even private schools for the children?"

"Children." He felt his heart skip a beat and speed up again, pounding against the wall of his chest. Cece might already be carrying his child. He couldn't let her go now, even if she wanted to be free. He was a man and she was his woman. It was as primitive and basic as that. His voice was low, raspy with urgency when he spoke again. "That's another reason you're going to have to marry me. That night we made love at the boathouse. We didn't use any protection. You might already be pregnant." He made an effort to control himself so he didn't frighten her with his intensity. "How the hell can I teach birth control and family planning classes if I can't even practice what I preach?"

"I want to have your baby," Cece said.

The words were simple, sincere. Their effect on him was devastating. He remembered her nakedness, the softness of her skin, the heat of her body. He remembered the way she surrounded him, took him in, held him close and gave back passion as fully as she received.

"God, Cece. Say you'll marry me as soon as we can get the license."

"And find a place to live." She laid her cheek against his, as shaken by desire and frustration as he was.

"Then it's settled," he said, touching her lips with a feather kiss. "We'll get married. As soon as I can scrape up enough money for a ring."

He felt her smile against his lips as the tip of her tongue darted out to tantalize the corner of his mouth.

"Don't worry about that," she said, her breath mingling with his. "I have just what you need. And it won't cost you a cent."

IT WAS SUNSET when Cece woke for the second time that day. She stretched her toes beneath the sheets of the king-size bed in their sinfully expensive hotel room overlooking Lake Geneva. Her foot brushed against Jeff's calf and she smiled to herself. He hadn't liked the idea of her paying for the hotel room, but she'd insisted and he'd given in with good grace.

Cautiously she lifted herself onto her elbow and looked down at the man sleeping beside her. The setting sun touched his chest with molten fingers of light. She laid her hand on him, feeling the crisp curling hair that covered his chest, the hard wall of muscle beneath, the slow, comforting, yet strangely exciting beat of his heart.

How she loved him. How she needed him. He made her feel whole and complete, in charge of her life. Together they could do it all, have it all. She could love and serve others, nurture the babies she helped bring safely into the world, care for the mothers and not be overwhelmed by their problems and their sorrows. Jeff's love and confidence in her would give her that strength.

"I love you, Dr. Baron," she said very quietly.

He lifted his hand to cover hers, but didn't open his eyes, although beneath the sheet, his body stirred and hardened and she knew in a few moments he would take her in his arms and make love to her again. And if he didn't initiate the loving, she would.

"I love you, Nurse Hayes," he said and waited for her kiss.

She looked down at their hands, fingers laced, two Tyler high school class rings gleaming dimly in the fading light. Exchanging them had been a whimsical gesture, but the commitment to the future together they represented was not. She moved her hand, touching the gold bands. Hers fit snugly on his little finger, just as she remembered it. His, she'd secured to her third finger, left hand, with a rubber band, just as she'd done in high school. She wondered if Gates Department Store still sold lengths of soft, furry angora yarn to wrap it with as she used to years ago. She giggled at her nostalgic thoughts.

"What's so funny?" Jeff asked sleepily.

"I'll tell you later," she promised, wiggling her fingers free of his grasp as she bent her head to give him the kiss he seemed to be expecting. She swept her left hand beneath the sheet to touch him more intimately still.

"Ouch," he said with a grimace as her hand closed around him. "That damn ring's cold."

"Is it?" she asked innocently, stroking him boldly. "It might be cold, but it seems to be acting as quite a stimulant down here." Jeff groaned a wordless reply. Cece's smile broadened. She felt very feminine and pleased with herself. She stroked him again. He groaned. "I knew there was a reason I didn't throw it away all those years ago."

"Throw it away? What are you talking about?" Jeff demanded, but his voice was ragged with desire and he didn't really listen to her answer as she closed her hand around him once more.

"Oh, nothing," she said, smiling still, as he pulled her atop him. "Nothing at all."

CHAPTER FIFTEEN

"ALL RIGHT, I give up. Margaret Alyssa looks just like Mom did when she was a baby," Jeff admitted with a laugh as he studied a handful of old black-and-white photographs of Alyssa at just a few weeks of age.

"I told you so," Liza crowed as she took the photos from his hand. She gathered up another handful from the pile she was holding on her lap. "I know you were all just humoring me when I said that after she was born." She flashed him a saucy, triumphant grin. "But I was right. I'm so glad I remembered this bunch of photos Cliff and I found in the attic at Timberlake before Granddad sold the lodge. I knew I could prove my point with them. It just took me a few days to recall where they were."

"Possibly because you're the world's lousiest housekeeper." Jeff couldn't resist needling her just a little.

Liza made a face. "And you're getting senile, big brother. How could you forget I gave the envelope to you for safekeeping?"

"You gave the envelope to Amanda, who kept it in her office for a while, then gave it to me for safekeeping. Why, I don't know, since we live in the same house."

"Well, you won't be living in the same house much longer," Liza retorted, changing the subject in the blink of an eye. "When are you and Cece getting married, anyway?"

"I don't know," Jeff admitted, looking across the room at Cece and Alyssa, who were busy admiring the baby Alyssa was holding on her lap. Celebrating their engagement was the occasion for this impromptu Friday evening gathering of the clan. "We haven't had time to set a date."

"Well, don't be as secretive as Brick and Karen Bauer. Having friends and relatives who run off to the county courthouse to get married without telling anyone spoils all the fun."

"Like sneaking into people's houses and taking all the labels off their canned goods and short-sheeting their beds?"

"Well," Liza said, having the grace to blush. "Brick's an old friend. And Karen needed loosening up."

"We're getting married as soon as possible," Cece said, overhearing their conversation. She gave the baby's downy blond head one last feather-light caress and walked toward them, smiling for Jeff alone. "No fussing over a big wedding. No showers and rehearsal dinners. But a church ceremony, I think. And both families."

"And if we're lucky, a weekend at the Wisconsin Dells for a honeymoon," Jeff said, half teasing, half serious.

"Oh, Jeff, how hokey," Amanda scolded as she sifted through the pile of photographs.

"That's just as bad as going to Niagara Falls for your honeymoon." Liza laughed and shook her head in defeat.

"Niagara Falls is too damn far away," was all he said. Cece didn't say anything. She only smiled and reached up on tiptoe to kiss his cheek.

"You are the world's last great romantic," she whispered, smiling again as she lifted her hand to touch the class ring she now wore on a chain around her neck, having replaced it on her left hand with her modest diamond engagement ring.

"I know." He touched his pocket, where, she knew, her own class ring was back in its familiar place on his key chain.

"Another wedding," Amanda sighed.

"Always a bridesmaid, never a bride," Liza recited wickedly.

Amanda pretended not to hear her. "And then another baby, or two or three in the family, and before you know it, they'll be calling me their spinster Aunt Amanda."

"It is sad that all the best men are either already taken or are your blood relatives," Liza said in mock sympathy, with a wink for Cece. "Right, sister-in-law-to-be?"

"Right," Cece agreed, giving Jeff a proprietary pat on his backside. "The best ones are off the market."

"Female chauvinists," Jeff growled.

Amanda ignored her sister's gibes. "Look, here's a picture of Grandmother at Timberlake," she said softly, so as not to disturb Judson. "She was beautiful. And she looks just like you, Liza, and the way Mother did at your age. Look at that dress. I wonder what color it was? And her figure! I wish I'd inherited that long, leggy Ingalls frame."

"You're a Baron, Amanda. Make do." Liza reached for the photo. "Margaret was very beautiful," she echoed, more loudly than Amanda as she studied the photograph carefully.

Judson had been sitting in the corner by the bay window, talking to Cliff about weather and fish and the best way to preserve the land along the lakeshore that he hadn't sold to the Addison Corporation when Timberlake Lodge changed hands. Now he got up and walked across the room, looking over Amanda's shoulder at Margaret's photograph. If her image still caused him pain, he hid it well.

"She was very beautiful," he said gruffly. "Very beautiful." He turned away.

The atmosphere in the room had changed perceptibly, like the sunny, late-September day that had faded into a rainy evening outside. Jeff wondered if he should open the bottle of champagne chilling in the refrigerator now, make a formal, if unnecessary, announcement of his engagement to Cece and lighten things up, or let them go on talking. Talking about Margaret and the murder, things they rarely discussed. Maybe it was time to clear the air. And maybe not.

Everyone was just too on edge. The grand jury had been deliberating for almost a week on the evidence the state had presented to prove its case against Judson. The longer they deliberated, the less likely they would be to clear his name. Amanda wouldn't admit to that, but she didn't have to. They all knew it to be true.

"Who's this hunk dancing with Grandmother?" Liza asked, holding up yet another photo, oblivious, because she chose to be, to the increasing tension in the room.

"I wish I knew." Amanda glanced over Liza's shoulder. "Mom, do you recognize him?"

Alyssa just shook her head, not even glancing at the picture Liza held toward her. "Mother had so many... friends...." She hesitated just long enough over the word for it to be noticeable. She remained seated by the fireplace, watching the flames, cuddling Margaret Alyssa to her breast. "I don't remember any of them."

"Don't even think of asking Granddad," Amanda hissed, snatching the picture away from her sister. "He's got enough on his mind without us waving a picture of one of Margaret's lovers under his nose."

Liza looked stricken. "I... I didn't think."

"It's all right," Jeff began, refereeing their differences, just as he'd so often done when they were kids.

The phone on the table at his elbow rang. He picked it up, expecting a call from the hospital, wondering what was wrong and if he'd have time to make a quick speech and pour the champagne before he left.

"Ingalls residence. Jeff Baron," he said. He listened briefly, then said, "Just a minute, please," and put down the receiver. He felt cold inside and sick to his stomach. "Amanda, it's for you."

She looked at the phone for a moment before rising to take it from his hand. After her clipped "hello," she listened silently to the voice on the other end. "Thanks for letting me know," was all she said before she replaced the receiver in its cradle. She looked at Jeff. There was worry and concern and a trace of fear in her eyes.

"Who was it, Amanda?" Alyssa asked, rising from her chair, still holding the baby in her arms.

"The grand jury brought in their verdict," Amanda said, getting right to the point. She took a step toward her grandfather.

"Oh, dear God, no," Alyssa said, her voice a mere whisper of despair. "No."

Judson turned slowly from the window where he'd been studying the rainy night to face them all.

"Well, girly?" he said with the faintest hint of a smile for Amanda. He stood tall and straight but his hands, thumbs hooked in his belt loops, trembled slightly.

"Apparently Phil Wocheck's testimony, whatever it was, was enough to turn the tide against you, Granddad."

"What could Phil possibly have told them?" Alyssa burst out.

"I don't know, Mom. I don't have access to any of the testimony."

"You're saying I'm going to have to stand trial for your grandmother's murder?" Judson's shoulders slumped as though under a great weight.

"Yes." Amanda looked past him at some demon of her own. "The grand jury brought down a murder indictment against you. And the D.A.'s office has handed the case over to the state attorney general's office. It's been assigned to Ethan Trask."

"Oh, hell," Liza said angrily. "Even I've heard stories about that guy. They say he never loses a case." She intercepted Amanda's quelling glance. "Well, almost never loses a case. What rotten luck."

"I'm way out of my league, Granddad," Amanda said miserably. "I think you'd better get yourself another lawyer. I'm taking myself off the case."

Judson shook his head. "No." His tone was stubborn, decisive. "I want you." He took Amanda's hands between his own, bent his head and kissed her cheek. "I won't have anyone else."

"I'm just a country lawyer!" Amanda seemed desperate to make him understand her limitations, real or imagined.

Judson smiled down at her. "You're a fine lawyer. My case couldn't be in better hands."

But he didn't say he was innocent. He didn't say he hadn't killed his wife. Jeff hated himself for the traitorous, fleeting doubt, but he couldn't stop it from searing its way through his mind. Cece stepped close, touched his hand, and the doubt disappeared, its darkness and pain banished by the light of her love and her trust.

"You can do it," Liza insisted, jumping up from the couch to give Judson a hug. "You can do it, Amanda," she repeated, her voice steely with resolve. "I know you can."

Amanda smiled at Liza's bravado. Judson still held her hands, and she returned the pressure of the embrace. "I'll do my best for you, Granddad. I promise all of you, I'll do the very best I can."

And now,
an exciting preview of

COURTHOUSE STEPS

by Ginger Chambers

*the eleventh installment of the
Tyler series coming in January*

Judson Ingalls is brought to trial for the murder of his wife. Is he guilty, as tough Assistant D.A. Ethan Trask is convinced—or innocent, as his granddaughter, Amanda Baron, acting as his defense counsel, believes? A battle of wits and wills ensues as the adversaries passionately clash both inside and out of the courtroom.

Watch for it next month, where Harlequin books are sold.

CHAPTER ONE

AMANDA SAW him across the lobby. He was standing in a cluster of people, but he was easily the most likely to draw the eye. Tall, dark-haired, in command—the set of his handsome features reflected a quick mind and a steely determination. The group he was with seemed to hang on his every word. Several individuals nodded; one left to do his bidding. He turned to a shorter man at his side, murmured something for his ear alone, then broke away from the small group himself. His walk was assured as he started across the room.

Amanda's heart rate jumped when she saw that he was coming toward her. She looked around for somewhere to hide. She didn't want to meet him like this! She wasn't ready! When she'd come to the courthouse in Sugar Creek, it was to tie up the last threads in a case that had nothing to do with her grandfather. She hadn't expected to run into Ethan Trask!

She sidled quickly toward a high rectangular table where other people were filling out forms. Picking up a form herself, she pretended to study it, but in reality she continued to watch the man . . . her adversary. His reputation had preceded him. He was the state attorney general's "Avenging Angel." When he was assigned to a case, he almost always won it. Brilliant, she'd heard him described. Merciless, as well.

She held her breath as he paused near her. Had someone told him that she was here? She spared a glance toward where he'd been standing and saw that the group had dispersed. No one was waiting to see what would happen next. Her blue gaze whipped back to the man and moved quickly over his angular face and strong, straight nose. She braced herself for his sharp word of greeting and the reactive flash of confident recognition that she would be no match for him.

Instead, his gaze lingered only briefly on her face before moving on. She was just another woman among many who had business in the courthouse. She might have been there to arrange bail for a boyfriend or to act as witness at a trial. He had no business with her, as far as he knew. No reason for recognition. Amanda remained frozen near the table. It was only when she saw him walk safely through the double doors of the building's main exit that she allowed herself the freedom to breathe again. Her heart rate took longer to settle.

She had known he was coming. *Everyone* knew he was coming; his picture had been in the *Tyler Citizen* on and off for a week. It was only a matter of when. Now he was here. In person. No longer a face in newsprint or a terrifying reputation to be feared. She had seen him, looked straight into his eyes, and she had discovered that this time reality was every bit equal to the gossip.

"Amanda...hello," someone called from a short distance away, drawing her out of her panicky thoughts.

Amanda looked up to see a fellow attorney struggling to contain an armload of notebooks and files. She forced a smile. "Sharon! Hello to you, too! I thought you were still visiting your parents in Florida."

Her friend grimaced. "I'm supposed to be, but I got called back. A custody hearing was moved up, so here I am. Have you heard? Ethan Trask is scheduled to set up his office in the courthouse today. Have you met him yet? Walk with me—I'm already behind schedule."

Amanda checked over her shoulder to make sure that Ethan Trask hadn't changed his mind and reentered the building. "No," she said, settling in at her friend's side. "I haven't met him yet, and I wish I never had to."

Sharon Martin glanced at her with compassion. "I don't envy you one bit. Neither does anyone else, with the possible exception of our usual showboater. He'd love to take on Ethan Trask. Winning or losing wouldn't matter, as long as he got plenty of media attention." Sharon hesitated. "Have you given any more thought to finding a co-counsel? I'd offer to help, but I'd be next to useless. You need someone who really knows their way around a criminal trial."

"I could always ask Larry," Amanda murmured dryly. Larry Richardson was the "showboater" Sharon had referred to. Not only did the man have an ego the size of Wisconsin concerning his abilities as a criminal defense lawyer, he also thought he was God's gift to women.

"Yeah, sure." Sharon's tone held just the right amount of sarcasm. "First he'd insist on being lead counsel. You'd have to do everything *his* way. Second, he'd inflate his fee. Third, you'd do all the work and he'd take all the glory. Fourth, you'd have to fight for your virtue every time you stepped into an empty room with him. And fifth . . . he wouldn't care nearly as much as you do about proving your grandfather innocent. Don't ask Larry!"

"I'll take your advice under consideration, Counselor."

Sharon, who looked tanned and rested from her week in Miami, ignored Amanda's teasing words. "The strain is starting to show, Amanda. Seriously, get some help. Have you thought of asking Professor Williams?"

Sharon and Amanda had attended the same law school in Illinois, and Professor Williams had been their favorite instructor. Several years ago he had retired and moved back to his family's longtime home on nearby Lake Geneva.

"I've thought of him," Amanda admitted.

They paused at the base of the wide, curving stairway that was the centerpiece of the graceful old building. Sharon glanced toward the upper floors. "I've got to go. Give him a call, Amanda. If our positions were reversed, I would."

Amanda waved her friend away and continued down a long hall that branched off the lobby. She had contemplated placing a call to Professor Williams on more than one occasion, but had hesitated each time because he'd been reported to be in ill health. And with all the upset about her grandfather's upcoming trial, she hadn't taken the time she once would have to pay him a friendly visit. She had been too busy trying to catch up loose ends so that she could devote herself completely to her grandfather's case.

As she neared the county clerk's office, a man who'd been slouching against the wall looked up and jerked forward. "Miss Baron! Could I have a word with you, please?" He pressed closer. "Would you give me a quick statement about Ethan Trask? How does your grandfather feel about his assignment to the case? Does he think he'll get a fair trial? Have you had second thoughts about representing your grandfather? Have you seen Ethan Trask yet? Have you talked with him?" He readied a notepad and a stubby pencil.

The barrage of questions set Amanda on edge. She still wasn't accustomed to such attention. Strictly a small-town lawyer, she handled small-town problems. The most notorious case she'd ever been involved with concerned a male dog of very mixed breeding that had fallen under the spell of a certain champion female show dog next door. Spike had displayed surprising versatility and enterprise in getting out of his backyard in order to pay his calls, and the show dog's owner had been furious about the little Spikes that had frequently turned up in his litters. He had sued the neighbor, whom Amanda represented, and the story had passed from local color to newspapers across the state. She had given a few quick interviews and been done with it. She and Rob Friedman, the owner and publisher of the *Tyler Citizen,* had had a few good laughs out of it. But ever since her grandfather's indictment, Amanda found little to laugh about.

She took a quick breath and said, "There's been no change in my grandfather's representation. He has every faith in my ability and in the state to give him a fair trial. As to Mr. Trask . . . he doesn't frighten either one of us. We're each still getting a good night's sleep."

"But considering Ethan Trask's reputation—"

Amanda flashed a naturally sweet smile. "I'll leave it at that. Now, if you don't mind, I have business to attend to."

The reporter held back as she stepped into the clerk's office. She might look cool and confident, which was the impression she very much wanted to give, but she felt far from that inside. If truth be told, her sleep patterns were awful. She kept having the same dream, that a monster was out to get her and, no matter where she took cover, always found her. From the drawn look of her grandfather, she suspected he was having much the same experience.

Amanda took care of her business as quickly as possible and made her way out of the courthouse. She had only one close call. As she was about to leave through a side door, she came face-to-face with the small, slender man who had been with Ethan Trask. She recognized him instantly. He had jet black hair, warm brown eyes and just the slightest trace of a Latin accent when he excused himself and stood aside for her to pass. He was not a handsome man. His nose was too large for his face, his mouth was too wide. But he held himself with such confident élan and had such quick charm to his smile that Amanda found herself smiling, too. Yet if he was in any way connected with Ethan Trask, he had to be dangerous.

Reacting instinctively, Amanda ducked her head and hurried away.

THE HALF HOUR it took for Amanda to drive from Sugar Creek to her office in Tyler included a quick stop at Marge's Diner, where she picked up lunch. Holding out the bag of food to her secretary, she teased, "Amanda to the rescue! Are you starving? That took longer than I thought. I fully expected to find you expired on top of your desk."

"Don't be silly," Tessie Finklebaum grumbled.

Tessie had been a legal secretary for longer than Amanda had been in the world. She'd seen everything, done almost everything, and was surprised by nothing. She had to be getting close to seventy, but she kept the date of her birth a deep, dark secret. It was as secret as the true color of her platinum-tinted hair. Each morning Tessie went for a two-mile "hike," as she termed it, and two evenings a week she attended an aerobics class. It was not in a person's better interests to call her "old."

Amanda pulled up a chair to her secretary's desk. The set of offices they shared was rather small, comprising her own office in the rear and the secretarial space in front. But she'd tried to decorate the place with a little taste, bringing a chair or two from home and cheerfully accepting Tessie's array of house-plants.

Amanda dug into the paper bag and divided its contents. She placed two tuna sandwiches, two bags of chips and two cans of soda on the napkins her secretary had spread on the desk. "I saw Ethan Trask today," she remarked easily.

Tessie fixed her with a piercing look. "You did? What did he say?"

Amanda grinned. "I didn't say I talked with him, I just saw him. Then I ran away like a craven coward. Tucked my little yellow tail between my legs and took off. What do you think of that?"

"I'd say you probably did the right thing. What was he like?"

Amanda leaned back. "Oh...tall, dark, handsome and terrifyingly competent. Nothing special."

Her secretary shook her head. "You'd better get yourself some help, young lady."

"That's what Sharon Martin said."

"You should listen to her. Ethan Trask will eat you alive."

"Thanks for your vote of confidence. I told a reporter I was perfectly assured of my ability."

"Are you?"

"I'm scared to death."

Tessie picked up her sandwich and started to munch. For a time they ate in silence. Finally, Amanda pushed away from the desk, her meal half-eaten.

"I'm going to make a couple of calls," she said. "If anyone needs me, ask them to wait."

"Sure thing, boss."

Amanda shook her head as she entered her sanctuary. For Tessie to call her "boss" was something of a joke. They both knew who was boss in the outer office, and it certainly wasn't Amanda. Tessie must think her in extreme need of a pick-me-up...which she was. Because joke all she wanted, she was truly terrified.

She had tried to tell everyone from the start that her grandfather should hire a lawyer more experienced with trial procedure, an expert in criminal defense. But no one had listened. They all told her she would do a great job. No one understood that criminal defense was an art form, just as was criminal prosecution. An ordinary, run-of-the-mill lawyer couldn't just walk in off the street, prepare a case of this magnitude and expect to win. She certainly couldn't. And if her grandfather ended up spending the rest of his life in jail because of her inability...

Amanda reached for her telephone index and punched in a number with the Lake Geneva area code. Ten minutes later, she had gained an appointment with the professor. After that, she punched in the number of the Ingalls mansion. Clara Myers, her grandfather's longtime housekeeper, answered the phone.

"Clara, hello, this is Amanda. I'm not going to be home for dinner this evening. Actually, I just had lunch.... Yes, I know how late it is. Would you please tell my mother that I'll speak to her when I get in, and tell Granddad... tell Granddad I might have some interesting news for him. No—" she quickly changed her mind "—don't say that last part. Just tell him I love him, and that I'll talk to him later, too."

She stared at the phone once she'd hung up. Then her gaze drifted to her rows of law books, which looked almost as pristine now as they had when she'd first received them, a gift from her mother and grandfather upon graduation from law school five years before.

Law, the body of rules that kept the fabric of society from coming apart... She had fallen in love with it when she was fifteen and one of her high school classes had gone on a field trip to the courthouse in Sugar Creek. She had watched the lawyers maneuver back and forth, watched as the defense team tried to use the cold and impersonal rules to the advantage of their client, watched as the state's representative held fast to the ideal of those rules. And from that day she had forgotten her earlier plan to become a veterinarian. She had haunted the library in Tyler, reading every book she could get her hands on that gave a view of the legal process.

She liked to think that, since becoming a lawyer herself, she had helped people. She hadn't won every case these past five years, but she had certainly attempted to. Most of her work involved technical expertise: what paper to file and where. Few cases actually went all the way to a trial. She tried very hard to mediate between people, to help them settle their differences before they resorted to further legal action.

Amanda sighed, her pretty face, normally so ready with the high-voltage Baron smile, unusually serious. The law *was* cold and impersonal, which meant that emotion held no place in judicial decisions. Just because a jury didn't like the way a defendant looked or behaved didn't mean they could take out their disapproval on that person by finding him guilty. Their decision had to be based solely on the evidence presented.

But in this instance, it was her grandfather she would soon be defending, and she wanted him to have every advantage that the system could offer—every bit of warmth she could stir in the jurors' hearts.

Her gaze moved to the newspaper clipping she had pinned to the wall earlier in the week—a picture of Ethan Trask. On it she had drawn the concentric circles of a target, with the bull's-eye the tip of his nose. At that moment, the tip had a dart sticking out of it. Not that she had made such a superb hit, though she'd tried for a quarter of an hour. She had ended up by marching over to slam the dart in at point-blank range.

Ethan Trask. The man she had seen so confidently issuing orders in the courthouse such a short time ago. The attorney general's "Avenging Angel."

"Oh, Granddad," Amanda groaned softly, beneath her breath, "if only it were anyone else!"